"I...

Fo... ...g to pass out. All the waiting, all the months, all the prayers, all the tears . . . she was dead. He knew it. The man on the other end knew it. That's why he was having such a hard time speaking, saying it . . . why Pyne couldn't make the call himself. The silence seemed to go on forever, finally Cody managed, "Yes?"

"My daughter . . . Sergeant Pyne said you could help."

"What?"

"My daughter, she's missing."

The flash of hope was only a flicker now. Later he'd realize that even then he knew what was left of hope was only imagined, but now he had to cling to it no matter how small. "Are you calling about my wife?"

"I'm calling about my daughter."

"My wife has been missing for three and a half months." He had to say it, and when he did he was surprised, for the emotion he hadn't meant to show gave odd dimensions to his voice.

"My daughter's been missing for two weeks." The man was crying. "She went on a honeymoon and they just . . ."

Cody hung up.

CRIES FROM THE DARKNESS

MICHAEL FISHER

Tudor Publishing Company
New York and Los Angeles

Tudor Publishing Company

ISBN: 0-944276-48-2

Printed in the United States of America

First Tudor printing—May, 1989

Chapter One

August, and it was raining. Cody woke up feeling lousy, but then he usually did these days. He looked to see what time it was, but he didn't have his watch on. He wondered where he'd left it and tried to remember going to bed the night before.

Overhead he could hear the rain pounding on the deck. Down the passageway Patrick was rattling around in the galley while Fats Domino was singing about the thrill he had found on Blueberry Hill. Cody knew it had to be Patrick; Damien didn't eat breakfast anymore . . . not for the last month or so. He'd really stopped eating it a couple of years ago when he was still a junior in high school . . . but then, in the first weeks after Ann had disappeared, they had all gotten up every morning at seven like she had . . . the three of them making breakfast in the tiny galley, together fulfilling her first chore of the day. Somehow it had helped keep a sanity, a sense of order.

"Dad?"

His mind had drifted to Ann again and he hadn't heard the boy approach. Pat was dressed like he had been most of the summer in cut-offs, tee-shirt, and white canvas deck shoes. Fats Domino wasn't singing anymore; the DJ with barely controlled hysteria was pitching an upcoming concert at the Forum. The world was back in the eighties again.

"I brought you some coffee."

"Thanks," Cody said and nodded where the boy should put it down. *He keeps the vigil,* Cody thought. *Of the three of us, he keeps the vigil, even down to the soft-rock radio station that Ann used to like. . . . Maybe when you're twelve you can hope more.*

"I'm making breakfast. Scrambled eggs and some of that Canadian bacon." Patrick's thick blond hair hadn't been combed yet this morning. Even so he was a pleasant looking boy, maybe a bit small for his age.

"Sounds great. I'll be right out."

The boy grinned his crooked grin, which was real, and left. He had always had that crooked grin. It curled up in the corner of his mouth like a cartoon character's and had nothing to do with his laugh or sense of humor, both of which were good and hearty but much more conventional. . . . The crooked grin was something else. It was quite spontaneous, and Cody had long ago surmised that it was meant to be secretive, for one only saw it when the boy was genuinely pleased with himself. It didn't occur to him that this morning the boy was happy because he'd made his dad happy, after the bad night last night.

Cody brushed his teeth and splashed water on his face. In a couple of days it would be September, the end of summer, the summer that was supposed to be the beginning of their dream . . . and now where the hell was it? He thought about showering and shaving but decided to wait until after breakfast. He knew he was depressed again and wondered, like he had a lot of mornings lately, if it was the vodka or the waiting. The vodka had been creeping up on him the last few months, though for a while he'd fought it.

As he stepped out of the small bathroom, his eyes caught a family photograph, and he became more depressed remembering the shouting of the night before. Damien, his older son, was dark and good-looking like Ann, with high cheekbones. At eighteen he was already six foot one, a good couple of inches taller than Cody. The shouting last night had been building for weeks. It was nearly the end of August . . . if they weren't going to sail around the world as planned, at least for now, then Damien wanted to go back to school. He'd be in his first year at Loyola.

"It's ready," Pat called from the galley.

"Right there."

But he didn't move. He felt cold inside. He had had too much to drink and had taken all his anger and frustration out on his son, shouting and cursing and telling the boy that he was being disloyal to his mother by wanting to go back to school. And now here, alone, he wanted to cry and tell Damien how sorry he was for saying all those things, and for a moment he remembered the boy when he was three, laughing, and hugging him. That was something else Cody had noticed in the last few months. His emotions had taken on wide and rapid swings, quick to anger, quicker the urge to cry, only laughter came harder . . . and all in the defense of a logic even Cody knew was mad, but couldn't abandon . . . that as long as nothing changed, as long as they could maintain the status quo . . . then Ann could come back and everything would be as it had been.

He sat on the bunk and wondered again if he really was going crazy. That would be the final irony,

wouldn't it? After all the years, all the whispers . . .
But he had never known such surges of guilt. Frustration. Such total helplessness. He loved Ann so much. He had been the Policeman, the detective, the one they used to say was one of the best. . . . For the thousandth time he remembered the last time he'd seen her.

"I'll be back in twenty . . . just need eggs and coffee."

"We're out of tonic."

"I'll get some." She smiled. By then she was stepping onto the jetty and moving away from him. The Mets had scored three runs in the first inning against the Dodgers and there had been irritation in his voice. She had smiled. He had been angry. She had smiled, but on the other side of the continent the Dodgers and the Mets, all hunched together in his $29.95 pocket-sized transistor radio, were playing baseball, but not the way he'd wanted them to play baseball.

That was his last memory of her. She had smiled. And now again, like it had been lately, it was hard for him to see her face. He was crying. Minutes had passed, and he knew that Patrick was standing there, but he couldn't help himself. He'd loved her so much and one day she'd gone to the supermarket and never came home. Disappeared without a trace. Patrick was crying now, too, and Cody hugged his son, and they hugged each other.

It was still raining when the phone call came. Pat had fallen asleep in front of the television and the phone had had to ring several times to pull him out of his sleep, out of his dream. In his dream he and Paul were becoming good friends. Oh, the rest of the guys, they seemed like nice guys, too, John and George and Ringo, but wouldn't you know it, his favorite, Paul, they really hit it off. The guys had been looking for a friend of theirs who lived in the Marina, but they couldn't find him and they'd run into Pat . . . and then his dream, which was becoming more and more vivid with every fleeting moment, was gone.

It was raining. The phone was ringing.

With Paul and John and Ringo and . . . it had been bright and hot. Mom had been there and the feeling had been warm and secure.

It was raining, harder now, the wind bringing the downpour in quickening waves. The man on the other end of the phone said he was calling about a woman. A missing woman. Sergeant Pyne had told him to call. It was a clumsy conversation, the boy awkward with his thoughts and questions, the man reluctant to part with any meaningful information. But desperately, above all else, Pat didn't want to break the connection. In all the weeks and months that his mother had been missing, with all the inquiries . . . this was the first time someone had contacted them.

"I'll get my dad, he isn't far . . ."

The man said he'd wait.

Pat was halfway out when he reconsidered. He darted back down the stairs and turned off the video tape. The Beatles, Paul and John and the others, were silent now. It wasn't bright and hot out and his mother hadn't been here in over three months.

"It could take me a couple of minutes to find him, but I know I will." The man said he'd wait. *Funny,* Pat thought as he ran down the jetty through the pouring rain. In that split second, the second time he talked to the man, there was a quiver in his voice that made it sound like the man was as desperate as the boy.

Pat had known when he said it that the "couple of minutes" was a lie, but he had hoped the man would wait. Pat knew he needed the time. He ran out of the Marina itself, then through a parking lot where a car backing out almost hit him. Pat had to fly sideways, and he landed hard on his elbow. It was bleeding, but the man driving the car never saw the boy he could have killed.

The Laundromat was a little less than a half mile from where their boat was moored . . . Pat made it in under five minutes. Cody was checking the clothes in the dryer when he saw his son.

They looked at one another . . . the boy soaked to the skin, a curl of blood snaked around his wrist . . . the man, father, former cop, former warrior . . . a hum of neon lights above them. "I fight housewives and old ladies now . . ." he had said in a recent drunken diatribe. "That's me, King of the Laundromats, King of the Supermarkets. . . . Show me the old lady I can't beat out of the best washer in the place. . . ."

The boy didn't have to speak. Cody knew why he was there.

"Hello . . . Hello."
"Yes . . . Sergeant Cody?"
"Yes. I'm not a sergeant anymore; I'm retired." There was no sound on the other end of the phone. He had the sense that he was sounding moronic. "But this is me; I'm Sergeant Cody." Still no sound. Panic. "Hello? . . . Are you there?"
"My name is Worden, Robert Worden . . . Sergeant Pyne told me to call."

Suddenly he realized how hot and muggy it was inside the cabin. Outside, the August rain seemed finally to be quieting. The spaces between Pat's nose and cheeks glistened. First pimples were on their way, he thought, and then felt a pang of desperation. Why were his powers of concentration so thin? Why was his mind wandering, now of all times?

"It's about a missing woman."

For a moment Cody thought he was going to pass out. All the waiting, all the months, all the prayers, all the tears . . . she was dead. He knew it. The man on the other end knew it. That's why he was having such a hard time speaking, saying it . . . why Pyne couldn't make the call himself. The silence seemed to go on forever, finally Cody managed, "Yes?"

"My daughter . . . Sergeant Pyne said you could help."

Madness.

"What?"

"My daughter, she's missing."

Madness slipping. The flash of hope was only a flicker now. Later he'd realize that even then he knew what was left of hope was only imagined, but now he had to cling to it no matter how small. "Are you calling about my wife?"

"I'm calling about my daughter."

"My wife has been missing for three and a half months." He knew now it didn't have anything to do with the conversation, but he had to say it, and when he did he was surprised, for the emotion he hadn't meant to show gave odd dimensions to his voice.

"My daughter's been missing for two weeks." The man was crying. "She went on a honeymoon and they just . . ."

Cody hung up. He knew as he did that he'd have

to talk to the man again . . . but not now . . . not right now.

"It wasn't about Mom." He said the words after some moments and before looking at the boy.

"It wasn't?" The boy had to ask. To be sure.

"No. It's about another woman. His daughter. Seems she's missing, too."

The phone was ringing again. The man and boy looked at one another. The air was hot and thick.

"Sergeant Cody?"

"Yeah."

"This is Robert Worden again; we were cut off."

"No, we weren't . . . I hung up on you."

"What?"

"I hung up on you."

Silence. Neither man had any further down to go. Neither broke the connection. There was a thread between them. They both knew it.

"Sergeant Pyne said maybe you could help me . . . Didn't he talk to you?"

"No."

". . . My daughter's missing. He said you used to be a cop. A great detective. He said you knew all the questions to ask about missing people. The agencies to contact. How to cover all the details the P.D. doesn't have time to do."

Silence. Then the man was crying again, uncontrollably. It blurred his voice. "I'm blind and I can't walk. I don't even know when I'm shitting. I was a motorcycle cop for fourteen years. Liquor store robbery, I caught a bullet in the spine. . . . My little girl's all I've got."

Chapter Two

The address that Worden gave him was in Canoga Park. With no traffic on the freeways the trip would have taken forty-five minutes. Today it took over two hours. The pavement was still wet and he had waited until the beginning of rush hour. He had waited for Damien. He had wanted to apologize. The eighteen-year-old did his best to accept. The words were spare.

The house was set back from the street a good hundred feet. Cody guessed the lot to be an acre. That was a popular size in the fifties and early sixties when land developers were trying to get people to move here to the end of the earth. A chain link fence tried to guard the property from the curbless street, but there was no gate across the entrance to the worn-out asphalt driveway anymore.

The driveway itself twisted its way through a front yard of waist-high weeds, along the way passing a rusted-out child's swing set, the shell of an old Studebaker, and a haphazard pile of lumber. ''A house of broken dreams,'' Cody thought and then drove away.

The bar he'd agreed to meet Pyne in was in a

shopping center five minutes from the house. The shopping center was flat and ugly, the kind the Valley seemed to have every square mile or so now. A giant supermarket commanded one end, a giant drug store the other. In-between was a string of a couple of dozen storefronts, each fighting for its piece of the American dream: Rose's Gift Shop, karate school, pool supply, "His and Her" haircuts, Gold Dragon Chinese Restaurant with a "take out" window . . . and then another broken dream, Nory's Jewelry Shop, the windows soaped, the "going out of business" banner faded from age . . . but not to worry, "Cookery Magic" will be here soon.

A swarm of kids, mostly boys, mostly on bikes, mostly shirtless or tank-topped were headquartered in front of the pizza parlor. The temperature was back up in the nineties, the air still heavy. Occasionally thunder rumbled across the sky.

Cody finally found a parking place near the Pioneer Chicken. The whole area was teeming with people. The parking lot, the walkways . . . fat women in tent dresses and thongs . . . old people, shuffling, eyes straight ahead, determined, determined . . . little brown babies, bellies hanging over their diapers, filthy and delighted, ice cream on their faces and bodies. *Where the hell did they all come from?* The question ran through his mind, but he knew the answer, and it was somehow unpleasant because somehow they all seemed like intruders.

He'd grown up in the Valley of the fifties. The Ventura Freeway only went to Sepulveda Boulevard then. In the summertime they had walnut fights and softball games, and a walk to the store meant neighborhood stores, a grocery, drug store, cleaners, hardware, and people knew people by first names.

Sometimes they bragged about the San Fernando valley being the fastest growing place in the country. The house he'd grown up in had been on a dirt road that turned into a foot of mud when it rained for more than a day, but that didn't matter because by then most of the paved roads had turned into impassable rivers . . . and of course, if it rained hard enough and long enough, they opened the dam, and fish could be seen moving down the bigger streets. . . . But this was the Valley of today; honking horns and two and a half million people—blacks and whites; Mexicans, a lot of them illegal; pocket communities of Vietnamese and Arabs, Chinese and Koreans—and all of them jammed together into more faceless and ugly buildings, the endless apartments thrown up so greedily at the end of the sixties, the beginning of the seventies, with hollow doors, fiber board walls, and shot plaster ceilings with their sparkles long grown dull.

"I was beginning to wonder if you were going to make it."

Pyne was rotund and in his late forties. He wore his hair in a crew cut that was the fashion of his high school days and carried an air of anxiety with him that had earned him the nickname "Little Mother" at the Van Owen Street Station. He was at one of the small tables at the back, where he had been throwing darts, drinking beer, and eating the free popcorn while he waited for Cody. Despite the air conditioning he was sweating heavily, and his coat was draped over the back of the chair so his service .38 revolver, which he wore on his hip, was clearly visible to all the other customers. Pyne, being Pyne, affected an attitude that he was unaware that his gun might attract attention, but Cody knew him too well. He also knew it was almost time for Pyne's annual diet. Every year the battle Little Mother waged to get his weight down to where he could pass the department physical seemed to become a bigger and more bizarre event. One year he spent three weeks locked up at UCLA on a liquid protein diet. Another year he carried scales everywhere he went . . . and everything that went in . . . and out . . . had to be weighed. *Poor bastard looks heavier than ever,* Cody thought.

"I've gotta be at a Scout meeting at seven thirty," he said, glancing at his watch as he put on his coat, then he hitched his pants saying, "Beth sends her love. . . . We want to get you guys out you know, you and the boys. Sunday barbecue." He had pulled himself together. He glanced nervously at his watch again. "Boy, I'm running short. . . . What'da ya say I call Worden and tell him we're on our way?"

"I need a couple of drinks first. I also want to know what this is about before we go over there."

Pyne sighed.

It wasn't until Cody was sipping his first double vodka-tonic that he understood why he had suddenly felt good. Just telling Pyne he wanted information on a case had relaxed him. He was comfortable, at least for these few moments, for the first time in months. It was artificial, but he didn't care. He had the sense of doing what he did—what he did well, what he had done up until five months ago when he had retired after twenty years. For just these few moments he was back in the world he had lived in so well and it didn't matter the circumstances or that Pyne was a little afraid of him, most of them were. It never had mattered to him. They had let him be, to do what he wanted to do, and as long as he didn't seek the glory, they didn't feel threatened, and they liked him because they wanted the glory for themselves. It was an unspoken bargain, and because of it they felt they controlled him, that he was theirs to use or show off . . . or if he ever got out of control, to destroy.

Cody was on his second drink when the fat man, still sweating, settled onto the barstool next to him. "I told Worden we'd be there in twenty minutes," Pyne said. "And I called Beth; she'll start the meeting for me." Then he ordered a beer and asked if there was anything else to munch on other than popcorn. He sighed heavily when he was told there wasn't. After some hemming and hawing he ordered a poor-boy sandwich, which had to be heated in a microwave that rested directly under a large, plastic, gold-and-red shield and helmet of a knight of old. They were in Camelot.

"Tell me about Worden."

"He's a real great guy, I checked him out myself. Motorcycle cop fourteen years. Three commendations. They gave him a medal of valor when he was shot. That was eleven years ago. . . . His old lady stuck it out for a couple of years, but it's pretty rough. Except for his arms, the guy can't move. He can't walk or see. Hell, he doesn't even know when he's shitting."

"Yeah, he told me."

The bell on the microwave rang, and Pyne's spirits were lifted. His grin became at once gossipy and salacious. "I guess when he lost control of his rear end, he lost control of his other equipment down there. That's probably why his old lady took off."

A bald-headed man had come through the front door while Pyne was talking, and a warning had gone off in Cody. He knew the man, but from where? The baggy clothes, the half shuffling walk, they were right, but something was wrong, something was out of place. The man looked around, his mouth half-open. Frowning? Disapproving? His eyes seemed to linger on the empty piano bar at the opposite end of the room. Boxes of paper goods were stacked on top of it. Something was wrong. Cody knew it. Something was out of place. His memory found adrenalin. The image of gunfire. Screaming.

Pyne ate voraciously.

The bald-headed man ordered a beer.

Cody felt for his gun, which hadn't been there for five months.

"What happened to Johnny?"

"Johnny who?" The bartender was in his mid-twenties and looked like he'd be more at home on a construction site.

The bald-headed man's voice gained an air of indignation. God he was sick of impertinent know-nothing people.

"The Johnny who owns this place. Who plays on the piano bar over there."

"Oh, him." The bartender put aside his concern for the Angels batting in the top of the eighth in Detroit. "He died."

The bald-headed man was stunned. "Died?"

"Yeah, couple of weeks ago. Just got sick. Couple of days later they took him to the hospital, couple of more days after that he died."

"Dead. My God. They know what caused it?" The bald-headed man was sixty-four and, though he looked ten years younger, at times like this he felt terribly mortal.

"Something to do with the pancreas. . . . I don't even know where that is," the bartender said and grinned.

"Dead," the bald-headed man repeated and twisted his finger unconsciously in his ear. Then he almost lost the bartender to the roar of the crowd on the television, but it was only the end of an inning and they went to a commercial, so the young man remained.

"I used to sing with him," the man said.

"That right?"

"I sing in a lot of places around the Valley. Over the hill, too. Suppose to go down to Redondo Beach later tonight."

"They pay you?"

"No. I just sing."

George. Cody remembered the bald-headed man's name was George, and in the same moment he knew what was missing. It was the wig. He used to wear a wig. It was brownish red and almost comical. And he did sing . . . in piano bars. He'd drift in late in the evening, ten or eleven o'clock, order a drink, and then linger hopefully within sight of the piano player, waiting to be called over, waiting for his chance to sing. And eventually it would come. The regular patrons knew him by name, and the older ones, the slurred, blue-rinse groupies, would tell him he sounded just like Bing Crosby.

Cody had seen George in several bars last year. George would sing; Cody would watch from a hidden place, shotgun in hand. He had been on stakeout. Six bad guys had been cruising the Saturday-night Ventura Freeway, swinging down, hitting bars that were close to an on-ramp, robbing, raping, killing. They hit eight places in eight weeks. The ninth week, Cody and thirteen other officers were waiting for them. It was a shooting gallery. Three bad guys were killed, two others wounded. The sixth one, the Judas, the one Cody had found and turned the previous Thursday, had lingered outside. Cody had never fired a shot that night, and he finally faced that night what he had known for a long time but had been avoiding: that he didn't want to be a cop anymore. It had changed, being a cop. Being a Policeman. Like the dirt roads and the softball games, the kind of cop Cody wanted to be didn't exist anymore. That night . . . The bloodbath . . . The guy's he'd been with, the "Special Squad," they had liked it. They had liked the killing.

"Been back East, New York, Boston, Maine. High school reunion. That's how come I didn't know about Johnny. He was a damn fine piano player."

"That right?"

"That's right," George said. He was starting to feel indignant again. The bartender moved off to fix another double vodka-tonic for the man at the end of the bar. George sipped his beer and wondered what time he should leave for Redondo.

"Tell me more about Worden." George was harmless but the adrenalin was still flowing. It didn't turn off as easily as it started.

Pyne took a breath. Red sauce patterned around his mouth. "When the old lady took off she left the girl behind. She was about fifteen then. Girl's taken care of him ever since. Even went to nursing school so she could be more help. Anyhow, about six months ago she meets this guy at night school. He's an accountant who wants to be a writer. They fall in love and want to get married . . . but of course there's the old man . . . you'd think it'd be a problem, but it isn't. The old man and this guy get along great. They sit and talk baseball for hours, and this guy being an accountant, he knows every statistic there ever was . . . maybe even invented a few of his own.'' Pyne paused long enough to blow his nose, finish his beer, signal for another, and take two more bites of the sandwich. He seemed oblivious to the food he sprayed as he started talking again. ''So it's all one happy family. What they work out is the kids will get married and instead of getting their own place they'll set up there. . . . That way the old man's disability can pay the bills and the boy can quit his job and try writing his novel full time.'' Two more bites, half a glass of fresh beer. Only the top and bottom end pieces of the bread remained. Pyne wanted to eat them, but he knew the discipline had to start somewhere. He put the end pieces on the cardboard plate and then pushed the plate away. He was sure Cody would notice.

''Worden said she went on her honeymoon.''

''That's right. That was almost three weeks ago. They were only supposed to be gone ten days.''

''Where did they go?''

''Kauai.''

''Hawaii?''

''Kauai,'' Pyne corrected. ''You ever been to the islands?''

''No.''

Pyne was at his best now; he liked being the keeper of knowledge. He explained to Cody as he might to his Cub Scouts, ''Hawaii has seven major islands. Oahu is the main island. That's where Honolulu is and about eighty percent of the population. The island of Kauai is ninety miles north of Oahu. It's the oldest of the Hawaiian islands . . . they call it the garden isle; it's really pretty. Beth and I were there a few years ago for a couple of days. We were on one of those trips where you do four islands in ten days.''

"The girl and her husband make it there?"

"Oh yeah, safe and sound. They checked into one of those hotels that caters to honeymooners and old people . . . or as they say . . . for the newlywed and nearly dead." He grinned, but Cody didn't return the smile.

"Then what?"

"Everything was fine for five days. The girl called her father twice a day. Once in the morning to tell him what they were off to that day, whether it was going to the beach or shopping or hiking or just going for a drive. Then at night she'd call him again and tell him all about whatever it was that they did, and he'd tell her about any baseball gossip he'd heard on the radio or anything interesting that happened, so she could pass it on to her husband."

"What happened on the sixth day?"

"She called in the morning like she always did. Told her dad that they were going hiking, but that it was an overnight trip. They were going to hike to some remote beach and camp there for the night. She told him she wouldn't be able to call him until late the next day. That's the last anybody heard or saw of them."

"What did the local police have to say?"

"Not much. They figured out which hiking trail they must have taken and organized a search. National Park Rangers got involved and actually did most of the looking . . . no sign of them. But apparently that trail is pretty scary in spots. There's cliffs and steam cracks and just a hell of a lot of jungle. Over the years there's been a couple of other people lost without a trace . . . but never two together. Of

course, then they figured they were honeymooners
. . . maybe they left the trail to, you know, get a
little . . . then just couldn't find their way back, got
lost, fell in a steam crack or over a cliff or God
knows what.''

Pyne paused and sipped his beer.

Cody knew the fat man was waiting for him to set
him up.

''What aren't you telling me?''

''Well that's the way they were going to write it
off. . . . I mean the Rangers were going to keep
looking, but the big search was over. They figured
one day they'd just find their bones or whatever else
was left. . . .

''Until?'' Cody was getting impatient for the point.

''Until they realized, the rental car the kids had
. . . it was missing, too. It wasn't in the parking lot
where they would have left it to go on the hike. It
wasn't at the hotel. They been looking about ten days
now . . . they can't find it anywhere on the island.''

''The car vanished, too?'' Cody's voice was hollow.

''Yeah, I thought that'd probably get you. I guess
that's what made us think about you in the first place
. . . why you might want to help . . . I mean it's the
way Ann disappeared, car and all.''

Cody felt cold inside; his ears were ringing. He
had the feeling of Ann. The feeling of guilt. But
why? What could he have done? But logic didn't
help. He had been the Policeman. Pyne never stopped
talking.

''This Worden guy, the captain had known him
when he came through the Academy. He kept calling
every day and crying. Wasn't there something we
could do? Couldn't the police on Kauai do anything
. . . ? I think they tried, the cops over there . . .

problem is the whole island's got a population of
about thirty-six thousand. I mean that's a bad crowd
at Dodger Stadium, so you can figure the police force
can't be more than a hundred or so guys, probably
only a handful of detectives, and God knows what
kind of training they've had.''

''You want me to go there?''

''We figured if anybody could find those kids it
would be you.''

Chapter Three

"They're going to have a night for Manny Mota," Worden said. Pittsburgh was at bat in the top of the second.

As advertised, the inside of the house smelled like someone who couldn't control their bowels lived there, and Cody knew the man had spoken to try not to cry.

"Line drive . . . base hit."

They were in the living room, which had long ago become his bedroom. Worden sat in the center of it, propped up in a hospital bed. He was a heavy man, and because of the heat was stripped to the waist. His skin was porcelain white and shiny from sweat. A swamp cooler pushed air through the house, but it couldn't do much good, not at this time of day, in this part of the Valley. On either side of the blind man were swinging hospital trays, both cluttered. Both had radios. The one closest to the wall, a shortwave, was dusty and the size of a small suitcase. The tray nearest Cody held Worden's baseball radio and his phone. The phone was designer-beige and grubby dirty.

A shortish, stoutish, fiftyish woman in a wrinkled print tent-dress and rubber thongs had let them in.

She told them her name was Mrs. Bowman. She was an R.N. and a neighbor, three doors down; her husband worked for the State and wanted to retire next year, but she thought he ought to go on for four more years and full retirement. Her oldest daughter was about to get married, and the Mexicans who she had hired to fix up the back yard for the reception had broken her sprinkler line in three places.

Pyne made a comical face to Cody as if he were going to pass out from the stench, while using his sincere voice. "Bob, I want you to meet Sergeant Ed Cody."

The two men shook hands. The blind man's grip was at once damp, flabby, and strong.

"I really appreciate you coming," Worden said.

There was a tremble in his voice. Cody sensed the invalid didn't want to let go.

"I don't know how much Sergeant Pyne has told you."

"Quite a bit," Cody said and slipped his hand free.

"Sergeant Cody has agreed to go to Kauai," Pyne piped in with the enthusiasm of a Cubmaster.

Worden began to cry. "Thank God . . . thank you. There's no way I'll ever be able to thank you enough."

"You don't have to," Cody said. His eyes, adjusted to the dim light, were scanning the room now. Photographs filled one wall. He moved closer to them and stepped back in time. A chubby, awkward little girl of eight or nine standing with her handsome policeman father. Same girl, braces now. Then the family portrait, the big framed oil done up from a photograph, and everyone looking rather artificial: Mom slick and pretty, with streaked blond hair and a deep tan; he still young and handsome, but a bit out of place in street clothes, and of course the girl, smiling, but still chubby, still a bit awkward, very much her daddy's girl.

"I know she's alive," Worden was saying. "I know it. Maybe it sounds crazy. But I do."

"High pop-up . . . oh, this one is a dandy, what you'd call a major league pop-up. Anderson's under it . . . and he's lost it . . . it hits the ground and both runners are going to be safe."

"She's alive. . . . My baby's alive."

Cody had seen enough. At least all he could look at or listen to for now. It was taking on a dreamlike feeling. All the photographs, all the words . . . the desperation, the hope in the blind man's voice, they were his; it was what they shared. And now, like so many other times in the last few months, he was having difficulty focusing his mind.

"Bullshit," Cody said.

"He must have lost it in the lights . . . it was way up there . . . and somewhere along the line he just lost it. Anderson's just lucky it didn't hit him on the head."

Cody's soft voice had frozen the other two men. But there could be no apology here. No embarrassment. Cody knew right now that he must only go on. It didn't matter that his ears were ringing and his stomach knotted up. He had to go on. He had to appear calm. He had to follow this case through, try to get some sense of accomplishment, try to stay on this side of sanity. "Your girl's been missing for over two weeks on a small island. The chances are both she and her husband are dead . . . just like the chances are my wife is dead. . . ." He knew his voice sounded hollow again. "That's the reality that you and I have to face . . . but that doesn't mean we don't go on looking for them. As long as we don't know for sure . . . as long as there's any remote hope . . ."

"And the next pitch is belted . . . long and deep and gone, and Pittsburgh jumps on top three zip."

"I want you to know where we stand. If you still want me to, I'll look for your girl, but I won't promise you any miracles. I won't give you any false hope . . . I'm all out of that."

For a few moments there was only the sound of the crowd from Dodger Stadium. *Life between pitches,* Cody thought. *Between innings and commercials. Between acts on television shows and smiling one-minute bursts of disaster on eyewitness news. That's all we have left anymore. Life in fragments, thirty or sixty seconds long. Is that all the longer we can think anymore? . . . Or just how long we can tolerate the pain?*

". . . Please find her," Worden finally managed.

A sense of calm came over Cody again just as it had in the bar when he had told Pyne to fill him in on the missing girl. "I'll need a recent photograph of her, and if I can get it, one of her husband."

"Wedding pictures came last week. Mrs. Bowman can find them for you," Worden replied. His voice sounded tired now.

"And I'll need to see her room."

"Why? There's nothing in her room that can have anything to do with Kauai."

"It's the way I work," Cody said. "I like to get a feeling for people. I never know what will help. It might be the colors she likes or just the way she hangs her clothes in the closet or just how she arranges her room. It might be something I can't even explain. I just know that sometimes it helps.''

He knew of course, that Worden was right. Under the circumstances it was remote that there would be anything in the girl's room that might help locate her. But he wanted to follow his routine, fulfill the rituals. His feeling of well-being was fragile. He sensed if he could get involved in this case, if, for just a little while it could cloak him from his own world . . . then just maybe he could help both Worden and himself.

The Bowman woman didn't stop talking all the way down the hallway. He heard about the Mexicans again and the sabotaged sprinklers. About Worden's daughter. She had known little Caroline since she was eight . . . and her husband, no one ever came right out and said it, but she was pretty sure he was Jewish. His name was Green, Martin Green; not much to tell from that, but still and all she was pretty sure he was, not that it mattered to her. Of course, they did spend the last couple of weeks before the wedding fixing up the master bedroom for themselves, painting, carpeting, buying some new furniture . . . doing all that work themselves and then planning on living here with Mr. Worden was a way to save a lot of money, and you know how those people are. Cody wondered with an inward smile why Mrs. Bowman's husband had decided to retire early if now he was going to have to spend his days at home with her. As he smiled at the mild joke, it struck him how long it had been since he had been able to smile about anything . . . and then he stepped off the edge.

He felt it the moment the talking woman opened

the door. The gray-and-white cat looked up from the aquamarine bed cover. The air was warm and stale with the smell of paint. But in that moment Cody stepped off into darkness. It was icy cold and deep inside was a desperate cry of fear . . . dark, pitch dark . . . and then he was back in Canogo Park.

"Her name is Calpurnia," Mrs. Bowman was saying with a smile. "It was so funny, she was part of a litter of kittens our Trixie had, and little Caroline, she couldn't have been more than fourteen then, thought she was a boy and named her Caesar, that is until . . ."

"Get out." His voice was soft but intense. His eyes weren't on her.

The talking woman had stopped talking. She didn't know what to do. There must be a mistake. She started again.

" . . . she had a litter of kittens herself. . . ."

"I said, get out." This time he turned his steel gray eyes to her. She didn't hesitate. He followed her to the door. Pyne was in the hallway.

"Don't go away," Cody told him and then closed the door.

Cody sat in the room for almost an hour, but the feeling didn't return. Death had been there. Death and more. It had touched him, but now it was gone.

Carefully, he now began to explore the room. After several minutes he went to the door. Pyne was still there, slumped against a wall, looking disgruntled.

"I want to know when they finished painting the room. Especially the windows," Cody said.

"What could that have to do with anything?" Pyne's words came out sour.

"Just do it." Cody had no patience. His eyes were

unrelenting, and after a moment the fat man hitched up his pants and waddled down the hall.

Pyne returned to find Cody sitting on the bed, petting the cat and looking through a photo album, which was one of a half dozen now laid out on the bed.

"They finished painting the night before the wedding. Mrs. Bowman remembers because her son helped them."

"That's when they did the windows?"

Pyne nodded. "Woodwork was the last thing they did. What's the big deal about the windows?"

Cody finished one album. He was restless. He knew he had a piece of the puzzle, but only one piece, and he didn't know what it meant, only that it was a piece of midnight somewhere on the edge of an eternity. He left the bed and moved back to the closet and started to look through it again as he talked. "Tell me, Pyne, if you were a burglar and you broke into this room, what would you take?"

Pyne scanned the room. "T.V., video tape machine, silver brush and comb set. Of course, I don't know what's in the drawers or closet."

Cody nodded to the bureau. "Top drawer. There's an envelope with three hundred and forty-two dollars in it. Next one down, some jewelry and gold coins maybe worth a couple of thousand." Frustration was audible in his voice. There was nothing in the closet, but he had known that the first time through.

"What are you getting at?"

"Look at the window."

Pyne was tired and hot. He had missed his early evening lasagna and now Cody was playing games. With a sigh, he waddled over to the window and then, after a moment, he looked confused. "It's been jimmied."

"And after the paint dried," Cody said. "That enamel would take a couple of days to dry . . . so what we have is, after the wedding, after the happy couple have taken off for the islands, someone broke in here, but to take what? Money, T.V., jewelry, they're all still here."

"There must be some mistake," Pyne said, not trying to hide his exasperation.

"No mistake. Those marks were made by someone who knew what he was doing. The question is, what the hell did he want? And what, if anything, does it have to do with the missing girl and her husband?"

"Oh boy," Pyne sighed, rubbing his face. "Do you always have to come up with some wild . . . I know Ann and everything . . ." He paused to try and straighten out his words and looked like a Cubmaster trying to deal with an idiot scout.

"Just like old times, huh Pyne?" There was tight, bitter humor in Cody's words. He moved across the room and started through the drawers again.

"Look, this is a simple case," Pyne was almost shouting. "A girl and her husband are missing on an island three thousand miles from here, and somebody making jimmie marks on a window here has nothing to do with it. It doesn't make any sense."

Cody's anger burst out. He wheeled, his words soft and cold and tearing. "Neither does a girl and her husband and their rental car disappearing off the face of the earth. . . . Or a woman going to the supermarket and never coming home. . . ." He broke off for a moment, and when he started again the anger was in control. "Or a guy up in Bakersfield who cuts up little girl's private parts, fourteen victims, and the judge gives him probation so he can do it again, and he does. . . . Or the handsome young college student who crisscrosses the country murdering people wherever he stops. . . . Or parents who torture and kill their babies. . . . None of it makes any sense, but that doesn't mean that it isn't happening . . . it's madness and it's all around us. Somehow the world's become filled with crimes without conscience or rules . . . it's goddamn madness."

"It's the times we live in," Pyne finally said after a few moments.

"Well, I've got a clue for you; they stink."

"I know," Pyne agreed so as to be agreeable. Then he added tentatively, "What do we do now?"

Cody knew he was being patronized again, but it didn't matter. "I'll try to catch a plane out tomorrow."

"There's one that goes directly to Kauai, but it's full; I checked," Pyne volunteered. "So you'll have to go through Honolulu and change planes, but that's no big deal . . . I can go in the other room and make the reservation for you if you like. The department will pick up your expenses . . . on the qt of course."

"Make it two seats. I'll have to take my twelve-year-old with me. I don't have anyone I can leave him with," he said, knowing it wasn't true. Damien was going away for the weekend, but he could watch Pat. He had in fact offered to take his little brother along. But Cody hadn't wanted to be alone. Not then. Not now.

For a moment the fat detective considered making an issue of the second ticket, but then decided not to. "Right."

"And Pyne," Cody said, stopping him in the doorway. "I want to stay at the same hotel and, if possible, in the same room the girl and her husband were in.''

Pyne sighed, the exasperation was creeping back. ''I'll do my best.''

It took Pyne almost thirty minutes to make the reservations. By the time the fat man returned, Cody knew what the burglar had been after. When he finally realized what it was, and realized how cleverly the burglar had almost accomplished his purpose, had almost gone undetected, Cody had for a brief moment been back on the edge of eternity again. And again, deep inside, the desperate cry of fear had been there, and he knew then he could never turn back.

Chapter Four

"Aloha, welcome to Hawaii."

The inside of the terminal was hot and muggy and already jammed with people when Cody and Pat emerged from the plane. It was a quarter to four in the afternoon. Three fat Polynesian men with bright-colored lavalavas and hairy chests and bellies strummed guitars and sang. Professional greeters held up cardboard signs and shouted over the babble of voices and the roar of jet engines to the passengers they were responsible for. Their muumuus and aloha shirts were from uniform shops; their smiles mostly born from the desperate chase. "Aloha, welcome to Hawaii." Leis had to be presented, names checked off, tour buses filled, and then maybe there was time for a cigarette, a cup of coffee, to put your feet up and hope the swelling went down, to get on the phone, and find someone who could come to the house between four and six and fix the garbage disposal. *How do I pay him? Hurry up the next plane is fifteen minutes early.* "Aloha, welcome to Hawaii."

Cody and Pat joined a forced march, down an escalator, down a long corridor, with crying babies . . . short tempers . . . all in search of the jitney bus that would take them to the Inter-island end of the airport.

Pat was dressed in his usual cut-offs, tee-shirt, and white canvas deck shoes. The flight from LAX had taken two double vodka-tonics for Cody; and a little over five hours. Cody had slept most of the way. It had been his first sleep in over twenty-four hours. It had been dawn before he had finally left Worden's, and by then he and the blind, broken man, who had once been handsome and young, had become friends. They had talked through the night and through the dark early hours of morning, of baseball and AIDS, of animal liberation and an old woman who was sure she had seen the ghost of Thelma Todd walking along the Pacific Coast Highway. Their conversation was, for the most part, inspired by the phone-in program that had come on after the baseball game. Worden told him he had called in to the program himself a few nights before to ask people to help find his little girl, but when they finally put him on the air he couldn't stop crying, and finally the host had yelled at him and made some rude remarks about drunks, and they cut him off.

And during the night, between phone-in topics and news and commercials, Cody had managed to get more information about the missing woman, her likes and dislikes and, as well as Worden could remember, what she and Marty had seen and done, the places they had gone to each day of their honeymoon. All this Cody elicited carefully with seemingly off-hand questions mingled into their conversation so as not to let Worden know his true purpose, and so as not to alarm him more than he already was. Cody made no mention of the break-in in the master bedroom.

Thunder rumbled across the Honolulu sky as they pushed their way onto the little bus.

"Whoever designed this airport just didn't have people in mind," Cody heard someone say with a certain humor. He thought it was the little man with the pixie smile who had squeezed into the seat across from Pat. Then the bus lurched to a start.

They waited in line for fifteen minutes to check in and receive their boarding passes for the flight to Kauai, and with still an hour to go before the plane took off, Cody found a coffee shop with a connecting bar. He bought Pat a soft drink and himself a double vodka-tonic . . . and then was surprised to discover he had no taste for a second.

The flight itself took twenty minutes. A blanket of dark clouds had been under them since they climbed out of Oahu, and so it wasn't until they had broken through those clouds in search of a landing that Cody got his first look at Kauai, and for a moment felt he was in a dream or a movie. He had never seen anything like it. The beauty captured him. The lush green island rose out of a sea of vibrant blues. Closer now, they saw stretches of white beach and beyond, giant fields of sugarcane moving gently and rhythmically with the breeze. They passed over a beachfront hotel; the landing strip was now in view.

"Gosh, look at the big grass," Pat said with amazement.

"It's sugarcane," Cody told him, and wished that Ann were here. For a moment he thought he was going to cry.

Unlike in Honolulu, the smallish Lihue Airport was crowded only with the passengers getting off the 737. Cody left Pat to wait for their luggage and went across to rent a car. Half an hour later, and five minutes from the airport, they spotted the Kentucky Fried Chicken they had been on the lookout for, and they turned left off of the highway and into the heart of the island's biggest town, which they found, to Pat's continuing amazement, only stretched a long block and a half. They passed a bookshop called The Garden Island Press, a Pizza Hut, a couple of car lots, an old movie theatre, and then the second landmark of their directions, a McDonalds, and Cody turned left again.

"It looks like something out of a Laurel and Hardy movie, except with palm trees," Pat said as they were passing the county building. It was an old and elegant cement structure with a red-tile Spanish style roof and a Greek-columned entrance facade

Cody smiled and realized the small-town island atmosphere had relaxed him.

"I'm Caleb Ho," the young man said, smiling and holding out his hand. He was dark and good-looking and at the moment was wearing an aloha shirt, shorts, and thongs. "Excuse the clothes; I'm on vacation this week and they weren't able to find me until an hour ago. If I had known earlier I would have met you at the airport . . ."

"That's alright," Cody said. He was less than impressed. *The kid looks like he ought to be on a poster encouraging people to come to the island,* he thought. "You're the investigating officer on the Greens' disappearance?"

The young Hawaiian's eyes seemed amused. "I was the first detective brought in. Later on, of course, a lot of the guys got involved. But I'm still coordinating all the information."

"I'd like to see what was left behind in their hotel room."

"I thought you might. I've got it ready for you,"

he said, and then he turned to Pat. "How about I fix you up with a soft drink and some magazines while your dad's looking through that stuff?"

"Sure, that'd be great," Pat said, after first darting a look to his father for approval.

"Third cubicle on your right," Caleb said, redirecting himself back to Cody. "I laid everything out for you."

Cody considered a moment and then moved off. Caleb and Pat watched until he had disappeared into the cubicle. Then the smiling Hawaiian said, "Come on," and Pat followed him through the complex of dull offices.

"You surf?"

"A little," Pat said. "I've got a boogy board, but it's at home."

"Well, if you're here long enough, I'll ask your dad if we can take off one day. I have a brother who's fourteen. He makes boards, does pretty good selling them, too. He won't mind lending you one for the day."

They had reached a waiting room. Caleb put some coins into the soft-drink machine. "Take what you want."

Pat made his selection and a can tumbled out.

"There's some magazines over there. You be okay if I leave you here awhile?"

"Sure," Pat said.

"Okay," Caleb said with a smile. "Then hang loose, huh?" He gave the boy the Hawaiian gesture of the loose fist with the thumb and little finger extended, but then saw the boy look confused. "You don't know what that means?"

"No."

Caleb grinned and repeated the gesture. "It's Hawaiian for hang loose . . . take it easy . . . relax. You try it.''

Pat did, a bit embarrassed. Caleb smiled. ''You got it . . . hang loose.'' He made the gesture again and then left the room.

In the third cubicle on the right, Cody felt nothing. He had been through the suitcases, the clothes, the assorted belongings of the missing couple, but he felt nothing. The fear and the sense of eternity he had felt back in California were missing here. Why? Because he was tired? Because everything here had been handled so much? Because it had been moved from the hotel room? It was odd, he thought, that he felt nothing, for after having gone through the items in the cubicle, he was almost positive that the same person who had broken into the house in California had been in the hotel room and been through these things, too.

''Find anything?''

Cody looked up to see the young Hawaiian in the doorway. ''Did you expect me to?''

Caleb considered and then, when he finally did speak, the ever-present smile faded a bit. ''I didn't know . . . I knew I couldn't find anything that seemed to make any sense, other than they just went hiking and then got lost, but that still doesn't explain what happened to their rental car.''

So there is a cop in there, Cody thought . . . *and better, one that admits it when he doesn't know everything.*

''Sometimes it's what you don't find that tells you what you need to know,'' Cody said.

The grin was back. Caleb was intrigued. ''What didn't you find?''

It was the question that Cody was waiting for. "First, tell me, how well are we going to work together?"

Caleb shrugged. "I've been told to help you any way I can."

"The missing girl's a camera nut," Cody said after a few moments, deciding that the young man was sincere. "There're a half dozen photo albums in her room back in California and a couple more boxes filled with pictures in her closet. The girl shoots everything . . . yet after spending five days of a honeymoon here, going to different places around the island every day, I can't find any evidence that she took a single shot. What's missing is photographs, or at least undeveloped rolls of film. They're not here or on your inventory list."

"That's because there weren't any," Caleb said. The smile was gone. He was unsettled by Cody's thinking. "Maybe she took whatever there was with her the day she disappeared."

"Maybe," Cody agreed. "But it doesn't make a lot of sense. Why haul around rolls of undeveloped film or photographs you've already had printed up?" And then he felt it . . . the same chill, the deep sense of fear. It was there for only a moment.

Caleb was looking at him strangely. "You alright?"

Cody knew he couldn't explain it to this young Hawaiian any more than he could to any of the others over the years. He was alone. Since the shooting, he'd always be alone. "There are two other possibilities," Cody went on. His voice was hollow, but he knew he couldn't do anything about it. "One is, someone broke into their room and took whatever film and photographs were there . . . "

"Jesus," Caleb said quietly.

For a moment Cody thought he saw fear in the young man's eyes. He waited until his voice was back to normal. "The other is, the photographs are waiting in some shop to be picked up after developing. If you could go through the phone book and show me the closest stores to the hotel that develop . . ."

"Let me check them; I'll know the people. It'll be easier."

Cody sensed the young man's discomfort. "You had no way of knowing she was a camera nut," Cody said, trying to let him off the hook.

Caleb tried a smile, but most of the fun was gone. "What tourist isn't? . . . I should have seen it, thought of it. Go on and check into your hotel; have a swim and a drink. . . . I'll be there in a couple of hours with the information."

This time it was Cody who smiled. He was beginning to feel comfortable with the young man. "Couple of other things to look out for . . . You're looking for photos put in by Martin or Caroline Green . . . but also, out of habit the girl may have forgotten and put them in under her maiden name."

"Right, I've got that here somewhere."

"The name's Worden . . . W-O-R-D-E-N."

"Anything else?" Caleb asked, now feeling like a schoolboy.

"Find out if anyone else has been asking about the photographs. If someone has actually picked them up, try to get a description."

Outside, it began to rain.

"Tell me," Cody asked as Caleb walked him and the boy through the police building, "what's the unofficial theory?"

"Drugs. There's a lot of stuff grown up in the

mountains, sometimes in the cane fields. We don't like to let the tourist board know, but it wouldn't be the first time someone has wandered into someone's crop and been killed for it.''

They moved outside now. Despite the rain, the air was warm and had the fragrance of flowers. Ann had always loved flowers. *Christ, I have to get a hold of myself,* Cody thought. But he didn't. Suddenly he was on the edge of the darkness again, and he could hear the deep fear calling for help. But why? Was it near? Was it because of Ann and the flowers? He was dizzy. He used the movement of getting into the car to hide it.

"What do you think?" Caleb asked.

Cody's ears were ringing, and then it began to subside. "I have a feeling it's not going to be that simple."

The heavens were opening up now. The tropical rains poured down on the young Hawaiian, making him look like a little boy standing in the shower. "See you at the hotel in a couple of hours," he said and smiled. "And don't worry about this . . . ." He meant the rain. "It'll be over soon."

Caleb sprinted back into the dull yellow police building. Cody backed up and then drove away into the sheets of grey rain.

Down the block, in his own rental car, the little man with the pixie smile watched and inhaled deeply as he touched the orange-glowing car lighter to his unfiltered Camel cigarette.

Chapter Five

The little man who was capable of the pixie smile
followed them to their hotel. He was exhausted, both
mentally and physically, and he had been afraid several times that he would lose them on the ten-minute
ride out from town. At one point it had been pouring
down so hard he couldn't see them at all. He had
momentarily panicked and stomped on the gas pedal
just as a giant cane truck had rumbled out onto the
highway in front of him as it crossed over to the
cane-field road on the other side. He had hit the
brakes, slid sideways, spun around, and nearly landed
in a drainage ditch . . . and then, as could happen on
the island, by the time he had straightened the car
out, the rain had dwindled to a fine drizzle. He drove
as fast as he could then. He dreaded the idea of
losing them, not because he wouldn't be able to find
them again—it was, after all, the only road around
the island—but because he was so tired, and there
would be a dozen or more hotels he might have to
check before he could sleep . . . for the man, Cody,
had to be dealt with. He was a sign of the growing
danger. It was so damn maddening. He had come so
far; he was so close; it was almost done, and then

that stupid little string had started to unravel. It never should have happened, but there it was, the unexpected he had always been afraid of. . . . He had tried to stop it first here on the island when he discovered it, then in the desperate flight to California . . . and now it had led to this. Cody, the ex-cop, here, looking for the missing couple. He couldn't let Cody find the hole, the mistake. Chances were no one would ever see it, but he couldn't take that risk, for what little he had learned about Cody in those frantic hours before the flight frightened him. And then he had spotted their car again, and he wondered if it was an accident that they were pulling into the same hotel the Greens had stayed at, and the fear inside him told him it wasn't.

The little man with the odd smile parked in a "no parking" zone. The sun was poking its way through the clouds. In the lobby, he leafed through some tour brochures while Cody and the boy checked in, and he wondered why a man like Cody would even care. The Greens were such boring assholes. She with that stupid high-pitched giggle, and photographs, always those damn snapshots . . . of everything. . . . Goddamn her camera, he almost said aloud in his anger . . . and shit, the husband wasn't any prize either, with his clammy body odor and cornball humor and endless baseball statistics. And the little man knew he found at least some satisfaction in what he considered the biggest joke of all . . . that they had really thought he was their friend.

Cody and the boy were moving now, suitcases and room key in hand, and the little man who was capable of a pixie smile stopped browsing through tour folders and followed . . . across a walkway overlooking the kitchen, down a long corridor with smiling tile frogs sitting atop room numbers. *Shit, does he know where he's going? How close he is?* The back of his neck was beginning to throb. Cody and the boy were moving past the stairwell, out of sight for a moment. When they came into view, the little man paused as if lost. *Shit, they're going in . . . the same room as the girl and her husband*. He remembered the big brown mole under her right breast and how hairy and disgusting it had looked on her fat body. Dammit, he couldn't let those jerk asshole Greens unravel everything, not now, not after all the planning, all the years and months the project had actually been in the works.

"Hi, you know where the ice machine is?"

The boy had come out of the room again just as the little man was passing it. The kid had an ice bucket in his hand and was so golden-tanned, his skin so smooth. The boy's appearance startled him.

"All the way down the hallway, I think," he said with his pixie smile, which always seemed to make everyone relax and inclined to like him, especially children.

The boy said, "Thanks," and moved away. The little man paused only a moment longer. Inside the room he could see Cody, shirt off, tanned, several scars, pouring a straight vodka.

The little man capable of a pixie smile found his way back to his car. He was right to have followed them. Cody had to be dealt with. But he realized now, it could be nothing overt, nothing that would draw police attention. But something to take him out of the action long enough for everything to be finished. It would be finished now, in the next few days. . . . Yes, Cody had to be dealt with, but not directly. Cuaresma. Yes, Cuaresma. He knew he couldn't

sleep until he had at least found Cuaresma. The little
man who was capable of the pixie smile had learned
a long time ago never to attack a strong man directly.
Always look for his weak spot and find a way at that.
In Cody's case it would be easy: the boy. The pretty
blond boy . . . and even as tired as he was, he
momentarily fantasized what it would be like to touch
him, hold him, caress him . . . and it made him think
of the other boy with warm arousal. The other boy,
oh, much smaller, but blond and pretty and so easy
to love; the other boy he had buried in the back yard
in Eagle Rock.

Cody sat alone in the room for almost thirty minutes but felt nothing other than a vague uneasiness.
This had been their room, but how many guests ago?
How many laughters? And parties? And maybe even
more honeymoon nights? He hadn't know what to
expect by asking for this room, but it was worth a
try, a try he had thought was going to pay off when
they first entered the room. Even during their approach down the hallway he had seemed to sense
something . . . and then it had all gone, leaving only
the vague sense of uneasiness.

With the ice cubes that were melting now he had
two more vodkas, showered, and then moved down
to the pool area below their window. Pat waved,
smiled, and dove off the pool's waterfall and swam
over to him. Caleb Ho had been right, Cody thought.
The sky was deep blue again, with only occasional
puffs of white clouds. The last of the sun was coming
through the palm trees. Beyond the pool area was a
lagoon that seemed to stretch the width of the hotel
grounds, and beyond the lagoon a string of cottages
made to look like modern grass huts, and all set

among rows and rows of coco palms. The aroma of flowers was in the air here also, and the beauty of the place was startling and tranquil for him. *A place where dreams are made,* he thought, and he felt he didn't belong here . . . not without Ann . . . for without Ann he was alone. Raw. Alone. A hunter and fighter in a world that seemed ever increasingly violent, a world with vanishing rules and decency and sense. He had taken her hand and tried to leave that world behind, and ever so briefly they had . . . and then she had gone and he was alone again.

"You ought to come in, Dad; the water's great."

He had half-considered a swim, which was why he had put on trunks . . . but not now. "Maybe later. Buy you a Coke?"

"No thanks. Maybe later," the boy said with a certain sense of disappointment, and Cody knew that the boy knew that the offer of a Coke had been motivated by his father's need of a drink.

Three young Japanese couples giggled past, each couple wearing matching tee-shirts. It was almost seven o'clock.

"Can I help you?"

He had reached the pool bar and sat down. "Joe" was the name on the bartender's nametag. He was Polynesian-brown, smiling and wearing the hotel's blue and white aloha shirt.

"Double vodka-tonic."

"Just get in?" Joe asked, making conversation as he made the drink.

"That's right. Staying in Kai I."

"Oh," Joe said and seemed to lose a bit of his smile before he put the drink down in front of Cody. "You want to put this on your room?" he asked, meaning the drink charge.

"Is that what the Greens did? Charge to their room?" Cody asked.

Joe looked thrown off balance; Cody pressed on. "I came from L.A. to look for them."

Comprehension dawned on Joe's face. "Oh, I see. . . . You a cop?"

"Ex-cop. Just doing this for a friend."

Joe started to wipe glasses as he talked. "The Greens were nice people. Usually came out here a little earlier than this every day. You know, after touring around the island or shopping or whatever they had done that day. She'd go swimming, have a few wines. He never did, swim or drink."

"They talk a lot to other people?"

"Mr. Green, he was funny. Sometimes he'd talk to anyone who'd talk about baseball. Boy, that guy knew everything about it, batting averages, pitchers, everything. Then, other times, he would just sit there by himself and write in a notebook. He was a writer, you know."

"The people he talked to, was there anyone special? Anyone he talked to regularly?" Cody asked.

Joe thought for a moment. "Nah, you know, just folks who'd come down for a swim or some sun . . . or a drink."

"So most of them would be in pool clothes?"

"Most, but not all."

Cody considered the answer and then asked, "Do you get to know most of your customers?"

He'd found a source of pride within Joe. "Oh, I try. It can be pretty hard; some folks only stay two or three days, but I try to learn my customers' names. It makes them feel good, huh? Like the aloha spirit."

"Then between those in the swimsuits and your

regular customers," Cody said, "you'd know pretty much who was a guest or not?"

"I guess so."

"What I'd like to know, then, is if you ever saw the Greens talking to anyone who wasn't a guest here."

Joe furrowed his brow and after a couple of moments shook his head. "That's a tough one. I mean the time they came out is a real busy time of day for me, you know?"

"Hey, Joe."

The bartender glanced with a smile at the source of the voice at the end of the bar, a couple in their seventies who were settling onto a pair of stools.

"Just another day in paradise," the old man called out with a toothy grin. It was obviously a familiar greeting from the pair, who were wearing matching Hawaiian prints, she in the muumuu, he with a colorful shirt above his white polyester slacks.

"That's right, Mr. Jackson. Two Mai Tais?"

"Rightyo Joe," Mrs. Jackson chimed in, sounding like she had already had several.

The bartender started to make their drinks.

"Just warmer-uppers," the man said. "We're invited to the cocktail party tonight."

"That's great, Mr. Jackson. You and the Mrs. will have a great time," Joe said. He checked his watch and announced last call, and it was several minutes before he got back to Cody with a fresh double.

"How about it? Remember anyone yet?"

"I'm sorry, no," Joe answered. "I was thinking about it while I was serving those other folks, and I kept thinking that there was something . . . but I just can't call it up, you know?"

"Keep trying. You know where to find me if you do."

"Sure."

Joe started to total out the register, which was next to Cody.

"Tell me, what do you think happened to the Greens?" Cody asked as he signed the check.

"I wish I knew," Joe answered. "My best guess is, they just got lost on the hike, you know, over a cliff or something."

"That doesn't explain the car."

"Yeah, I know . . . but my guess is some kids grabbed it for a joy ride and they ran it off another cliff or just left it in a cane field."

"Am I too late for a Coke?" The pool water dripped off of Patrick. His smile was always engaging, but now seemingly more so with his left eye turning in ever so slightly as it did when he was tired. His voice, which hadn't changed yet, had a certain tremble of naiveté that was natural to him. And it was part of his charm and uniqueness that he was a boy totally without wiles.

"Your boy?" Joe asked.

Cody nodded.

"I'm closed, so it's against the rules," Joe said with a sense of conspiracy as he filled a glass first with ice, then with Coke. "So if you tell on me, I'll get in trouble."

"I won't," Pat said with sincerity.

Joe smiled and put the glass down in front of him. Cody made a move to pay, but Joe stopped him.

"On me," he said. "I liked the Greens."

Night came, and with it the beating of the ceremonial drum. A young Hawaiian man, stripped to the waist and wearing only a lavalava, ran through the field of coco palms with a flaming torch in his hand, and as he ran he whirled the torch through the air in a swooping circle over his head. Every time it touched the ground, a pod was set afire. Twenty, thirty, forty, finally eighty little fires danced and lit up the field of coco palms. All through this, a voice on a loudspeaker told of how the hotel was on ancient grounds that Hawaiian royalty had lived on and how the Hawaiians had never told time by day, but by the nights. Cody and Pat watched the show, and finally the young Hawaiian, still running, still with the torch in his hand, arrived at an outrigger and got in. Then, as it was paddled down the lagoon and as the drumbeats faded, the big crowd in the dining room applauded . . . as did those outside.

Cody and Pat were outside with a number of other onlookers, many who had come from other hotels just to view the show. It was a small sea of bright muumuus and shirts and white polyester pants, and it was a happy crowd, relaxed and romantic. Not far from them, three pigs turned on six-foot spits.

''So much for the house of bricks.'' Pat grinned.

The man named Cuaresma watched as Cody and the boy drifted back toward the lobby. Though no one paid particular attention to him, he did not fit in at the hotel. He was short and stocky and sported a diamond on his left nostril. His grey work pants were grimy, his aloha shirt faded. He broke wind and crumbled an aspirin tablet in his fingers and then tried to pack it onto the tooth that was hurting so damn bad.

Pat was asleep on the floor in front of the television when the phone rang. Cody had dozed off himself. He was overtired and had had a strange and disturbing dream. He couldn't make sense of it; he only knew it had something to do with Ann.

He answered the phone on the second ring, still half asleep.

"Yes."

"Sergeant Cody?"

"Yes," he said again, coming awake, recognizing Caleb Ho's voice.

"It's Caleb Ho . . ." His voice was shaky. "I'm in the lobby. I've got what you wanted. The photographs."

Chapter Six

"Sorry I'm late," Caleb said as Cody sat down.

It was a little past ten thirty, and they were in the hotel's lounge bar. Like the main restaurant, it had an open-air window that ran the length of the room and looked out on the lagoon. A group of four Hawaiian musicians were playing reasonably contemporary music. Several couples, in colorful tourist attire, were dancing romantically.

A waitress seemed to have followed Cody to the table. The troubling, jumbled dream he had been having about Ann when he was awakened was still with him, and having slept, he had lost his taste for alcohol. He ordered a grapefruit juice. Caleb ordered a light beer.

"Elvis Presley used to stay in one of those," the young Hawaiian said, referring to the "grass-hut" bungalows on the other side of the lagoon.

Cody had the dull headache of a mild hangover. The world wasn't quite in focus. *What the hell is he talking about?*

"He used to stay here all the time," Caleb went on, smiling. "Sometimes when he didn't want anyone knowing where he was. He even made a picture here once."

"Is that right?" Cody replied, maintaining his link with the ongoing world around him. The night air had been cool when he came down from the room, but now he was feeling warm.

"Yeah, I don't remember it. I was only a little keiki then, but my dad was in the movie as one of the extras at a big wedding, only I think they cut his part out."

"That's show biz, huh?" Cody said dryly, trying to regain control of the conversation.

"Yeah," Caleb said. His voice was tight.

It was then that Cody sensed something was wrong. The young Hawaiian was avoiding the moment. Cody's headache was beginning to throb, and in the cool night air he was sweating. "You said you had the photographs."

The waitress brought the drinks, and Caleb's voice was artificially cheery, and suddenly Cody came out of the fog. He was hot and sweating, sitting in an open room with a couple of dozen people in darkened shadows behind him.

"They even made some *Fantasy Island*s here, with Ricardo Montalban and that little guy."

Cody could wait no longer. The hairs on the back of his neck were tingling; he could feel himself being closed in on. He leaned over the table with one hand beneath it; his words were hard and icy. "I've got a Walther automatic pointed at your belly. If you've set me up, you're dead, right here, right now."

Caleb went pale. He looked like someone had kicked him in the testicles. He had a hard time finding the breath to speak, and before he did, Cody knew that he had misread the situation.

"I haven't set you up for anything. I'm only trying to help."

"Why the runaround?"

"I just thought I'd try to find something out before I gave the pictures to you," Caleb said weakly.

Cody settled back in his chair. "Don't ever play games with me. If you want to know something, just ask it straight out."

The last words came out rather strangely, for Cody's gaze had drifted . . . Ann was on the dance floor. His head was pounding again, and he was starting to feel dizzy. She was in a bright-green-and-black dress, and the man with her wore a matching shirt and white polyester pants. He was balding and looked like Cody's childhood memory of Adlai Stevenson. Cody was on his feet now. The band was playing "Picnic," and every turn and every look, the closer he got across the polynesian room, it was her. He was on the dance floor now, and people were moving awkwardly around him, staring at him. The bandleader was looking to the bar for help. There was no doubt where Cody's attention was trained, and finally the 1952 and 1956 Democratic candidate for president stopped and turned his gaze on him.

"Is there something you want?"

And in that moment he saw that it wasn't Ann. The eyes were the wrong color, and now, this close, it didn't look like her at all.

"I'm sorry," Cody said, his voice echoing in his ears. "I thought you were someone I knew. I'm sorry." Then there was nothing else to be said. He wheeled and moved off the dance floor; past Caleb at the table, straight to the bar, which was empty of customers but had two bartenders and several waitresses to serve the room.

"Double vodka-tonic."

The bartender seemed unsure for a moment and

then mixed the drink and brought it to him. A moment later Caleb joined him and dropped three packets of photos on the bar in front of Cody. Cody consumed half his drink in one pull before he glanced at the packets and then, finally, turned to look at the young Hawaiian. The cool night air was drying the sweat on his forehead, the pounding was almost gone.

"I'm sorry about what happened at the table."

"It's alright," Caleb said.

Cody finished the drink and signaled for another one. "The lady on the dance floor, I thought I knew her."

"Think it was your wife?" Caleb asked timidly.

So they had warned them about the crazy man they were sending out, the great detective who couldn't even save his wife, find her, who couldn't even save himself.

"Yeah," Cody finally said as the barman brought his next double.

"Jesus, I'm sorry," Caleb said, and his voice quivered, as if he shared a piece of Cody's pain.

Cody sipped his drink, and neither of them spoke for several minutes. A tiny Filipino couple, ancient, and impeccably dressed in formal clothes, appeared on the dance floor. Their movements were as perfect as their clothes, and soon the other couples backed away and let the tiny, smiling islanders enjoy their place in the spotlight.

"If it makes you feel any better, I have a Walther with me, but it's upstairs and packed in a suitcase."

Caleb grinned. It was a genuine grin, and Cody now knew why he reminded him of Patrick.

"If you promise not to tell anyone . . . I'll tell you, I almost messed my pants over there when you said you had a gun pointed at me."

They both grinned, genuine grins. On the dance floor, the ancient couple got a round of applause. The bandleader introduced them as regulars who lived nearby. More applause.

"What did you want to find out before you gave these to me?" Cody asked, indicating the photographs. He was feeling better now, the heart rate slowing down. He was doing his job again.

"I wanted to know how you knew that someone else would be looking for these." There was no smile on Caleb's face. He wanted to learn from Cody.

"I didn't for sure," Cody said, and he opened the first packet of photos and started to look through them. "It seemed logical, and if someone had been, it finished a pattern . . . and now you're telling me someone was looking for them."

Caleb still didn't understand. "At three of the shops I checked . . . including the shop here at the hotel."

"Did anyone see the person asking for the photos?"

"No. The inquiries were made over the phone."

"Figures," Cody said. "When did the calls come?"

"As near as I can pin it down, the first calls asking about the pictures came two days after the Greens were missing."

"There was more than one call?" Cody had become alert, looking away from the photos, back to the young Hawaiian.

Caleb smiled. "I'm glad to see that something surprises you. The more I talked to those people in the shops, the more I got a spooky feeling. Each of the shops got a call from a man on the second day the Greens were missing. . . . A couple of days after that, they got a second call; a woman calling herself Mrs. Green, asking if her pictures were ready."

Cody absorbed the information for a moment and then started through the second packet of twenty-four shots. There had been nothing in the first group that had jumped out at him, only beaches, mountains, a lighthouse, a pair of boys fishing off a bridge . . . "But nobody had pictures for the Greens?" he asked abstractly.

"No," Caleb admitted with a blush. "It was like you thought; she put them in her maiden name . . . only I forgot to ask about Worden the first time; that's what took so long. I had to get a guy out of a party to come back and open his store."

Cody smiled slightly and sipped his drink, he appreciated the young Hawaiian's honesty.

"You said it was the end of a pattern," Caleb reminded. "What pattern?"

"The pattern is, someone is afraid of some of the photos that Mrs. Green took . . . and not just these, but others, too. And it stretches three thousand miles, from here to California." The second twenty-four snapshots were much the same, tourist spots, more beaches, a comical pose in front of a waterfall, an open-air shopping area overlooking the ocean, a geyser of water.

"Tell me about California," Caleb asked, sounding like a boy asking to hear a ghost story.

"I was in her room in California last night. While I was there I realized that someone had broken into it—broken into it after the couple had left on their honeymoon. What bothered me was I couldn't figure out what the thief had taken. There was money, jewelry, a T.V., and V.C.R. . . . all left behind. It wasn't until I went through her photo albums for the second time that I realized four snapshots had been removed."

"Jesus," Caleb said. "You mean pictures she'd taken before she came to Kauai?"

Cody nodded. "And whoever took them was cute about it. The girl was very methodical about the way she laid out her albums. The pictures that were taken were from several pages of a big picnic, church or community sponsored, something like that. . . . Instead of just taking the photos and leaving holes, the thief replaced them with pictures from other pages, other albums . . . they were all outdoor shots, but if you looked closely you could see they weren't from the picnic."

"But why?"

Cody shrugged. "Someone she knows. Someone she's photographed. Someone who doesn't want any connection with her to exist. . . . Any idea who these people are?"

He handed Caleb a half dozen photos of a group of people at the outdoor shopping area. The young Hawaiian squinted in the bar light and then recognized someone. "That's Evan Hannibal and his wife Lillian. She has a table she sponsors out there that sells coral necklaces and stuff like that to raise money for the whales or something."

Cody had thought there was something familiar about the tall white-haired figure, and looking closer now he recognized the man *Time* magazine had called "the Great American Poet" several years back. "Which is his wife?"

Caleb pointed to a handsome woman somewhere in her forties. Much younger than her elderly husband, she had striking long dark hair that was blowing freely with the wind and was wearing a lavender dress that seemed almost to glow against the deep blue of the Pacific behind her.

"What about the other people with them?"

Caleb squinted again. There was a lean, almost cadaverous-looking man who seemed hopelessly out of place in a huge Hawaiian shirt that looked like it could belong to the much bulkier Evan Hannibal. Near him was an elephantine woman who looked to be well into her sixties even with a head of flaming red hair and who, despite the sunny day evidenced in the picture and the shirt-sleeve attire of the others, was wearing a tweed suit. They all seemed to be in a good mood. A muscular, sandy-haired young man was laughing. Even the little man with the dark brown, neatly slicked-down hair had a smile on his face . . . a pixie smile.

"Look at this guy," Caleb said with a grin. "He looks like one of those cement elves that people put in their gardens."

Cody did look. "I've seen him before."

"Where?"

"I don't know. Somewhere recently. Do you know him?"

"No. This other guy, though," he said tapping the cadaverous figure, "I've seen him around. Last couple of years he's come with the Hannibals when they come to the island."

"How often is that?"

"Oh, two or three times a year. They stay a month or two at a time."

"How long have they been here this time?"

Caleb sighed and thought for a moment. "Couple of months at least. I remember they were here for the Fourth of July. They had a big ceremony at this hotel. Evan Hannibal was part of it, read one of his poems and all that."

Cody stared at the picture for a couple of moments. Nothing was adding up. "What about the other two?"

"The lady with the red hair, she's a friend of Lillian Hannibal's, even before the marriage to Hannibal."

"What do you mean?"

"Before she was Lillian Hannibal, she was married to a guy named Auerbach for a few years, until he died . . . the blond-haired guy," he said tapping the muscular, sandy-haired young man, "he's Mrs. Hannibal's stepson, Auerbach's son by his first marriage. He was only a teenager when his father died. . . . A few years after that she married Evan Hannibal, and they been coming back to the island several times a year ever since."

"They have a house here, then."

"Yeah, you could say that." The smile was still there, but with a hint of bitter sarcasm. "It's a place called 'Kamalani,' about fifty acres, it's own private beach that runs about half a mile . . . big rambling house with some guest houses, flower gardens that magazines come out to photograph about twice a year."

Cody decided to wait to explore the source of the bitterness. Instead, he studied the photographs again. The little man with the pixie smile troubled him, and then it came back. "He was on the plane today from Los Angeles . . . at least I think he was. I know he was on that little bus that takes you across Honolulu Airport. He made a funny remark about how whoever built the place didn't have people in mind."

"You can't think these people had anything to do with the Greens' disappearance."

"Why can't I?"

"Well, I mean . . ." Caleb laughed nervously. "He's Evan Hannibal. . . ."

"And she's Mrs. Hannibal." Cody finished the sentence for him. "You didn't seem so warmly disposed to them when you were talking about the house they're living in . . . what'd you call it?"

"Kamalani, and that's different," Caleb said and didn't disguise the fact that Cody had touched on a sensitive area, and then he tried to soften it with a smile that didn't quite work. "The Hannibals are some of the most respected people on the island, and I guess their houseguests would have to qualify that way, too . . ."

"Right," Cody said dryly and sipped his drink, then he handed the young man nine of the photographs from the first packet. "These all seem to have been taken at the same place."

Caleb studied them and after a moment nodded. "Anahola Beach."

"Doesn't look too crowded. See anyone in these shots close enough to recognize?"

Caleb looked again and finally shook his head. "No."

Cody selected four more photographs, these featuring the pair of boys fishing off the bridge. "I think we can eliminate these two. They look pretty dangerous, but I'd give them a pass."

Caleb wasn't enjoying the humor. Cody relented. "The rest of the roll is around a lighthouse. Like the beach shots, there's no one close enough to be recognizable. In fact, in all three rolls, the only people featured in any shots, besides the Greens themselves, are the Hannibals and friends."

Caleb considered and finally uttered the familiar, "Jesus."

"Maybe it's a mistake," Cody said. "Maybe the Hannibals and their friends have nothing to do with it. But someone was trying to get their hands on these pictures before us . . . and right now the Hannibals and friends are our only candidates. If they're as honest and upright as you think they are, they won't mind answering a few questions about a pair of missing honeymooners.''

Caleb finished his beer and signaled the bartender. ''Two more of what he's drinking.''

Cody smiled. ''Afraid of what your boss is going to say?''

''The thought had crossed my mind.''

''Get me the Hannibals' phone number and address; I'll do the rest. I'll be real polite and make an appointment.''

''It's not that easy, I'm supposed to . . .'' Caleb was talking before he was thinking, and now, not knowing how to get out of it, he just stopped.

Cody finished for him. He'd been there before. ''You're supposed to keep me under control, take me out, walk me through a trail the Greens were supposed to have disappeared on, and eventually put me back on a plane and send me home . . . only it doesn't work that neatly anymore, does it? You know it and I know it . . . but if you try to explain it to your boss he's liable to blow a gasket: Photographs? What the hell does that have to do with the missing couple? Not to mention that the Hannibals are the most respected people on the island and you don't want to harass them on some cockeyed scheme that this guy Cody cooked up . . . didn't they tell you even his own people think he's half crazy?''

Caleb sipped heavily from his double vodka-tonic, then coughed, gagging on it.

''Go home. Tell them I told you I was tired and wanted to rest a couple of days before I started looking for the Greens. . . . I'll find my own way to the Hannibals.''

"No, you won't," Caleb said after a moment. "The number's unlisted; it'll take a little digging. Can you wait until morning? If not we could probably go bang on the Hannibals' door now.''

Cody grinned. "Pat and I will be having breakfast across the way, about nine thirty. . . . What about your boss?''

"I don't want to think about that right now," Caleb said after some thought and a small smile. "See you in the morning." Ignoring the rest of his drink, he moved off into the night.

On the dance floor the ancient Filipino couple danced alone, and elegantly, to "Now is the Hour.''

Upstairs in Kai I, Cuaresma packed some more aspirin onto the aching tooth. The blond boy slept at his feet. Cuaresma knew what had to be done. His instructions were clear. The goddamn tooth was driving him crazy. Shit, the boy was stirring. Cuaresma backed to the wall. He knew if the boy awoke he'd have to kill him here, before he could cry out.

The last song had been played, the last dance, danced. The ancient couple in the impeccable formal wear had stolen into the night. Cody watched other couples strolling back to their rooms along the lagoon and he thought of Ann and the dream he had had earlier in the night, and it still troubled him and he didn't know why.

Chapter Seven

He slept the rest of the night without dreams and woke a few minutes before sunrise. Through the window near his bed the sky was soft blue and offered up a bouquet of gently stirring coco palms. He felt both relaxed and strange, and after a moment realized that he didn't have a hangover. He sat up.

"Hi," Pat said.

Cody had moved the boy onto the bed last night when he had come in, but now he was back lying down in front of the T.V. again, scrunched up with a blanket and pillow, watching cartoons and eating the last of the fruit in the basket the hotel had left in the room.

Cody felt good and knew it was more than just lack of a hangover. It was the tranquil picture out the window, the whole surroundings, the aroma of flowers in the air last night, the people he had met. Most had been friendly. Most had been smiling. Somehow they seemed to exist without the big city armor of anxiety and aggression.

"What about that swim?"

"Now?"

"Yeah," Cody answered in a mischievous tone.

"I'd rather not," Pat said with a yawn, "I'm tired."

"You're a wet blanket, is what you are," Cody said with a grin.

He swam twenty-nine laps before he gave up on his quest for fifty, and as he hung on to the side and caught his breath, he tilted his head back and looked up at the gently swaying palms and the blue balmy sky. He was the only one out in the early morning, and the world seemed his alone, and he wished Ann were here, that he could bring her here, that they could stay here and never have to go away . . . and now beyond the palms he saw that the rich greens stretched to a mountain. It was the Sleeping Giant, he remembered. Pat had told him the story on the drive out from town. The giant had been the great protector of the Menehunes, the island's legendary little people. But one day he had fallen asleep on top of the mountain just as invaders were sweeping onto the island. His little friends tried to wake him by throwing stones at him, but giant that he was, the stones they threw were only pebbles, and one caught in his throat, and he choked to death. The Menehunes buried him where he lay, and his profile can still be seen. Cody swam back to the shallow end under water and wondered in a desperate pang if he was to be a modern Sleeping Giant, lulled to sleep and unable to act at his time of greatest crisis . . . and suddenly he was angry that Ann wasn't here and angry that she had disappeared and angry that he had been so helpless. "God damn it," he hissed as his head broke the water, and a gardener who had appeared looked at him and then looked away and started to work.

*　　*　　*

They were driving through the town of Kapaa when he first sensed that they were being followed. Both sides of the main street were crowded with businesses, mostly in rundown one- and two-story buildings from the 1920's or earlier. He needed to be sure about his feeling. He pulled over in front of a park, on the other side of which waves were lapping up a small beach, and pretended to check a map. The old white convertible, which had pulled out of the hotel parking lot only seconds after they had, rumbled past. Then, a block later, it pulled into the parking area for a hardware store. It was a clumsy move. After some moments, a white-blond-haired man got out and moved to the trunk and opened it.

Cody pulled away from the park. He passed the white convertible but couldn't get a better look at the white-blond-haired man's face. The man was wearing an aloha shirt and light-colored slacks. A block later Cody turned left and started up a winding hill road. The houses they passed were small and pretty, many of them the same vintage as the buildings in the business section but much better cared for. Shrubs and brightly colored flowers were everywhere, and behind them the deep blue ocean grew ever larger as they climbed . . . and finally, moving around one of the curves near the crest, Cody spotted the white convertible starting up the hill.

Mass started at eight. The walls of the church were made from volcanic rock and reached up about ten feet to where there was an open window, which stretched around half of the building and could only be closed by dark brown wooden shutters. The roof was made of corrugated iron and was supported by exposed steel girders, on which families of birds had made their homes. The fact that they flew around and chattered during that service didn't seem to bother any of the parishioners. Cody had selected a pew where he could keep an eye on the road. The white convertible had rumbled past, belching smoke, as they had walked from the parking lot to the church.

It was a narrow road without much traffic, and from the church, which was situated in a natural hollow, it was impossible to see down it any distance, but he had to be alert. His mind was working. No one knew why he was on the island except Caleb Ho and, of course, the rest of the police force. Could he trust them? Were the police some how linked up with the missing couple? . . . with the burglary in California? . . . the searching of the room here? If they were, what chance would he have of staying alive if he started to unravel this case . . . ? And maybe he already had with the photographs last night, with asking to see the Hannibals. And then he remembered the little man with the elflike smile. He'd been at Honolulu, and he'd been in the photographs with the Hannibals. But how would he know who Cody was . . . what he was after? And then Cody realized that everyone was on their feet. The priest and altar boys and lectors were coming down the aisle now, and music was playing, and voices were singing about a Hawaiian Madonna. As Mass went on he kept an eye on the road and glanced about the church itself and he saw that the bandleader from last night was now leading the church group of musicians and singers. Then he realized what seemed odd to him. The music was pretty, actually melodic, and he wondered when the last time had been that he had enjoyed the music at Mass. His childhood? That long ago? They played and sang with obvious joy from the back of the Hawaiian church, and their instruments were mandolins and ukuleles and violins. . . . Who the hell were those people on the mainland who had taken over the music at Masses with their bad folk songs in a style outdated in the 1960's? Who were they with their guitars, and as he had seen recently, bongo drums . . . with their unsmiling faces, standing on the altar as if it were a stage?

"On the night he was betrayed . . ." The priest's words lept out at him in the middle of his thoughts. On the night he was betrayed. On the night he was betrayed, and he wanted to scream and strike out, but at who? Who had robbed him of her? Who had stolen her? Who was following him today in a white convertible . . . ? And he knew he was mixing all of his dark thoughts together, and he knew that they didn't mix and there would only be confusion.

Pat went to Communion. Cody remained in the pew. He couldn't bring himself to go. At first when Ann had been missing he had tried going every morning like she had so often. But there's only so much hope . . . there were only so many prayers . . . and so much damn despair. Behind him now they were singing about the Hawaiian Madonna again. The birds flew and chattered and tended their young, and the statues of Mary and Jesus and Joseph each had fresh flower leis around their necks, and he didn't go to Communion, as he hadn't gone for a couple of months now, but for the first time he felt ashamed.

They were eating eggs Benedict when Caleb arrived. He was in pale yellow slacks, a nicely pressed silk aloha shirt, and cream-colored shoes.

"You look like one of the guests," Cody said.

"My Evan Hannibal visiting clothes. My mother wanted me to wear a jacket and tie, but I compromised to this by promising to get his autograph for her,'' he said with a twinkle in his eye and then added with a certain pride, ''We have an appointment at Kamalani at twelve thirty.''

''Do they know why?''

''I was kind of vague.'' Caleb grinned. ''It was Mrs. Hannibal I talked to. I told her there were some people that we were looking for who had been near there, and I wondered if they wouldn't mind looking at a few pictures for us.''

''She seem uneasy at all?''

''She asked how her dear friend the chief was . . . and then said it would be much more convenient if we came by later in the week . . . but I was my normal charming self and told her we were anxious to get this cleared up and it shouldn't take more than a few minutes . . . and finally she said that of course she'd be more than happy to give any assistance . . . but I had a feeling she wasn't happy, let alone more than happy about it.''

Cody glanced at his watch.

''Before you get to thinking we have a lot of time, we don't,'' the young Hawaiian said. ''I thought you might like to see the place where the pictures of the Hannibals were taken . . . and then I kind of promised your boy that I'd get my brother to take him surfing, if it was okay with you, and I kind of got it set up . . . I mean, they're sort of waiting for him.''

Cody glanced at Pat, who had suddenly brightened. He and Caleb looked like a couple of school boys in on a scheme. ''Can I, Dad?''

Cody managed a grin. ''I'll think about it while you get changed.'' He handed the boy the room key.

''I'll be right back,'' Pat said, trying to impress with his efficiency.

"Brush your teeth."

"I will." And he was off.

Cody watched the boy until he disappeared out the far end of the dining room.

Caleb was still selling. "It'll be real safe. I know the beach they're going to, and there's life guards . . . and my sister will be there, too."

Cody turned to him; his eyes were cold. "Think hard . . . it's important. Anybody at the police station know that Patrick is going surfing with your brother today?"

Caleb's face clouded. Finally he said a simple, "No."

"Then he can go." Cody softened. "I appreciate your looking out for him like that."

"No problem . . ."

"I shouldn't have brought him. I should have left him with his older brother . . . I was followed this morning, on the way to church."

"Jesus. By who?"

"Man, very blond, white convertible, about fourteen or fifteen years old. Didn't get the license. The point is, besides you and the rest of the department, who knows I'm here, and why . . ."

"I don't know . . . no one." The young Hawaiian seemed rattled.

"Don't worry." Cody smiled. "You passed last night. Besides, you don't have to have anyone follow me, you already know where I'm going."

Caleb seemed relieved, then remembered and pulled out one of the photographs of the Hannibals and friends at the open-air shopping area and handed it to Cody. "I've got a couple more names to go with these. . . . The red-headed lady is . . ." He hesitated long enough to straighten out some scribbled notes, then grinned as he looked back to Cody. "My aunt works for the island paper, writes the society section . . . Carmel Beecher Van Kueren. Like I told you last night, she's a friend of Mrs. Hannibal's going way back to even before she was Mrs. Hannibal . . . anyway, she writes books about the secrets of the pyramids and cosmic forces of the universe, stuff like that. Every once in a while when she's on the island she gives lectures. My aunt said she went once but couldn't make sense out of anything she said."

Cody considered. "Does she make her living this way? Or does she sponge off the Hannibals?"

"I don't know. My aunt says she's pretty well respected for that kind of thing . . . and Mrs. Hannibal's supposed to be big in that stuff. The Van Kueren woman has a church somewhere in Los Angeles, 'The Spiritual Institute of Cosmic Teaching.' " He was having a hard time reading his writing. "That's about all on her anyway."

"Who else?"

"This guy." He pointed to the lean, cadaverous-looking man in the too-large aloha shirt. "Name's Nelson Hobart. For years he used to have a pretty famous boys' choir, appeared in movies, on T.V., stuff like that, the Hobart boys' choir . . . but as far as my aunt knew, for the last four or five years he hasn't done anything but live with the Hannibals . . . both here and in California. When he first started coming over with them, there was talk he was going to organize a new choir that would tour with Hannibal while he gave his readings . . . but nobody talks about that anymore. Now he's just writing his memoirs."

"What about our little friend with the elflike smile," Cody asked.

"No luck . . . my aunt didn't know him. She hadn't even seen him before."

"You did good," Cody finally said after staring at the pictures for several more minutes, then added, "We have five out of six: the Hannibals, her stepson, Van Kueren, and Mr. Boystown . . . all we have to do now is to find out who our elf is."

"You really still think the Hannibals and their friends have something to do with the Greens' disappearance?" The note of incredulity was back in Caleb's voice.

"I told you last night, I don't know . . . but right now they're all we have to hang on to . . . them and the man in the white convertible that was following me, even if he did disappear once we went into church."

"He didn't follow you back?"

"No," Cody said, but his mind was re-examining all the pieces, turning them upside down and sideways, only there weren't enough pieces yet to make any sense . . . photographs carefully stolen in California, more photographs pursued here, the Greens vanishing, their room searched here, and now the man in the white convertible.

Caleb offered to drive, but Cody said he didn't want to confuse anyone, so they took his rental. It didn't take long to prove his notion. They were just crossing the bridge over the Wailua River when he spotted the white convertible in the rearview mirror, and in that moment he knew that the Greens were dead. He could feel the cold; it was a dark and heavy pressure on him, dirt or rocks; a dog was barking, a small one, Pekingese, something on that order . . . then the sound gave way to an air horn, and Caleb yelled and pulled the wheel toward him and the rental swerved out of the way of an oncoming tourist bus.

"Sorry," Cody managed.

"You want me to drive?"

"I'll be alright," he said. But his hands were shaking, and he pulled over to the side and got out and made his way into the cane field. He was hot and sweating. His ears were ringing, and he threw up everything in his stomach . . . and he was crying now and moved further into the cane because he wanted to be alone. He couldn't let Patrick find him; he had to be alone . . . because he knew now it wasn't the Greens he had seen cold and dead, it had been Ann.

Chapter Eight

Voices.

"Dad?"

"Sergeant Cody?"

The spider was the size of his fist. It looked like a giant daddy longlegs.

"Dad, where are you?"

The sun was hot, the day growing sticky. He was up to his ankles in wet red dirt. The spider was moving now, up the green stalk of sugar cane that reached well above his head. He looked at his watch; sweat stung his eyes. As near as he could figure, he'd started his flight twenty minutes ago. Why? It seemed so empty now, like a dream slipping from memory, a dream that no longer made sense.

Voices. Voices.

"Patrick, don't you get lost on me," the young Hawaiian's voice was beginning to lose its composure.

"I won't."

"What do you think happened to him?"

"Sometimes. . . ." The boy's voice dropped off, then after a few moments he finished, "Sometimes he thinks about my mom."

He had seen her cold and dead. . . . He'd felt it

inside of him. The little dog barking. The little dog barking. He had seen her face . . . but . . .

"Dad?" Patrick's calling voice was closer now.

He stood silently, his feet deep in red mud, the spider perched above him. All of his energy, all of his emotion had been taken out of him, and now he began to feel them build up again. Seeing her like that . . . it was what he had been afraid of all these months, what he had been running from, what he had been drinking for . . . to block out thought, realization of what he knew, what had to be true . . . but why here? The question screamed inside his head, and then he knew. It was this island. Lush, green, and tranquil, it was this island. He and Ann had never been here, but it reminded him so much of her. After so many months he had started to relax, to let his guard down . . . and he had forgotten to be afraid of the silence.

"Hi, Dad." Patrick was standing next to him wearing his cut offs and tee shirt, white canvas deck shoes now covered with red mud. Cody had the urge to cry but didn't. He knew he was regaining control.

"Hi, Pat . . . I'm sorry, I wasn't feeling well."

"It's okay."

". . . See my friend," Cody said, indicating the spider.

"Wow."

"They can't hurt you." The young Hawaiian had joined them quietly, coming up behind Patrick. He had taken his shoes and socks off and had rolled his slacks above the knees.

"You've been through these fields before," Cody said.

Caleb grinned. "I've played in these all my life, since I was a little keiki. I used to collect these guys too, but my little sister, she was scared, so I had to let them all go.''

As he spoke he reached out his hand and nudged the giant spider until it left the stalk and crawled onto and up his arm.

"Oh gross," Patrick said and meant it.

The young Hawaiian laughed.

They went back to the hotel so Cody could change his slacks and shirt, and not a word was spoken of the sudden detour. Instead, Caleb talked of surfing and got Patrick to talk about the surfing he used to do in California, most of which was when they lived in Playa Del Rey.

"Is that near the beach?"

"Right on the beach. We used to own a duplex there before we sold it to buy the boat. We used to live upstairs, and the guy we rented out to on the bottom, he used to write for T.V., *Magnum, Moonlighting,* all those shows.''

They passed through Lihue ten minutes after leaving the hotel. There was no sign of the white convertible. It didn't make sense. Cody wondered if anything would ever make sense again.

Their ride took them through a series of swaying cane fields and tropical forests and picturesque little towns, and Cody's mind drifted back to the blind Navajo woman in Flagstaff almost nine years before. He had found her foul-smelling, drinking in a cheap bar near the railroad tracks. She knew who he was when he sat down, and she laughed at him and told him he felt dirty being there, and stupid, and then she had asked who had sent him to her, and then answered the question before he could. "Trapper, that silly soft man.''

Trapper was a professor of parapsychology at UCLA. Cody had been working with him since a couple of weeks after the shooting . . . the night he had been dead . . . the night of terror, almost eight months earlier. Cody had been back on the job almost half that time, but he was still trying to cope with the "gift" that the shooting had left behind, still trying to cope with sanity.

"Put your hands on my eyes." Her accent was heavy, her words slurred from drink. Merle Haggard was singing on the jukebox, and another Indian, a fat man with a baby face, about thirty, started to throw up on the floor halfway down the bar. The customers were all Navajo, seven of them, all drunk. It was two o'clock in the afternoon, the fifteenth of the month. They were drinking their bi-monthly government checks.

"Put your hands on my eyes, God damn you. You don't want to touch me, but you need what I can tell you. Maybe I make you do more. Maybe I make you make love to me in the back of Jimmy's truck."

Others laughed. Cody put his hands on her eyes. Her body odor was worse than he had first thought.

"You want to cry," he said quietly.

She belched and was angry. "You not supposed to tell me, I tell you."

He saw a little Indian girl, about three.

"I'm sorry," he said. She was very pretty. "I'm sorry for you."

"God damn you, bastard, God damn Trapper, soft bastard." She pouted and finished her drink and told him she wanted a beer, and a whiskey and Coke. He ordered it for her. She drank the beer down, still pouting, and finally spoke without turning to him.

"How did you get hurt? Bad pain in head. I see

gunfire. Big orange fire.'' The words came out like a string she was pulling, never knowing how far it would reach.

"I was shot in the back of the head. Left for dead," he said. The words hurt to say, but he had to say them, face them as often as he could until it wouldn't hurt anymore.

She drank half of her whiskey and Coke. "I see you on your knees, hands tied behind you . . . very bad men . . . When you wake up, long time . . ."

"Four days. The bullet cracked my skull but didn't go in, went around inside my scalp."

"Four days, and then you wake up and you see things."

She didn't talk for several minutes. The bartender splashed the floor with water and then squeegeed it and the vomit out onto the sidewalk. The baby-faced man was drinking a beer.

She turned to Cody and put her hands on his eyes. She held them there for several moments and then pulled them down and asked for another beer. He ordered it for her. "You very lucky," she said. "You see very little." She laughed, but there was no humor, only a mocking of herself. "You see little, only sometimes you see a leaf; I see the tree. Sometimes you see a bird; all the time I see the sky . . . you afraid you crazy; I want to die. All time I see people mad; I see people gonna die; I know when people gonna shit their pants . . . Old David over there, Old David, he going to shit his pants; he thinking about it; he too drunk to go to toilet. I try to make breakfast for my husband. I used to have husband, handsome man. . . . But after I start to see things all different thoughts come into my head, never stop, like I get ten radio stations all at once in my head. I can't think; I can't make my husband breakfast; he call me fat crazy pig. . . . All these things I see, they never stop; that's why I drink all the time I got money; that's why soft Trapper want to make studies with me. So you come to me for help, only how can I help you? I live in hell.''

"Does drinking help?''

"Sometimes . . . Only can drink when I have money.''

"What else helps?''

". . . Anything to stop the silence so you can't think. T.V., radio, loud . . . all night, even when you sleep.''

She was crying now. He ordered her another whiskey and Coke. "If I see only what you see, I laugh; I still have my husband. You see only little, only sometimes. I see everything. You see only shadows.''

He left her long enough to put money in the jukebox and think. Several more customers had come in, all Navajo. There was a black-velvet painting of J.F.K. over the bar. The bartender was beefy and white, with a short-sleeved checked shirt and neatly parted thinning hair.

"Can I ask you one more question?''

"Old David shit his pants. Look, I bet you can see it on the floor.''

He could.

"You want to know about my baby girl. How come I know so much I can't save her life. Because of all the things you see, you can never trust any of them . . . they might only be part of what is going to happen, or did, or maybe it was stopped.''

"But your own little girl?''

"Worst of all, can never trust what you see for people you love. Too much in your head already about them. Too much thoughts, what you want, what you are afraid of . . . it gets all turned around. Never know. Never trust.''

Never know. Never trust. Caleb had swung the car off one two-lane highway and onto another and immediately into a tunnel of hundred-foot trees that stretched for at least a mile. He had seen Ann dead, cold and dead in a dark place, somewhere nearby a little dog barking. Never know. Never trust. The drunk, blind Navajo woman's words were all he had left.

Chapter Nine

"You must be our young Inspector Ho." Lillian Hannibal's voice carried with the confidence of a rich woman dealing with a tradesman, genial but firm, smiling but not to have her patience tried. They were moving toward her across a pale lawn that stretched the better part of an acre from the elegant white frame house to the secluded half-moon beach. A hundred yards up, a cluster of banana and palm trees decorated the banks of a small river, which emptied into the same Pacific bay, and beyond, in all directions, there were no other homes to be seen. Kamalani was a private island on an island, with the ocean at its front, and as a backdrop, giant banyan trees and patterned gardens with bubbling fountains and blossoms of white and gold and bright reds and blues . . . and all this was layered symmetrically into the gently climbing slopes of the property until, abruptly, a mountain, with huge craggy fingers and in its own electric emerald hues, shot straight up. Near the top, where the piercing blue of the sky jumped out again, a silent waterfall fell.

Here, nearer the house, a white trellis covered with scarlet- and champagne-colored bougainvillea bordered a patio half the size of a basketball court. And there on the patio was the Great American Poet himself, surrounded by his faithful entourage and set off by larger-than-life marble statues . . . Michelangelo's David, Venus de Milo, and a half dozen other unclothed Romans and Greeks Cody didn't know by name. Among the still living, he noted Carmel Beecher Van Kueren with her enormous figure and bright red hair. The cadaverous Nelson Hobart sat alone, away from the main group, his hands upraised as if conducting an invisible boys' choir. In the center, of course, his fine white-gold hair playing gently in the breeze, was Evan Hannibal. He sat at an umbrella table, as if posed, listening to the man nearest him. The speaker had tufted grey-and-black hair and wore a three-piece suit. Close by, a moon-faced man in a salmon leisure suit listened intently. Missing, Cody noticed, were Mrs. Hannibal's sandy-haired, muscular stepson . . . and the little man with the pixie smile.

"Welcome to Kamalani," Caleb said for only Cody to hear. "Once upon a time it belonged to a Hawaiian king who, thinking it was the most beautiful spot on the island, gave it to his people."

"They seem to have lost a bit of their control of it," Cody said wryly.

The smile returned to Caleb's lips.

Twenty minutes before driving past the "Private Property" and "Trespassers Will Be Prosecuted" signs, they had dropped Patrick off at Caleb's house. The young policeman still lived with his mother, two younger brothers, and two sisters. It was a small well-worn house in a neighborhood of small well-worn houses. An overgrown hibiscus crowded the red dirt driveway where the aging family station wagon resided, and there had been a scratchy, fat dog named Bambi and an old tire hanging from a pine tree branch. The walls of the house, like the church's, were made out of volcanic rock. "All the houses around here were originally built for cane workers," Caleb had told him. "The volcanic rock was the cheapest material they could get; luckily it also turned out to be the strongest."

They paused now as they reached the white Rolls Royce. Lillian Hannibal was almost on top of them. She was in a silk Muumuu-style dress that was obviously tailor made. The colors were pastels, dominated by shades of lavender and soft purples. Around her neck, surrounded by diamonds, she wore a large cut Amethyst. The purple stone caught Cody's eye; it had almost a rose tint to it.

"And you would be Sergeant Cody, all the way from Los Angeles," she said with a hint of irritation.

She was laced with expensive perfume, dressed and jeweled for the big scene. *But why?* Cody wondered. *For us? Or is she always like this?*

"Right on both counts," Caleb answered Mrs. Hannibal. Try as he may, Cody knew the young Hawaiian was intimidated by the rich woman.

"And you are Mrs. Evan Hannibal," Cody said, trying to take control of the conversation.

But she had no intention of letting him and instead fixed her eyes on Caleb as she indicated the group on the patio: "As you can see, and as I warned you, we are having quite a full afternoon. . . . I finally got through to one of your superiors, though apparently it didn't do any good. . . . He told me what you are supposed to be helping Sergeant Cody with. . . . He was going to try and stop you from coming out here." She paused long enough to sigh with impa-

tience. "Since he obviously didn't, I will assure you
as I assured him that none of us here at Kamalani
know anything about the missing honeymoon couple
. . . frankly, why you should have thought so in the
first place is beyond me . . . but now that you have
come out here, satisfied your curiosity, I would ask
that you now leave as quietly as you came."

She was doing her best to end the audience before
it began. The firm smile never wavered, and Cody
knew what she reminded him of now—a nurse, a
head nurse who is only happy with complete authority and control.

"The photographs in the paper weren't very clear,"
Cody said. "I wonder if you might look at a couple I
have."

Her eyes went to him. The anger in her voice was
cold. "I thought I just told you . . ." But she saw it
was no use. Her words trailed off. Cody had the
photographs out, showing them to her—the wedding
shots. She couldn't miss them; they were the big
ones, the eleven by fifteens. The plump daddy's girl
was all grown up and still a bit awkward in her white
gown, but somehow the smile was radiant, and she
was everyone's little girl.

Lillian Hannibal glanced at the photos quickly and
tried to look away, and then couldn't take her eyes
from them for several moments. "No. . . . As I said
before, I've never seen them."

But in those flickering moments Cody sensed a
soft spot. Instinct chased it. "That's odd. A day or
so before they disappeared you were looking right at
them."

Lillian Hannibal paled. "I don't know what you
mean."

"Don't you?"

For a moment he thought she might split open, or faint, or cry. He didn't know why or what she might have to hide, but as a cop, over the years, he had questioned a lot of people, seen the same look a lot of times . . . and apparently some things never changed. Even here in Alice's Wonderland, with giant statues and cascading waterfalls, she was lying . . . and as soon as he knew it, he felt it again . . . again he was on the edge of eternity. The feeling was not as strong as before, not as strong as it had been in the girl's room, or even outside the police station. But it was there, with the deep fear, calling for help.

"No," Lillian Hannibal said finally, her strength creeping back. He had let precious seconds slip by. In the hot Hawaiian sun, he was cold. He couldn't let her get away. He had to refocus his mind before the moment was gone. . . .

"But they took these," he said and showed her the photographs taken by the Greens at the open-air market.

Now it seemed she was teetering on the edge again. She took the photos and examined them. It was several moments before she spoke, and when she did, authority, or at least the facade of it, was fighting to return. "They're at Spouting Horn. I have a table there to raise money for the Marine Animal Protective League."

But something about her tone said she was scrambling for solid ground . . . why? Cody pressed by saying nothing, just staring at her inquisitively. Suddenly he realized that the sense of eternity and the crying fear were gone . . . only a memory now . . . and then he wondered if it had been real a moment ago, or was it just something he had wanted to be there. And once again he wondered if he was crazy. Why was he badgering this woman? She was prominent and famous. Her husband was more prominent and more famous. . . . No . . . no, he wasn't crazy, at least not completely. She was lying. He knew that. He had to hang on to that. That was true, and he knew it from twenty years experience.

"Sergeant Cody, my husband is a very famous man. People are always taking photographs of him. I can hardly be expected to notice everyone of them." She was at home now. Comfortable. Lying, but comfortable.

"So what you're saying is, you didn't see them . . . even though you seem to be looking right into their cameras." He tried to make her position sound as imbecilic as he could, and for a moment she was uncomfortable again, but then the strength returned.

"We look to be some distance away. . . . I'm sorry I can't help you. The fact is, we just didn't see them. And having said that, I have told you all I can, which is exactly what I told you it would be in the beginning. Now, once again, if you will be so kind as to show yourselves out."

"I had hoped to talk to all the people in the picture."

"That's impossible. I'm not going to have my husband and his guests disturbed."

"We wouldn't take much of their time."

"You won't take any of their time."

"The missing girl's father is an invalid. He's worried about his daughter."

"My husband and his friends saw nothing, I've told you that."

"No. Actually you told us what you didn't see."

". . . Good day, Sergeant Cody . . . Detective Ho, I expect I'll have another conversation with your superiors. I won't be very complimentary."

She turned and started for the patio. It was Cody's voice that stopped her. "Mrs. Hannibal . . . I was a policeman for twenty years; I have a lot of friends, too . . . a lot of them in the news media. They always like a good 'man bites dog' story . . . you know, something unexpected. They'd probably make it sound pretty sensational that America's best-loved poet, America's grandfather, wouldn't help a blind and crippled man find his daughter by answering a few questions."

She said nothing for several moments, and he wasn't sure it was going to work. She had lied to him. He didn't know why, or about what, but she had lied. The question was, how far would she go to keep up the defense. Could the others on the patio be trusted to hold up their end? Did they have to? And how important was her husband's reputation?

Important enough.

"You are a very annoying man," she said finally, and the voice was ice.

It was Evan Hannibal himself who spotted them first as they approached the patio, and he rose to greet them with his famous smile. "Two handsome, formidable young men . . . you must be the local gendarmes my wife told me might appear." His voice was melodious, his manner theatrical, and there was a twinkle of humor in his eyes.

The same couldn't be said for Carmel Beecher Van Kueren. She was also on her feet now, standing motionless in her great bulk, studying them with a gaze that reminded Cody of an evangelist's.

Across the patio, Nelson Hobart had taken time off from his invisible boys' choir to pay attention to their arrival. And even from a distance, Cody could see that he wore a toupee and that it made him look slightly ridiculous, for it was chestnut in color and at least twenty years too young for his aging face and neck.

The man with the tufted hair and the moon-faced man in his salmon leisure suit had little interest in the policemen and sat in their chairs with the impatience of people who have been interrupted in the middle of an important conversation.

"Almost right," Lillian Hannibal said with a glowing smile for her husband. She had shifted gears nicely and now was the cordial and gracious hostess. "You see they're not both local policemen. Sergeant Cody has come all the way from Los Angeles."

Hannibal arched his eyebrows as if performing. "Ahhh. Good old L.A. is where we live most of the time, don't you know . . . ? And what brings you to our beautiful Kauai?" He sounded the name of the island almost musically, as if explaining the name to a foreigner.

"These two," Cody answered and offered Hannibal the large wedding photos.

The old man seemed surprised but took the photos and then had to put them down on the table as he fumbled for his glasses. Lillian stepped in and helped, as a doting mother might for a child. She was at least forty years younger than her husband, and as he examined the wedding pictures, she explained to him both who the couple were and the fact that they had taken some candid shots of them at Spouting Horn. Finally, Hannibal moved his glasses down his nose and looked to Cody.

"I am afraid I am at a loss as to how I might benefit you."

"I'm not sure myself," Cody responded. "All we

know is that the girl and her husband disappeared on
this island, that the police have been unable to come
up with anything in the conventional manner . . . I'm
just hoping by checking and rechecking everything,
that we can come up with someone who saw them
and maybe noticed something out of the ordinary
. . . any scrap of information.''

"Sergeant Cody has made this trip as a favor to
the girl's father. It seems that he's an invalid and
depends on her night and day.'' Lillian Hannibal
spoke the words with a hint of pathos, as if to elicit
an emotion from the old man. It did. . . . He received the words solemnly, pushed his glasses back
up his nose, and restudied the photos . . . and Cody
wondered if Lillian knew she had just made a bad
mistake.

"Carmel, Nelson, come have a look. You were
there that day,'' the Great American Poet said with
the proper dramatic tone.

"I don't need to see them. I remember the couple
vividly.''

It was Carmel Beecher Van Kueren who had spoken, and her voice itself had startled him as much as
her words. It was a deep bass, almost a man's. She
glided toward them like a New Year's float, and
Cody noticed pastry crumbs at the corner of her
mouth. So did Lillian Hannibal, who patted them off
and asked, with what Cody thought was a little too
much concern, "You saw them, dear? This honeymoon couple at Spouting Horn?''

Hannibal handed the huge woman the wedding
photos and pronounced to Cody, as if reciting a line
of poetry, "I fear I cannot help you . . . I saw them
not.''

"Their pictures mean nothing,'' the enormous
woman said after glancing at them.

"But these are the people who disappeared," Caleb interjected. "A moment ago you said you remembered them vividly."

"But I do." She was looking at him, but her eyes seemed far away. It was the evangelist's eyes, only now alive, in sight of the vision, and Cody remembered the lectures this woman gave, where people like Caleb's aunt came away not understanding what the hell she had been talking about. "I realized it the moment it was said that they were a honeymoon couple; it explained everything. . . . Don't you remember, Lillian? It rained the morning we were to go to Spouting Horn, a torrential downpour. We thought we might be housebound for days. And then, in the early afternoon the clouds parted unexpectedly, and the sun shone through the still-wet air, and around the house was a shimmering halo of rainbow."

"I remember, I remember," Lillian said, and she did, and her eyes told Cody that she believed. There had been a mystical experience; Carmel Beecher Van Kueren had experienced it and Lillian had been there. She, through the huge woman, had also touched it.

"Do you remember what I said?" the enormous woman asked.

"You said," Lillian said with a fervent smile, "that this must be like the day when the veil was lifted from Isis."

"I meant after that," the big woman corrected.

"Oh," Lillian said, but apparently didn't remember.

"I said . . . that today we will encounter something . . . something good and wonderful." The fat woman with the man's voice talked at a rapid clip, so many words to be gotten in, so many thoughts. "And then we got to Spouting Horn . . . and all at once I told you I thought I was going to faint . . . I was so overwhelmed with the feeling of love and warmth, all fusing into an almost magnetic field of happiness.''

"Yes, I remember now. Everything she is saying is true," Lillian stated. "We had to go back to the car to sit down."

"I'm not sure I understand," Caleb said. "Did you or didn't you see the honeymoon couple?"

"With my eyes, I don't know. It's certainly not the memory image I retain of them. But they were there. I can vouch for that. I felt them with the power of their love for one another."

"You felt this because they were honeymooners?" Caleb asked, wearing a mildly astonished expression, and then added, "This island is filled with honeymooners. There are thousands here every month."

But the huge woman seemed off on another plane of thought, and so Lillian came to the defense. "What you must understand is that Mrs. Van Kueren is a most extraordinary person. . . . While all of us, every minute of every day, are on the receiving end of the cosmic program that links us, not only to every other living thing, but to the sun and planets and the faraway stars, most of us only catch rare glimpses of the great mysteries and truths, and when we do we call them premonitions or instincts . . . ESP. Mrs. Van Kueren, on the other hand, is world-renowned for being highly sensitive to all the cosmic forces around her . . . which of course has led her down the path to a great many of her spiritual insights. When a very strong cosmic force, such as the love of these honeymooners, passes close to her, it can be like a great moon pulling the tides. She can be deeply affected."

"I didn't see them," Nelson Hobart said, leaning in and taking a quick glance. His eyebrows were sparse, and he had used an eyebrow pencil to fill them out. His tone was at best argumentative. ''I don't like people who take pictures of me or my friends without asking. I think it's rude as hell.''

''I can understand that,'' Cody said. ''But you didn't take a very good look at them.''

''Good enough,'' Hobart snarled. ''I don't like looking at people's faces. They're usually stupid,'' he added, looking directly at Cody.

''Really. Well what part of people's bodies do you like to look at?'' Cody asked, as if the answer might be lurid. He didn't like Hobart, and there was the off chance that the question might provoke the man to reveal the source of his anger.

''Is that supposed to be funny? I don't think it is, and I think you've wasted enough of our time.''

''Nelson, I'm sure the young man meant no harm,'' Hannibal beamed. ''He is after all a fellow Angelino, don't you know?''

Hobart sulked.

''Well, sergeant.'' Lillian Hannibal was using her head-nurse voice again. ''You have the answers that you came for. Except for Mrs. Van Kueren, none of us were aware of your missing couple.''

''I don't suppose you picked up any other cosmic forces from them,'' Cody asked the fat woman. ''Like where they might have disappeared to?''

''No,'' she answered with her deep bass and a smile, and Cody imagined that without her clothes she must look like Jabba the Hutt.

''I don't suppose either of you gentlemen were at Spouting Horn that day,'' Cody asked, directing the question at the tufted-haired man, who up until now hadn't been paying particular attention. Now, both he and the moon-faced man in the salmon-colored suit looked up.

"No." The sterness had returned to Lillian Hannibal's voice.

Evan Hannibal seemed a little confused until he realized who Cody was talking about, then the smile returned to his face. "Oh, no, these gentlemen are all the way from the East Coast. They just arrived this morning."

"New York?" Cody asked, pressing the opening.

"Boston, if it matters," the tufted-haired man said. "I'm Mr. Hannibal's attorney."

He had nothing to lose. He might as well keep pushing. "Boston, you live in a beautiful city, Mr. . . . ?"

"Crocker, Abraham Crocker."

The lawyer was almost as unpleasant as Hobart. But Cody was after information, so he put on a simple smile and stated, "And this must be your partner," referring to the moon-faced man in the salmon leisure suit, realizing Crocker would have to think him an idiot to believe they were in any way connected on a regular basis. But it was the moon-faced man who rose to the bait, standing and offering Cody his card.

"Lyle Tibbet . . . Farmer's Bank, Billings, Montana."

"Billings, of course, is my husband's hometown," Lillian explained curtly.

The moon-faced man's card had the word "President" under his name.

"That's very interesting," Cody said, then took one of the Greens' snapshots from his shirtpocket and wondered how long he could go on pushing. "I guess that leaves us with just these other two gentlemen who were with you at Spouting Horn."

Not far.

"Sergeant Cody," Lillian Hannibal's voice was definitely unpleasant.

"Mrs. Hannibal, you've all been very kind with your time, and I realize I can't ask to speak to the two gentlemen in the picture if they're not here. . . ."

"They're not," she said, overriding him crisply.

"Could I ask if they are still on the island?" Her only answer was a glare, so he went on. "I understand the young man in the photo is your stepson . . . a Stephen Auerbach." He deliberately read the notes clumsily from the back of the picture.

"My stepson, Stephen, lives here at Kamalani year-round. He happens to be scuba diving today," she said precisely.

Evan Hannibal, who seemed oblivious to the tension between his wife and Cody, had taken the photo and was studying it. "The other fella there," he said, tapping the man with the pixie smile, "is Alex Polk. I think he's off shopping today, isn't he?"

"Gone to an art show over in Lihue."

"Ah," Evan Hannibal replied with an arched eyebrow.

"This Alex Polk," Cody asked, "does he live on the island also?"

Nelson Hobart laughed derisively.

"Mr. Polk is a houseguest," Lillian answered in a voice that said there was no more.

"Returned from the mainland last night," Hannibal said melodically. "Another Angelino, don't you know?"

"He must like to travel," Cody said with a smile. "I mean, he was in the photo that the Greens took a couple of weeks ago . . . and now he's back again."

The statement left them all silent. The old man looked confused; Lillian, tight-lipped.

"What part of Los Angeles did you say he was from?" Cody went on enthusiastically.

"Pasadena," the old man said after a moment, and the confusion was gone, the twinkle back.

"Eagle Rock," Nelson Hobart corrected, spitting out the words as if living in Eagle Rock were an offense. "He only teaches in Pasadena."

"Right," Hannibal chuckled. "Alex is a professor . . . American history, don't you know. And well he ought to be, being a direct descendant of our illustrious eleventh President of these United States, the right honorable James K. Polk himself. Of 'fifty-four forty or fight,' if you remember your school days."

"I remember." Cody smiled and realized that he liked the ancient poet. He seemed, for all his posturing, at least to be genuine. . . . And then, from when he was fourteen years old, came a wisp of memory. "I remember also . . . 'In the dark, dark night I am afraid to go. Afraid of what I might find, afraid of what I might not . . .' "

Cody paused. He couldn't remember it clearly anymore, and after a moment the poet went on with the stanza he had written fifty-some years before. ". . . but go I must into the black, as others have gone ahead, for others will follow and fall again, and others will fear and fear . . . until one of us finds the light."

Chapter Ten

"You think she's lying."

"I know she is."

They were moving across the pale lawn again, this time away from the patio. Cody had left the wedding pictures with Lillian Hannibal with the request that "if by chance" either her stepson or Professor Polk, with his pixie smile, knew anything about the missing couple, they'd give him a call at the hotel.

"How?" Caleb asked.

But Cody's mind was working on the problem of how to go back. He needed to, just for a few minutes. On the patio he had pushed as far as he could against Lillian Hannibal without being thrown out, but it wasn't enough. He had to go back, see inside the house, and right now every step was taking him further away. . . . Then he knew what to do and smiled for a moment and paused awkwardly in his walk. Caleb paused also, looking a bit confused.

"How do you know she's lying?" Caleb tried again.

"She told me," Cody said and then turned and waved to those on the patio. He knew there was no point in trying to explain everything to the young

Hawaiian anymore than there had been to any of the others in the past. "First, when she almost broke apart when I showed her the wedding pictures."

"Yeah, I saw that," Caleb said.

On the patio, only the man with the tufted hair wasn't watching. All the others saw Cody wave, but only Evan Hannibal returned the gesture . . . and then Cody fell down.

"Jesus, what's wrong?"

"Actually . . . nothing," Cody said with a slight grin for Caleb's benefit, slowly pulling himself into a sitting position. "Except I want to have a look inside that house."

"Jesus," Caleb repeated.

The moon-faced banker and a Filipino houseman who had suddenly materialized were hurrying toward them, so Cody spoke quickly and only for Caleb to hear. "The second way I knew she was lying is that before I came here I read everything that had been reported about the missing couple—in both California and island papers. Not one of them mentioned the fact that the girl's father was an invalid."

"You mentioned it."

Cody grinned. "I didn't mention it. I hit her over the head with it so we could talk to her husband . . . but what did she add to it?"

"That her father depends on her night and day?" Caleb offered the answer after a few moments, and then only tentatively, not sure he had made the true discovery.

Cody nodded to let him know he had. "And how did she know that? She could have assumed it, I suppose. But why not assume that the man lives with a loving wife who takes care of him? . . . Or in a hospital or nursing home? Why assume that his daughter, just married, took care of him day and night?''

''Mrs. Hannibal is standing by to call an ambulance if you are in need of one, sergeant,'' the moon-faced Montana banker called out as he and the houseman neared.

''No . . . I think I'll be all right,'' Cody answered with a rather dazed look. ''If I could just have a place to rest a few minutes out of the sun, perhaps some washroom facilities . . . old injury. Took a bullet in a drug raid one night.''

''Oh, of course. Yes, I see. We'll help you to the house. I think that's the best thing to do.''

His sincerity was staggering, and Cody fought smiling. *He's no doubt Billings' man of the year,* Cody thought. *Mr. Republican. Head of the Kiwanis.*

Caleb watched, amazed, for help they did. The Filipino houseman, five foot two, and the Billings banker, at least a foot taller . . . one on each side, they guided the wounded warrior back to the house. Caleb trailed behind and realized that his police life would never be quite the same again.

''In here will be best,'' Lillian said. She was herself, at her best . . . in charge. She let them into a spacious, impeccably decorated room. The walls were white, the floor a dark polished teak. One wall sported a screened window that ran the length of the room and looked out onto a fern garden and bubbling fountain. ''He'll be comfortable here,'' she said and saw him deposited on a white wicker lounge with Gauguin-style cushions.

''Would you like some ice water, sergeant, or perhaps something stronger?''

"Water would be just great. I'm sorry to put you to so much trouble."

She didn't reply. She wasn't sure if he was sorry. The Filipino houseman disappeared to retrieve the water.

"This is my husband's writing room when we're on the island," she told him eventually as he rested and recovered.

It looks more like a museum, Cody thought. Everything was perfectly in place, from the highly polished floor to the books in the bookcases, the flowers in their vases, the palms in their tubs, the ivory and brass ceiling fans turning gently in the tropical air . . . and of course the Great Man's desk, with a blank pad of paper, a half dozen old-fashioned ink-pens, and a bottle of ink sitting nearby. It was all so seemingly casual . . . and yet it looked like an artist's impression of the way a great writer's desk should look.

"Is he working on something now?" Cody asked.

"My husband's always writing, composing," she said with an indulgent smile. "It's not like being a policeman, Sergeant Cody, or a butcher or baker. Being a great poet is not something one retires from . . . it's part of his fiber, his every living breath." The look of the true believer was back, her eyes beaming.

"Part of his cosmic forces," Cody couldn't resist. But he kept a straight face, and she couldn't be sure.

"Yes," she agreed.

He decided he was beginning to understand their married relationship. She was the keeper of the sacred flame. The curator of a national treasure. It was a grand relationship, which of course assured her of her own place in the sun. It wouldn't even have to end when he died. She could go on for years if she chose to, talking about his genius and his cosmic force and showing off impeccably decorated "writing rooms."

Except for his trip to the restroom, she stayed with him for the fifteen minutes he was in the house, and when he said he was fit again, she instructed Caleb to drive his car across the lawn to the patio to make it easier for the visiting policeman.

When the car came, Evan Hannibal wished him another hearty goodbye. Nelson Hobart scowled. Carmel Beecher Van Kueren looked as if she saw dark clouds approaching. The man with the tufted hair, Hannibal's attorney, was angry and was directing his words to the moon-faced banker. "For Christ's sake, we're talking about four million dollars . . ." And as they drove away from the patterned gardens, Lillian's stepson, the sandy-haired Stephen Auerbach, watched from where he had been hiding among the ferns.

"She never left you alone." Caleb hadn't spoken until they were passing through Kamalani's gates back onto the public road.

"I saw enough," Cody answered, then added, "but it will be better for you if I don't say any more."

They rode in silence for almost a minute. On the ocean side they could see surfers, and Cody thought about Pat and then almost instantly of Ann. He felt depressed again, and the feeling that he wanted to cry passed through him, and when it was gone he knew he wanted a drink. A stiff one.

"You don't need help?" Caleb asked finally.

"Not the sort a career-minded young policeman should be getting involved in."

"What can I do?"

"Forget it."

"I don't want to forget it." For the first time, Caleb was pushing hard. It was the tough side all cops have to have. Somehow it surprised Cody.

"For probably the only time in my life, I'm involved in a case that's really something." The young Hawaiian went on. "I knew it when those people at the shops told me about other people calling and asking for the Greens' photographs, days after the Greens were missing . . . now you've convinced me Mrs. Hannibal is lying. Why she is, I don't know. But something weird's going on at that house . . . I want in."

"It could all blow up in our faces," Cody said after considering for a few moments. "Evidence-wise we haven't got anything to tie the Hannibals to anything."

"We've got enough that you're going to break into their house and try to find more."

Cody grinned. "My my, what devilish thoughts they put into young policemen's heads these days."

"That's what you went back for isn't it? To see if they had an alarm system? Get the general layout of the place?"

Cody let the grin go. The young Hawaiian had to know what he was letting himself in for. "We're talking about America's best loved poet and some very important people. If I'm wrong, they'll just call me a half-crazy ex-cop and I'll go back to my boat in California . . . but you and your career . . . they'll tear you to pieces."

"I'm willing to take my chances," Caleb said.

They rode in silence for some minutes, and for the first time in a long time Cody didn't feel alone.

"Think that professor has something to do with it?" Caleb asked tentatively.

"You don't miss a lot," Cody said, and it was a compliment.

Caleb shrugged, trying unsuccessfully to hide the fact that he was pleased with himself. "I mean, he went back to Los Angeles after the pictures at Spouting Horn were taken . . . that could put him there at the right time to have broken into the girl's room."

"Pull over here," Cody said, indicating a group of shops. The young Hawaiian obeyed, and Cody asked, "Do you have any contacts in the local telephone company?"

"Yes," Caleb said, after thinking a moment.

"Then maybe we can find something out without my having to break into that house," Cody said, "or at least find something out that gives us a better reason to. . . ."

"What do you want?"

"You brought it up yourself, the phone calls from 'the Greens,' days after they were missing, to those three shops . . . those calls had to be made from somewhere."

"You want me to find out if they were made from Kamalani?" Caleb stated.

Cody nodded. "If they were, the telephone company's billing computer will show it . . . and those shops are twenty miles away, there's gotta be a dozen places to get photos developed closer to Kamalani."

Cody felt good, and he realized it was because he was beginning to feel like a cop again. He left the car and moved to a bank of pay phones, which were the reason he had asked Caleb to stop.

As he punched out the number, and then his credit

card number, a little girl he guessed to be five watched him from the doorway of a scrimshaw shop. She was wearing a brightly colored bathing suit. Drips of ice cream ran down her front, which was understandable because her face and, in fact, the hand in which she was holding the melting ice cream cone were also covered with the mess. It was her dark hair and pigtails that made him smile. They reminded him of pictures of Ann when she was a little girl. "Hi," he said. But it only made the girl disappear into the shop. A small lizard darted along the wooden walkway.

He found Pyne on the second call. He was at home. He was barbecueing, Beth said, and then she went to call her husband to the phone.

A half a minute went by and then there was a loud clattering. "Goddammit, someone's got to watch the fire." He could hear Pyne shouting, and even from three thousand miles away he could tell the fat policeman was bombed. It seemed odd. He couldn't remember Pyne being drunk. Little Mother usually liked his calories in solid form, fries and sandwiches, cakes and chips. He considered hanging up and waiting until tomorrow.

"Hello?" The word was slurred and too loud.

"Sound like you're having a good time."

". . . Who is this?"

Christ, he should have waited until tomorrow.

"Cody." Silence. "I'm calling from Kauai."

"Oh yeah." The fat man remembered. "Did you find them yet?" His words were still sloshy, but there was something more, an emptiness. He wasn't Little Mother or the happy Cubmaster today.

"Not yet. I need some help."

"Do what you need. Whatever you spend we'll find someway of getting back to you."

"I need some names checked out."

"Oh boy, Cody. What are you talking about? What crazy scheme do you have cooking up now? I can't take any more of that stuff about someone breaking into the girl's room over at Worden's. . . . I can't take that shit to the captain." His voice sounded at once belligerent and desperate.

"You have something to write with?"

"Shit," the fat man whined, and Cody could hear him rummaging around for some seconds.

The little girl came out of the scrimshaw shop again and stared at him until he smiled. Her face and hands were clean now. "We've got kittens."

"Do you?"

"Yes. Six of them in California. My mother hates them, but my dad says we can keep one, but I'm not suppose to tell my mother that."

"Someone hang up the phone." Cody could hear Pyne shouting, and a moment later there was a click.

"I'm in my office now," Pyne said, his voice still slurred from drink but also drained now, more than before.

Cody remembered the windowless room, the Formica desk crowded with papers, the turquoise couch, and the paintings of wide-eyed children on the walls.

"I've got a pencil."

"The man's name is Polk. P-O-L-K. First name, Alex, or Alexander. Early forties. Five foot six or seven. Maybe a hundred and fifty pounds. Dark hair. He's supposed to be a professor of American history at a college in Pasadena. I don't know which one."

"What does he have to do with Worden's daughter?"

"I'm not sure yet. Run a check on him. And since the missing girl and her husband both went to night school, check that out, too. . . . See if their paths ever crossed.''

Pyne sighed heavily. Neither man spoke for several moments. Finally it was Cody. ''What's wrong, Dan?''

''Nothing.'' But his voice said the dam was about to break, and after several more moments of silence it all started to come out. ''I think I've got cancer; there's blood in my piss.''

''Have you gone to a doctor?''

''It only happened last night. I thought maybe it would go away, but I knew it wouldn't. I couldn't sleep all night. Three or four times I had to take a pee, and I was afraid to go . . . my son hates me. He's fifteen years old and smokes pot, and he hates me. He calls me an asshole. He tried to attack me with a baseball bat once. What the fuck's the point of anything anymore?''

''Call a doctor; there could be other reasons.''

''How do I call a doctor? I've got a houseful of people for a barbecue. What am I supposed to say? Party's off. I'm dying of cancer. I have piss in my blood . . . blood in my piss,'' he corrected himself. ''Do your boys hate you?''

''No. There's times they're not too happy with me.''

''I bet they never called you an asshole or tried to hit you with a baseball bat . . . what's the whole point? . . . There aren't any other reasons. My father died of the same thing. . . .''

Again neither man spoke. This time the silence lasted for almost a minute.

''This Polk . . . I'll check him out,'' the fat man finally said. The emotional boil had been lanced. He didn't sound drunk anymore. ''Do you really think he has something to do with breaking into the girl's room at Worden's place?''

"I'm pretty sure it was someone on this island."

"Oh boy," Pyne said, but he didn't have the heart to get upset at the man he'd just made his confessor . . . "Anymore names?"

Cody thought about giving him the others, but decided against it. "Not today. He's the only one I don't know anything about."

Again there was a silence.

"Shit, I'm only forty-eight years old."

Chapter Eleven

Corona.

Juan Corona.

He buried some of his victims alive. Why did he think Ann was buried alive? Why did it keep coming back to him? The dark place? Her? The little dog barking? Dark and buried, the ground closing in. Alive for minutes? Hours? Days? And water. If it rained, the wet would seep in, making it harder to breathe, harder to move, so much easier to die . . . in fear . . . fear so unfair. Fear. Abandonment. Fear in the darkness, crying out for help. He wanted to throw up, but he didn't want to leave the phone booth. The connection was broken, but he needed to be alone. Pyne had thrown him back into a deep depression, and he desperately wanted a drink.

And then he knew why he had thought of Corona . . . Juan Corona. It had been hot and sticky that day in Haywood, too, just like it was now, inside the glass booth. He'd flown up from L.A. to see a rapist who wanted to make a deal, end his pain, get out of jail, turn state's evidence on his former friends. Corona had been there in the courthouse, too, in another waiting room, waiting for his attorney, waiting for another retrial. Hoping to end his pain. Hoping to get out of jail. Hoping to blame his twenty-five murders on his dead brother. What a guy. A real champion. A man ahead of his time. A serial killer on the crest of the great American wave. It seemed so strange to see him just sitting there, this living prophet of mass murder. Eleven years in prison, eleven years since the first headlines, and now he was just a paunchy brown-skinned man, well into middle age. He seemed so ordinary, so inconsequential. Did he have bad breath? Hemorrhoids? Did his joints ache when the weather turned cold? Did he dream of his murders? Of his joys? Of his madness? Of his hacking human beings to pieces with a thirty-inch machete? Who could have guessed, this ordinary looking man . . . Who could have stopped you, Corona? Who? The law? Not the law. You were the first sign, weren't you? The dawn of modern American madness, of crimes beyond the law, beyond reason and even the human decency recognized by other criminals . . . you were the dawn. So tell us, how are you and all the others who have come after you to be dealt with? How do we stop you in the vacuum beyond law and reason, in the vacuum of madness? How do we stop you without first joining you, and once we have, how do we ever go back?

"I want to see where they disappeared, the trail they were suppose to be hiking," Cody said as he opened the door of the glass booth. He'd known from the beginning that it was something he'd have to do. This seemed like a good time to get it out of the way. He didn't really expect to find anything that the investigators before him hadn't found, but it was part of his routine. Procedure. Filling in the boxes. Crossing the *t*'s dotting the *i*'s. It made him feel like a cop again, and that was good because it helped numb the other feeling.

Caleb had been standing there for a minute or so, having finished his own call.

"Sure," the young Hawaiian said, but he seemed unsettled. "My friend from the telephone company is going to go into work tonight and try to get the information for us."

Cody managed a wry grin. "Beginning to bother you that you and your friend are technically on the edge of a criminal conspiracy?"

Caleb smiled. "We were thinking of going right from this into gunrunning . . . it's just that the hiking trail is all the way on the other side of the island. It could take us an hour and a half to get there."

"By car, yes, but I'd like to go by helicopter. Don't worry, I'll take care of whatever costs there are . . . the view from the air will help give me a sense of the land." That part was true at least. Sometimes, in some cases of missing people, Cody had found that observation, not only of the immediate surroundings, but of the land as a whole, could help clarify patterns for him . . . but he also knew that there were other reasons why he wanted to go by helicopter . . . vague, half-formed, dark reasons he wasn't capable of facing yet.

The helicopter picked them up in Poipu, near one of the lush hotels that, along with seemingly endless clusters of condominiums, crowd the southern point of the island.

"It can be pouring rain back in town or back at your hotel and ninety-nine times out of a hundred it'll still be warm and sunny here," Caleb told him. "It's also the best surfing on the island."

Patrick confirmed both counts, reciting the same information he had learned from Caleb's younger brother, Derek. They had spotted the boys on the beach and had a few minutes to talk to them before the helicopter appeared. As promised, Caleb's sister was there to keep an eye on them. She had already made Patrick put on his shirt and wear it even while in the water. "He looked like he was beginning to burn," she said. She looked to be about twenty-five, and her name was Maile. She was beautiful. She wore a mesh, red-and-white KAUAI football jersey over the top of her two-piece bathing suit. Cody felt close to her; he didn't know why. Maybe it was because she was taking care of his son. Maybe it was her smile. Maybe it was the island. He felt attacted to her and then felt guilty as he thought of Ann . . . and the dark place and the fear and the little barking dog were coming back . . . and then the helicopter was there, coming down over the tops of the palm trees.

"You and Patrick will have dinner with us tonight?" she asked.

"Yes, I think we'd like that," he answered.

Cody had never been fond of helicopters, and as the airship, whose normal business was to show tourists the scenic wonders of the island, swooped sideways up into the sky, he was glad he'd had time for a couple of double vodka-tonics in the hotel bar.

He had gone there to make another series of phone calls, chasing something that had been nagging him. At Kamalani he hadn't been able to think of a good way to go after it. By the time he'd reached Poipu, he'd decided to just go for it the best way he could,

even if Brooklyn was light-years from Boston. . . .
On the fifth call, he tracked down the man he was
looking for, a police detective named Bobby Cormier.
A half dozen years earlier Cormier's fourteen-year-
old daughter had run away from home. He had been
sure she had headed for the bright lights of Hollywood, and he had needed help finding her. Cody had
helped. But then, when they did find her, at first it
wasn't pleasant. Ann had made the girl stay with
them. She and the girl had long talks and lots of
crying and walks along the Playa Del Rey surf . . .
and after a week or so, the shouting between Cormier
and his daughter wasn't there anymore. They went
home to Brooklyn together and Bobby had said,
"Any time, anywhere, all you have to do is call
me." So Cody did. The debt was old, but Bobby
Cormier's memory was good. He would take sick
leave and tomorrow fly up to Boston and, hopefully
without causing too many ripples, nose around and
try to find out about four million dollars and why
Abraham Crocker had flown all the way to Kauai and
was angry with Evan Hannibal's moon-faced banker
about it.

At Cody's request the helicopter flew the long
way, along and around the coast. As before, he said
he wanted to get a sense of the land. But much more
strongly now, he sensed there was something there
that he wanted to avoid, something inland, near his
hotel. What? Why? He didn't know. He wasn't ready
yet.

Then, nearing Lihue, they had to swing inland
temporarily to avoid the airport's airspace. They passed
over a shopping center—the Sugar Mill—backyards,
rooftops. At a park a barbecue was cooking, smoke
curling up and over the softball game in progress,

and he thought about Pyne, the fat man in California, afraid he's dying, afraid to find out . . . and then Cody knew why he wanted to fly only along the coast. He was afraid, afraid of what was inland, afraid of what might be there . . . and more afraid of what might not be.

They touched down in Hanalei a little past four, in a park near the water. Cody had read that the north shore was considered one of the most beautiful stretches of land in the world. It was all of that and more for him. He found it startlingly beautiful, from the rough green mountains cloaked in mist, to the paddy fields and rivers. He saw the long white beaches and palm trees, the blue-green ocean, and now, touching down, he caught sight of a grove of pine trees that circled the bay. It somehow seemed unreal, the evergreen trees one doesn't associate with a tropical island, there, set out against the bay, and for some moments he was relaxed, and he wished Ann were there. He felt at home here.

"Some of my relatives go back a hundred and fifty years around here, growing taro, rice." The young Hawaiian had to shout to be heard as they climbed out of the helicopter. "A long time ago this used to be one of Kauai's biggest seaports . . . big clipper ships used to bring the missionaries in and take the rice out." This last part he added with a smile, trying to make it sound as if he found a certain humor in the history, but the edge of tension had returned, the same edge Cody had noted when he first mentioned Kamalani.

A squadron of boys on bikes, ranging in age from about eight to twelve and wearing only bathing trunks or cut-offs, swooped down to watch. Most of them were Hawaiian-brown with shiny black hair. But it was a blond-haired boy with a deep tan who said something in pidgin, which Cody couldn't understand, that made all the others laugh and even Caleb grin.

"I think they find us amusing," Cody offered as they moved past.

Caleb's grin grew. "That's close enough."

And Cody laughed.

"That's my cousin Victor," Caleb said, indicating a man standing next to a dusty black pickup truck. In the back of the truck a pair of kids, a boy and a girl, were climbing around, laughing and playing. "He'll take us the rest of the way, to the end of the road."

Victor, who sported a goatee, was a stocky man, somewhere in his thirties, and had a round face that when relaxed formed a natural smile. He was wearing shorts, a tank top, and a baseball cap that almost got knocked off when he and Caleb greeted each other.

"This is my friend from California, Ed Cody," Caleb said, making the introductions. "My cousin Victor and his keikis, Tommy and Leilani."

"I'm glad to meet all of you," Cody said, and the children giggled while he shook hands with smiling Victor.

"The first missionaries came here in the 1830's. They built grand churches and were dedicated to saving all of our heathen souls . . . whether we liked it or not."

They were passing an old, well-restored church. The three men sat in the cab of the truck, the two kids in back, along with a funny-looking white dog with a black circle around his eye, who had appeared suddenly as they started to drive away. Barking madly and running alongside, it had managed to keep pace until suddenly it lept upon the hood of a parked car and then into the bed of the passing truck. What Cody found most remarkable was that none of the others seemed to find anything out of the ordinary.

"Somewhere along the line the missionaries decided material wealth wasn't good for us, so they relieved us of it . . . and since about the only thing the people had was the land, that's what they took . . . the hell of it is, they still have it."

"I'm afraid my little cousin only sees the bad side of the old missionaries," Victor said, trying to smile, and Cody realized this was a long-running dispute between the two.

"I just see what's there," Caleb answered his cousin, and it seemed for a moment he wanted to stop but then couldn't resist going on for Cody's benefit. "Just go downtown; you have the Wilcox Museum, the Wilcox Hospital, the Wilcox this, the Wilcox that. They came here preaching love and charity and ended up stealing a good part of the island . . . and they're not alone. Try the Robinson family; they have huge holdings throughout the islands. . . . Jesus, they own Niihau; they own an entire island . . . but of course they're great humanitarians. You know what they raise on their island? Hawaiians . . . about three hundred of the last pure Hawaiians . . . and the people who live there aren't allowed to leave except for medical purposes, and then they're closely supervised. And you and I, ordinary people, we can't go there at all unless we have special permission. You understand what they're doing? They're running a zoo. They came here a hundred and fifty years ago to save our souls, but they're still treating us like we're less than human.''

They rode in silence the rest of the way, Caleb having apparently vented enough steam.

They stopped about fifty yards from the end of the road, which was crowded with parked cars and tourist buses, one of which was doing its best to turn around at the moment.

''Can we play on the beach?''

''Please?''

The boy and the girl were used to working together, their questioning voices rising at the end of each sentence, which Cody had noticed was a prevalent speech pattern on the island. The odd-looking dog, meanwhile, had asked no one's permission and had jumped out and run off as soon as the truck had come to a stop.

''Be careful,'' Victor said to his children, and they bounded out happily. Cody noticed for the first time that the boy had a deformed leg and moved with a rolling limp.

''Hey *bla*,'' Caleb said to Victor after Cody had climbed down ''I'm sorry for getting on my soapbox.''

''*Aole* pilikia,'' Victor responded with a warm grin and tousled Caleb's hair.

''My cousin's a very religious guy,'' Caleb said as he and Cody moved down the road. ''He and his wife are Mormons . . . good people. I shouldn't get him upset.''

''I can see why so many people come here,'' Cody said as they reached the actual end of the road, and for the first time he had a good look at the gentle beach.

''You snorkel?''

''I have.''

"The reef out there, you'll find fifty or sixty kinds of tropical fish, all colors."

Cody enjoyed the view several moments longer before getting back to business. "Where do we find the trail?"

"Right behind you," Caleb answered and pointed to a rough green cliff that rose several hundred feet.

Cody followed his gaze. "Where I come from they call that a cliff."

Caleb grinned. "It's just like that for the first quarter of a mile or so, then it gets better . . . about five miles from here is where it really gets a bit scary. . . . There are parts of the trail that are no more than nine inches wide along the side of a cliff . . . and if you make a mistake it's about four hundred feet straight down." The young Hawaiian had been smiling until his eyes caught Cody's.

"It doesn't make sense," was all Cody said after several moments. It didn't. At least not in the mental image he had of the awkward daddy's girl. Oh, he could see her here, taking photos, her endless photos, wading in the water, and even strolling along a nature trail, but an easy one, not this one . . . not climbing a cliff, not unless it was a hell of a lot easier than it looked from here.

"I'll need a little time," Cody finally added.

"Sure," Caleb nodded.

Cody followed the sign and found the beginning of the trail at the base of the cliff and started to climb. It was late afternoon, and the heat of the day was over, but it was still warm and muggy enough to work up a sweat. Higher and higher along the difficult trail he climbed. He didn't pace himself, and the sweat poured off his body and made his shirt cling to him. He had been a fool; he had assumed that a trail was a trail was a trail. Higher and higher, and now, above the palm trees, he could see the rolling outcroppings of the uninhabited part of the island. If it had been a painting he wouldn't have believed it actually existed.

Caleb reached the summit several minutes after Cody. Cody was glad to see he was breathing hard, too.

"Not exactly an easy climb."

Caleb smiled. "I like coming up here. I used to come up here a lot when I was a keiki . . . after my dad died, we kids spent most summers with our relatives on this side of the island."

Neither spoke for several minutes. The view was almost overwhelming, tranquil. No wonder a boy would come here and dream of his father gone.

"They never came here," Cody said simply.

"The Greens?"

Cody nodded. "I don't think they ever meant to."

"But they told everybody they were going to. They even told her father."

"I know," Cody said. "That's the part I can't make out. Why lie to him? He's blind and crippled, three thousand miles away . . . but they did; they must have. In my mind I've gone through everything I've seen of hers . . . her clothes, her knicknacks, her photographs. The girl wasn't athletic."

"Then at least something makes sense," Caleb said, but he looked sheepish. "They didn't have a permit. People who are going to camp out overnight on this trail are supposed to get a permit in Lihue."

"Why didn't you tell me this before?"

"I didn't think of it. I told some of the guys at the department when I originally found out, but they said it didn't matter. They said a lot of people probably camp up here without permits . . . and besides, they had told so many people they were going to . . . people at the hotel, guests, people who worked there.'' The young Hawaiian was talking out of weakness. He felt like a schoolboy again.

But Cody wasn't paying attention to the words. He knew now. He knew why he had wanted to avoid the inland part of the island near his hotel. He got to his feet and felt dizzy, but it didn't matter; he had to go down. He had to face his fears; his terror, and he knew if he found something it would be terrible . . . and if he didn't, for him, infinitely worse.

''The cane field this morning, where I stopped and ran in . . . I want to go there. . . . I want to search it.''

Chapter Twelve

They flew low over the cane field, the giant green stalks flattening and rippling in their wash. They had been searching just a little more than five minutes when the giant greens danced open and revealed the top of a blue Toyota.

Nearby they found a spot on the cane road wide enough to land the helicopter. From there they walked in, Cody and the young Hawaiian, shoes off, pant legs rolled up, through the red mud. Later Cody would calculate that where he had stopped moving that morning, where his son and Caleb had caught up with him, had been less than fifty feet from the car. The death car. The dusty blue tomb.

They were naked, what was left of them, the honeymoon couple. So happy. So much ahead of them. . . . The summer Hawaiian sun had turned the blue Toyota into an oven, and in the weeks and days they had been there, the heat, combined with their own natural body gases, had caused their bodies to bloat to extreme proportions. The skin was almost black now and cracking with fissures, like overripe melons.

Caleb staggered into the cane and disappeared for a few moments.

Cody wanted to cry and laugh. The fear, the desperate crying for help he'd first sensed when he walked into the girl's room, was here. This was it, where the awkward daddy's girl, so afraid, oh, so afraid, had been thrown into the endless black eternity.

"You don't want to be a cop anymore."

Caleb didn't answer.

They decided against using the radio on the helicopter. They didn't want to run the risk of making the news public, not yet. So they walked out to the closest hotel where Caleb could phone in. It was a smaller hotel than the one Cody was staying in a mile or so down the road, not quite as nice, but closer to the water.

Caleb opted for the pay phone in the laundry; he thought it would give him privacy. Cody commandeered the bar phone and talked the hotel operator into placing a collect call to Brooklyn. He warned Bobby Cormier that the game had changed. . . . He had to be careful; there could be a double murder connected to the trail Cody had set him on.

"Miss," Cody called to the barmaid. "Another one for me and one for my friend."

Caleb shook his head. "No, we should go back. . . . I should be there when the others arrive."

"Trust me, you need this one."

After a moment, the young Hawaiian gave way and sat down. His legs were trembling.

"Tonight, maybe not until tomorrow morning . . . but sooner or later the people you work for are going to start asking questions. You've got to live here the rest of your life. In a few days or weeks I'll go away and maybe never come back. So what I'm saying is, don't back yourself into a corner . . . but the longer you can stall the answers, the longer you can avoid talking to them about the visit to the Hannibals, or the photographs, the better chance we'll have of getting to the real bottom of this.''

''The Hannibals are too respected,'' Caleb said. His voice was tired, his emotions drained. ''The department won't believe this could be connected to them. . . . I don't know that I believe it anymore myself.''

''Really?'' Cody was suddenly angry. He'd been fighting this all his life. People, either too stupid to understand or those who just didn't want to face it anymore, wanted it to go away, leave them alone. ''What about the photographs? The ones missing in California? The ones people were trying to get a hold of here? The ones only the Hannibals and their friends are in? . . . Including Professor Polk. Polk, who has been to L.A. and back since the honeymooners took those shots.''

''It's not enough. A lot of people go between here and California.'' Caleb's voice was almost a whine. He was the latter type. He just wanted them to go away.

''When did it not become enough? When cops-and-robbers on Kauai turned into an ugly double murder?''

''We don't even know it's murder yet.''

''Oh, it's murder all right, kid. You were in the bushes barfing your stomach out—I don't blame you for that—but while you were at it I took some careful looks through the windows. For the record, there's a small bullet hole behind the lady's ear. . . . The question for the autopsy will be if she was shot before or after her breasts were cut off . . . charming, right?'' Cody was hitting him hard because that was all he could do. If he lost Caleb, he knew it could all slip away, and he didn't want to let it. No. Not this one. He wanted this. He had his teeth in. He wanted to rip this one apart. This one could vent all the anger and frustration he had built up over the months since Ann had disappeared . . . he couldn't lose it, not and hold on to any sanity of his own. . . . Only right now the young Hawaiian looked like he was ready to throw up again. Cody softened, just a bit . . . ''You're lucky living here. Here on this island, this kind of murder, it knocks the shit out of you when it happens . . . but it's a once-in-a-lifetime crime here. Where I come from, murder and madness have become a way of life. In Los Angeles we average three murders a day . . . from crimes of passion, senseless gang killings, all the way to the sick and the bizarre, and they're the worst . . . and they're the ones whose numbers keep growing. You think you're a cop, so you're tough, and you think it doesn't phase you, but one by one, over the years, they strip it away from you, the parts that make you human. Over the years they tear at you piece by piece, until finally you're down to raw nerve and bone, and you find you're yelling at your wife and yelling at your kids, and you drink too much, and sometimes you think how pleasant it would be to just place your service revolver in your mouth and pull the trigger, because then it wouldn't hurt anymore.''

Caleb managed half his drink. He looked steadier now. He looked afraid now.

Cody went on. ''We've opened a can of snakes, and we don't even know what they look like or what they're after. If I had to guess now, I'd say it has something to do with four million dollars . . . and I'd say someone out at Kamalani has something to do with this. Maybe it's little Professor Polk, maybe it isn't . . . but if I had to guess now, I'd say Lillian Hannibal has seen those kids dead. . . . I think that's what was in her eyes today when I showed her the wedding pictures . . . that's why she almost fell apart.''

"You want enough time to break into their house?" Caleb asked. His voice was resigned.

"At least that much. Whoever did this is smart. They're a can of snakes that can slip away. Disappear forever given the cover. Their natural cover is Evan Hannibal and crowd. Like you just said, they're much too respectable for any cop counting on his pension to try and tie in to a murder, let alone a sex murder. . . . If I'm right, that's a second cover. . . . For some reason, whether it's the four million or not, the Greens had to die. But the killer or killers are cute; they decided to make it look like something else. If they get away with it, your nice little island will be in a panic for the next few weeks, waiting for the sex maniac to strike again. Then after a while, when nothing happens, they'll figure it was just another tourist, and of course that'll make everyone feel better . . . knowing it wasn't one of their neighbors, knowing that their wives and sisters and daughters will be safe. Meanwhile, the real killers, the can of snakes, will have gotten clean away.''

Caleb finished the drink. Its taste didn't bother him like the night before. There was a slight hesitation in his voice. "What if you're wrong? What if you get into the Hannibals' house and find nothing?"

''Then I'll go back to California. And me and what happened to the Greens will only be a bad memory.''

The light was almost gone when the emergency vehicles arrived. The chief and the deputy chief showed up along with a dozen or so other cops, and the coroner, of course. There was an odd silence, Cody thought, like they were all moving through a dream. They were barefoot. Those who weren't wearing shorts had their pant legs rolled up, slogging through the red mud. The islanders weren't used to this kind of murder. It was monstrous. And though the official inspections of the bodies hadn't proved this a murder yet, it had been inferred, from their own conjecture, built up over the days and weeks the couple had been missing . . . and of course from the report Caleb had phoned in. ''We think we found the Greens. The license plate on the car matches. We haven't opened it yet, but they look to be naked. In the back seat. Dead. Jesus, so dead.''

A couple of four-wheel-drive trucks had been brought in. As night overtook them, their headlights, some jury-rigged spotlights, and a dozen flashlights were all that stood between them and the darkness. The contrasts were extreme: glaring light, pitch black shadows.

They discovered that the blue Toyota was locked, all four doors. Finally, a uniformed policeman was told to break a window with the butt of his gun. It wasn't easy. It took four or five blows before a hole was punched in the shattered safety glass. Then, because of the stench from within, it was twenty more minutes before they could break out enough of the window to unlock one of the doors. By then, everyone near the blue Toyota was wearing a surgical mask.

At that point Cody moved away. He knew it would be hours before they finished here, and he needed to rest. He had too much to do before dawn not to. He found his way back to the cane road and slipped into the back of a police car.

Years ago he had learned how to grab short periods of sleep, deep, restful periods. It was a combination of relaxation and concentration, focusing his mind, eliminating all thoughts and emotions . . . eliminating and eliminating until all was gone and he slipped into the peaceful darkness and it swallowed him. Tonight it was difficult, with so many thoughts racing. Ann, dear Ann. He'd been so afraid, like Pyne, like the awkward daddy's girl. . . . He'd been so afraid that what he had seen this morning had been Ann, dead, in the dark place, not able to come back. Dead and afraid. He knew that he'd first seen the Greens this morning . . . but then the image had changed to Ann's. He thought of the old, blind Navajo woman laughing at him. . . . That's what he had been afraid of all afternoon . . . what he had been afraid to face . . . if the honeymoon couple hadn't been there in the cane, then it would have to have been Ann he had seen, somewhere in the world, dead . . . dead—or was he really mad? Did any of it make any sense? And the Navajo woman was drinking her drink and laughing. Maybe he was mad. Maybe there was a sex maniac. Maybe he was mad, as everyone had whispered for so long. It wouldn't be the first time he had lurched into the wrong direction on a case. He thought of Patrick laughing, and he smiled, and then Carmel Beecher Van Kueren

filled his vision, the enormous fat woman talking
with garbled words about cosmic forces and the . . .
Isis . . . Isis, the lifting of her veil . . . Nelson
Hobart spinning in a circle, his ratty toupee hovering
off his wrinkled head . . . Patrick laughing, and
through Patrick he saw Ann and he loved her, and as
he did he slipped over the edge and the darkness
swallowed him.

Caleb was shaking him by the shoulder. It took
several moments to clear the sleep away. By his
watch he figured it had been over two hours since he
had gotten into the back of the police car.

"Do the Hannibals have a dog?" Cody asked.

"I don't know," Caleb said. "Is it important?"

"I'm not sure." Cody frowned. As he awoke he
had seen the flashing, snarling teeth of a dog, but he
didn't have time to try and sort it out.

"They want to know how we knew to search
here," Caleb said.

Cody climbed out of the car. It looked like most of
the group had moved back to the cane road. The
coroner's wagon rumbled slowly past them now.

"They always want to know . . . until I tell them."

"What do I tell them?"

". . . It was a hunch," Cody said finally. "All
good cops get hunches."

Caleb lingered. He wished there was more, but
when he realized that there wasn't he moved off
down the cane road, past another police car, toward a
thick Asian-looking man who was talking to what
looked to be several reporters. But there were no
lights, no T.V. cameras. *What a nice island,* Cody
thought. *They'll be here tomorrow, over from Hono-*

*lulu no doubt . . . but tonight, at least, the poor
honeymoon couple will have that shred of dignity
left; they won't be center stage for the happy news,
between false-teeth cleaners, underarm sprays, and
the modern world's answer to the court jester, the
jovial weatherman.*

The thick Asian man finished his conversation with
the reporters and then listened to Caleb for several
moments, considering. Then he started across to Cody.
Cody thought he looked like a Hawaiian version of J.
Edgar Hoover, big head, rimless glasses. He was
wearing shorts and a Hawaiian shirt. He paused in
front of Cody for several moments before speaking.
It was as if he were observing an interesting species.

"You want to inform your people?" he asked
finally.

"Sure."

He stared at him a moment longer, then the Hawaiian J. Edgar Hoover turned and moved off, seemingly aimlessly, back into the cane.

It was almost midnight when they got to Caleb's
house. Patrick was asleep on a mat in front of a silent
T.V. with Bambi, the fat, scratchy dog, curled up
next to him.

Maile was the only one up. She was in the cramped
kitchen correcting papers. She was a schoolteacher.
Third grade, Caleb informed him. She asked if they
would like anything to eat, and they both realized
that they were famished. Cody hadn't eaten since his
eggs Benedict that morning. Caleb hadn't eaten at
all.

She scrambled a dozen eggs with Portuguese sau-
sage and made toast. Patrick woke up and came out.
Was he hungry? "Pat's always hungry," Cody said,
finding a smile to match the boy's.

Maile smiled back, but only out of form. There was no friendliness about the smile anymore. This afternoon on the beach she had been open and pleasant, but it was different now. He had brought death into the house, like he had so many times before, into so many homes, so many families. He was the carrier, the bearer of dark, unwanted things. She didn't want to be near him any longer, and he wondered how long it would be until she felt that way about her brother.

A half hour later, Patrick was curled up and almost asleep on the back seat of the rental car. Cody and Caleb stood on the red dirt driveway.

"Tomorrow morning they want to go over my logs with me . . . everything I've done since you arrived."

Cody managed a smile. "You've been keeping logs on me?"

Caleb shook his head. His smile was tired. "I was suppose to. . . . I've got to go in and write them."

"Don't leave anything out."

"You mean it?" The relief on Caleb's face was obvious.

"By the time you go in in the morning I'll know if we were right or not . . ."

"You're going in then, the Hannibals' house?"

"Let's go back to where we started this afternoon. For your sake . . . you never asked that question."

Cody pulled the rental car through the overhanging hibiscus and out onto the two-lane road. Across the way, a funeral home sat, dark, a shiny fifteen-year-old hearse parked on the lawn.

Nearby, Cuaresma sat in a pickup truck, parked

deep in the shadows of a gas station. He packed a crumbled aspirin on the tooth that was on fire as he watched Cody's rental car turn onto the highway that would take him back to the hotel. *I never should have started,* Cuaresma thought. *I never should have gotten involved.* Murder. And now he couldn't stop. They wouldn't let him stop. God that tooth was killing him.

Chapter Thirteen

The first drive through, Cody discovered that the sprawling hotel parking lot was full. The dawn would bring Labor Day, he remembered, last day of summer, last day of fun . . . last day of hope for a blind and crippled ex-cop in Canoga Park.

Since Patrick was sound asleep, the second time through he parked in a no-parking zone near the entrance closest to their room and carried the boy up. As he did, he realized that it must have been five years since he had last carried the sleeping boy from car to bed. . . . That had been a Sunday, too. They had driven down to San Diego, to Sea World. It had been hot and crowded, but it had been a good day. The boys had had fun . . . and for the first time in a couple of months so had Ann. For the first time, she had relaxed and smiled and laughed with real laughter . . . for the first time since the miscarriage.

The baby they had lost had been a girl. They had both wanted one, but Ann had especially. And then, when they had lost the baby, he had almost lost her, too. She had hemorrhaged. The doctors had seemed helpless to stop it for more than a few hours at a time. For days he had trembled on the edge of eter-

nity with her, afraid to breathe, afraid to cry, afraid
so much that he'd lose her . . . a thousand prayers, a
thousand beggings. Relatives had consoled him. Even
fat Dan Pyne had come to the hospital, wanting to be
his pal, wanting to help, full of homely platitudes
about life and death. He had wanted to punch him in
the face. Funeral signs had lept out at him as he
drove home to shower, to change clothes, to clear his
head. Funeral signs, billboards, mortuaries, they had
always been there, but he had never seen them before, never paid attention. Old Father Concannon
came, he had baptized her when she was a baby and
now he gave her last rites. Once she had even stopped
breathing. . . . And then slowly, ever so slowly, she
had started back. . . . He had always known that he
had almost lost her then . . . but now, for the first
time, carrying his sleeping son, he wondered if maybe
all that time since had just been a gift.

The message light on the phone was blinking. He
put Pat on top of the bed, took the boy's shoes off,
and then drew the other half of the bedspread over
him to act as a cover.

Who would have left a message? The question
nagged him. It seemed a bit too quick to be hearing
back from Pyne . . . unless he'd come up with something startling about the pixie-smiling Professor Polk
. . . or unless he had somehow heard about the Greens
being found dead. He hoped it wasn't that. He knew
he had to inform them in California about the discovery of the bodies, but not just yet. Not until he'd had
a chance to crack the case open. Not until he had had
a chance to look around inside the Hannibals' house.

"Front desk." It had rung eleven times.

"Kai I. My message light is on."

He had to wait another half minute.

"Mr. Cody?"

"Yes."

"There's a message and an envelope in your box."

Cody considered asking who they were from, but decided against it. "I'll be down in a few minutes."

"Mahalo."

He hung up, got to his feet, and realized how tired he was. He wanted a drink. It was one thirty in the morning and he needed to get at least another hour's rest before going out to Kamalani. First, of course, he had to go down to the front desk . . . and before that, he needed to move the car. He satisfied all positions by mixing a drink and carrying it with him, vodka and tonic, half and half. One drink would help him sleep, he reasoned . . . and yet, by the time he had finally found a space in the back parking lot, he had finished the glass and badly wanted another.

Fatigue ached across his shoulders. The grotesque image of the dead honeymooners depressed him. He knew he shouldn't have any more to drink if he was going to function effectively in the predawn hours and yet he knew he desperately wanted another drink, and another and another. He wanted to blot it all out, make it go away, put himself into a deep sleep and not wake until ten or eleven, maybe even noon . . . then have a big breakfast and a swim. He wanted to laugh and go horseback riding with his son, make it so there were no dead honeymoon bodies rotting in the paradise sun . . . and no crazy people talking about Isis and cosmic forces and . . . Jesus, maybe it was they who were crazy. Maybe he was the sane one and the rest of the world was mad, and he smiled because he realized he'd picked up Caleb's "Jesus."

Jesus. As long as he'd gone that far, maybe it was

actually Jesus, God, who had gone mad. What other answer could there be? Why was it so often he stood alone, battling, battling against ever-increasing enemies? . . . battling to protect the principles of his boyhood while all around him the whole world had gone mad. His boyhood . . . ? Was that it? His boyhood, the root of his beliefs, was that his problem, the cause of his madness? Had he stayed in his boyhood while the rest of the world had grown up . . . ? But if so . . . then who was really mad? His boyhood had been a better place. Drugs, pornograpy, child abuse, and violence were not champions then. Who the hell was mad?

"Here you are, Mr. Cody."

He was a lean, good-looking Hawaiian in his late twenties. He looked sleepy. The tag on his aloha shirt announced that his name was Lance.

Cody thanked him and started back for his room, unfolding the message as he walked. It was handprinted on a piece of hotel stationery.

> *"Mr. Cody: I don't know if it will help, but I remembered something last night about the Greens that I didn't remember when I talked to you. If you are interested, I'll be on duty from 11 AM to 6 PM at the pool bar tomorrow (labor day).*
> *Joe (the bartender)*

Cody recalled asking the bartender about people he might have noticed with the Greens, people other than hotel guests. Maybe it would be something. From experience, probably not. But maybe . . . Then his ongoing thought process stopped, and he suddenly felt cold inside.

He had opened the envelope, which had simply said ''Mr. Cody'' on it. Inside was a Polaroid picture of Patrick, asleep on the floor of their hotel room, in front of the television. He knew what it meant before he read the note that was with it. The note was made up of cut-out letters and words from magazines.

WE CAN GET THIS CLOSE TO YOUR BOY
NEXT TIME HE WILL DIE
SAVE HIM GO HOME BY FIRST PLANE
DO NOT COME BACK
DO NOT GET CUTE
TELL THE POLICE AND *I WILL KNOW*
SAVE YOUR BOY BEFORE IT'S TOO LATE

He ran the rest of the way back to the room, ears ringing, heart pounding. How long had that envelope been waiting for him? A few hours? All day? Was it already too late? He wondered how long he had been out of the room, how long Patrick had been alone. Had he over-stayed his time? His fingers seemed too big for the key, and then the key seemed too big for the lock. Open . . . finally. . . . Hurried movements. Have to look . . . afraid to look . . . relief. It was all right. Patrick was still asleep where he had left him. Safe. Safe.

He checked the room. Closet. Shower. No one there. He needed a drink. No, first the toilet. Diarrhea. Christ, he felt like someone had driven a train through him. He made a drink, a double. It was gone in moments. He poured another. His hand was shaking. Christ, his whole body was shaking. He knew he had to stop drinking. He had to deal with this. Knowing he'd regret it, he poured the rest of the fifth down the sink—the sink made out of a giant seashell.

Christ, madness. The life of his sleeping twelve-year-old son had been threatened, and he was standing in front of a sink made out of a seashell. Just another day in paradise. Just another day in paradise.

He had saved the fresh drink. He'd sip it. But first the Walther. It was still there, top shelf in the closet. He loaded it. He didn't know where to sit. The chairs in the room were too reclined. Too "vacation." They went with the giant seashell sink. He wanted to pace. He didn't want to pace. He sat on the floor, gun between his legs, drink in his hand. He wished he hadn't dumped the rest of the vodka in the sink. He remembered the bottle of wine that had come with the complimentary fruit basket left in the room. He'd drink that next. It was better than vodka, not as strong. But enough, enough. Christ, the adrenalin was flowing; he didn't know how to stop it. He was angry, so goddamn angry. He wanted to scream at the top of his lungs. At who? At the whole fucking world. At whoever did this. It was like Ann all over again, the same sense of rage—helplessness. They had threatened Patrick. They had threatened his little boy, his private part of the world! What kind of monsters was he fighting? The sons of bitches. The sons of bitches. He'd kill them. He knew then that he'd kill them. He sipped heavily at his drink. It was half gone. His heartbeat was slowing.

Had he crossed over the edge? He knew he'd kill the people who had threatened his child. Oh, he had thought of it before, fantasized of brutally beating and killing anyone who might have stolen Ann, hurt Ann. But not until that moment had he known he would really do it. Had he finally crossed over? Was his boyhood finally to be left behind? . . . Yes, if it had to be. They had finally pushed him too far.

He spent the better part of the next hour on the phone. Using "800" numbers, he managed to book himself and Patrick on a seven A.M. flight to Honolulu, and then onto a connecting flight to L.A. at nine thirty. He had no intention of going on to L.A. with Patrick, but he was being careful. He was alone again. Like a threatened animal he had to be alert for every sound, every shadow. He could trust no one. Anyone who could have gotten into the room to take a picture of Patrick while he was asleep was certainly capable of listening in on his phone calls or gaining access to a computer that could check airline reservations. So, for all the world, he was leaving. Only he would know he wasn't . . . only he, but the bastard who had threatened his son would find out. The bastard who had crossed the line. The bastard who had attacked his family.

"Front desk."

"This is Mr. Cody in Kai I. I'd like a wake-up call for five forty-five, and then have my bill ready. I'll be checking out when we come down."

"Yes, sir, Mr. Cody."

It was less than three hours until he had to get up. He realized he hadn't finished his drink, had never opened the wine. He had no desire for it now. He was working now. He was at war now.

His mind zeroed in on the only time the photograph of Patrick could have been taken . . . when he had been called down to the bar by Caleb, and the suspicions were back again. Why was the young Hawaiian so late in getting back with the honeymooners' photographs? Was it really because he had forgotten to use the name Worden when he called the shops the first time, or was it because he needed to get other people into place, into motion? And what was all that bullshit about *Fantasy Island* and Elvis Presley? He had explained it away then, but this was now. His sleeping child had been threatened. And who was the guy in the white convertible? The police were the only people who knew why Cody was on the island. The police. The note said, if he went to the police, "I will know." So who could he trust? Could he trust the young Hawaiian? He wanted to. He liked him, his family, they reminded him of his own. They made him feel comfortable, relaxed. Maybe they were supposed to. . . . He was alone again. He had been right in the first place. There was no one he could trust.

He knew he must sleep. He lay down next to his son. The Walther went under his pillow. He closed his eyes and tried to concentrate, to clear his mind, to find the nothingness. The plan to visit Kamalani, the Hannibals, to slip into their house in these predawn hours had been abandoned. Their time would come. He knew that. Everyone's time would come, until he had the bastards who had done this. But first he had to get Patrick out of the way, to get Patrick safe. Safe . . . and he thought of Ann, and she wasn't afraid anymore, and then nothingness swallowed him.

Cuaresma waited forty minutes after the last light had gone out in Caleb Ho's house. The whole side of his head throbbed in pain. The aspirins weren't helping anymore. He opened the half-pint of whiskey and took a mouthful and tried to hold it on the side of the bad tooth. He opened the door of the truck and got out.

The door made more noise than he had counted on. He stood motionless for another minute. There was no sign of alarm. He had to pee. He did—right where he stood, in the street. It seemed funny, he thought, that a shiny hearse should be parked on the lawn almost across the street from where he was going. Funny. Very appropriate.

He wished he'd never gotten involved in this. But there was no stopping now. He lifted a five-gallon can of gasoline out of the bed of the truck. The throbbing seemed a little better. He swallowed the whiskey and started across the yard.

As he had expected, the front door was open. He stepped inside and paused, trying to adjust his eyes. Maybe it was the pain that made him lose his concentration, but he didn't see the dog until it was leaping at him. He yelled and jumped back, and teeth tore into his arm. There was nothing else to do. An orange flash exploded from his gun. The bullet ripped the top of the dog named Bambi's head off. The sound woke the household . . . and that's when all hell broke loose.

Chapter Fourteen

A ringing phone was pulling him out of the darkness, and in those first few moments he realized how deeply asleep he had been. It had rung three times that he was aware of before he managed to pick it up. He shouldn't have been that deeply asleep. The mists were fading, and with their retreat the feeling of danger began to fill him again.

"Wake up call, sir. It's a quarter of six."

He mumbled something in reply and hung up, and then suddenly the memory of the photo and the threatening note came back. He felt for and found the Walther under his pillow, still there, still loaded. He was on his feet next, gun in hand, moving, head pounding. He shouldn't have fallen so deeply asleep. He felt lousy, but then he usually did these mornings. . . . Relax. The latch chain was still secure on the door. Relax. Patrick was still sound asleep. Relax. But not for long, he knew, for outside the sky was pale. Dawn was on the way.

Madness.

A ghost of himself stared back from the mirror over the giant seashell sink. . . . *Christ, is that all that's left . . . ?* He felt the stubble of his beard and realized how filthy he was, how filthy he felt. He found some clean clothes and took a shower. All the dried sweat and grime and red mud from yesterday washed away . . . but not the image of the dead, bloated honeymoon bodies, or the photo of his son and the note that came with it . . . and in that moment he had to pull back the shower curtain and make sure the Walther was still there on the ledge, next to the giant seashell sink. He wondered about Bobby Cormier and the four million dollars, and about fat Dan Pyne and whether he had found anything out about the pixie-smiling professor. *Dammit,* he thought. He had wanted to be in and out of the Hannibals' house by the time he called Pyne. And he wished he could call Caleb. He wanted to trust someone, to be able to count on someone. But he knew that was a luxury he couldn't afford, not until Patrick was clear of all this—not until Patrick was safe.

"Pat . . . Pat, time to get up."

"What . . . ?" His voice was still half in sleep.

"We're going home. Got to catch a plane."

The boy's eyes opened, and he sat up and tried to be alert. "Going home?"

"Going home," Cody repeated. "Plane leaves in an hour. Better hurry and get dressed."

He's a good-natured boy, Cody thought. *Not a complaint.* He was up trying to find his clothes, still in a sleepy fog. *Christ, who could threaten to kill a child?*

"Lillian . . . Lillian."

The sound of his voice startled her at first. It sounded so old and uncharacteristically thin.

"Lillian." Louder this time, with full resonance.

Theatrical and melodious. The very walls seemed to resound with his tones, and it restored for her a spark of courage that she desperately needed now. She had slept in fits and starts, finally rising an hour ago to come here to her meditation room. And here she had knelt, sometimes trembling, sometimes praying, surrounded by her statues and pictures . . . of Krishna and Christ and Buddha and the Virgin Mary, of Isis and Brahma, and of Mother Teresa and St. Germain and the Great Pyramid . . . and more, saints and prophets. The candles were lit and the chimes sounded softly in the gentle breeze of sunrise . . . and yet, all this, but still no solace. Not this morning. Not today. Not until this last horrid, squalid battle had been won . . . or lost.

"Lillian, come quickly."

And this time she did.

Her gown was flowing, silk and lavender. She called out as she approached the door, "Evan, is something wrong?"

But one look at his face told her nothing could possibly be wrong . . . the Great American Poet was beaming. He was eighty-five years old. His sight was dim. His memory sometimes played tricks now, and that worried him, and he tried to hide it from others. . . . But this moment he was so happy. He looked like a small child who had just been coddled by a loving mother.

"I've just had the most remarkable dream," he said.

"The boy?" Lillian asked with a hopeful smile.

"Yes," he answered and couldn't stop smiling, and for a moment, before going on, he even giggled. "We were at the Hollywood house, and I looked out the window, and there he was by the fountain, like he was the first time he came.'' He paused now, seemingly caught up again in the image.

Carmel Beecher Van Kueren had appeared in the doorway. ''Tell us everything you remember,'' she said gently in her man's voice . . . and while she spoke her enormous girth glided over to the old man's bedside and turned on a dictation-sized tape recorder. ''What was he wearing?''

Hannibal closed his eyes and swayed back and forth for several moments, and then the smile again lit his face. ''At first, black. Just as he did before.''

''You mean when he actually appeared at the house?'' Carmel Beecher Van Kueren wanted to be precise.

''Yes. Yes . . . silk. Fine black silk, and the shirt clung perfectly to his delicate little torso . . . and the sleeves ballooned just a bit . . . and there was something else.'' He squinted. Difficult memory, damned memory, don't slip away. . . . It was back. ''A crescent. . . . Later it changed, first to a sun, a brilliant golden sun . . . and then to a phoenix, all in diamonds, of course, but by then his clothes were white. . . . No. No. The phoenix was no longer diamonds; they had changed to sapphires.''

The two women exchanged guarded but excited smiles.

''Slowly.'' The enormous redheaded woman guided him. ''Keep the progression from the beginning of the dream, from when he was in black, by the fountain at the Hollywood house.''

He closed his eyes again and nodded several times before speaking. ''He wasn't sad like he had been on the visits.'' This recollection brought a smile to his face . . . and a smile of revelation to the faces of the women.

"He seemed very happy to see me and started speaking rapidly in French, and I had to stop him and say, 'I'm sorry, but I only speak English,' and he laughed, and his laughter was like the sound of tinkling glass bells. Then he said, 'You never were good with languages, were you? Not in all the passages of time . . .' And then he didn't say anything . . . but I had a sense of being with him in ancient Egypt, long before the Pharaohs, in a ceremony with gold and flames . . . and then again I was with him in ancient Greece . . . and then again in France, in times of turmoil, bad days for the royalty . . ."

The old man's brow furrowed. "And then he said he had to leave me, but that I would be with him at the dawning. . . . He said, 'I must leave before I can return.' . . . and I knew he was going to the Himalayas. . . ."

He paused for several moments, and no one in the room spoke. Finally the furrowed brow relaxed again as he smiled, and he laughed and went on. "And then we were here . . . walking among the flowers. I was still an old man like I am now, and he was in white . . . silk, white, and the crescent had become the brilliant sun. 'Join me,' he said . . . and I said, 'Yes, I want to join you. . . .' "

Again the old man laughed, this time in true delight. "And then I was a boy again, like he was—I couldn't have been more than seven or eight—and we were both running in the surf. We were wearing only some kind of white gossamer loincloths, and they furled and flapped in the wind, and the water splashed cold on our bodies, and we were laughing

. . . and I was so happy . . . and then the landscape began to fade . . . and I was an old man again. He looked up at me and seemed to be a little afraid, not terribly afraid, but just a little, and he said, 'Save me,' . . . and he came up into my arms, and I said, 'I will, I will,' . . . but then he was gone and I was afraid that he hadn't heard me . . . but then I saw him again, and he was smiling. His golden sun had become a sapphire phoenix and he was smiling, and I knew that he knew that everything would be all right, that we would join him, that he knew we would pay the four million dollars, and we would all join him.''

The white convertible was following them again. Cody had pulled out of the hotel parking lot about ten minutes past six. Patrick, riding in the front seat next to him, was dressed in his cut-offs, tee-shirt, and white canvas deck shoes.

Then, just like the day before, they were crossing the bridge over the Wailua when Cody spotted the convertible in his rear-view mirror. He had expected it. He would, in fact, have been badly disappointed if it and its white-blond-haired driver hadn't appeared. . . . He wanted, of course, to spin the car around, force the convertible off the road, beat the living shit out of the white-blond-haired son of a bitch, stick his gun in his face, and make him tell what he knew. But he couldn't, not with Patrick there. He couldn't force the action and worry about the safety of his son, too. There would be others involved. There had to be. The white-blond-haired driver was too clumsy to be operating on his own. Just the way he followed them both yesterday and now established that. He was either too dumb to realize that Cody would spot him

. . . or he didn't care. It could have been considered brazen if it hadn't been so awkward . . . but whoever killed the honeymooners had been anything but awkward . . . or dumb . . . or clumsy. Whoever killed them had been vicious and rather clever, if not outright smart. Whoever had killed them had gone to California and stolen pictures out of the dead girl's bedroom. Cody thought of the little professor again and his funny little smile. He had gone to California and come back. Why? Was he the one smart enough not to attack Cody openly, but to threaten him personally? An attack would have brought everything out into the open, would have convinced even the dullest of police brass as to his line of investigation. This way whoever had done it had bought time. Not much . . . but maybe enough for four million dollars.

No, he couldn't move on the white-blond man yet. It had to be this way. Right now, whoever killed the honeymooners would know that he had checked out of the hotel and was on his way to the airport. Whoever killed the honeymooners would think they had the situation under control, and that was good. He wanted them to think that, and if he pulled off what he hoped to, the element of surprise would be in his favor.

The only question was how far the white-blond man would follow them—just to Lihue Airport or all the way to Honolulu to make sure they got on the connecting flight to Los Angeles? He hoped all the way.

By the time they got to Lihue Airport, the sun had come up hot, and the parking lot was already jammed with Labor Day traffic. Cody parked in a car-rental "return space" and for some minutes lost track of the white convertible and its white-blond driver.

They were third in line to check their car in . . . or at least make an appearance of doing so . . . when Cody spotted him again. The white-blond-haired man was lingering in front of the terminal building, laughing and chatting off and on with different porters in their uniform aloha shirts, while, of course, keeping an eye on them. Stupid. The son of a bitch really was stupid. He and the porters were much too friendly, much too familiar to be just casual acquaintances. . . . Now even if the bastard didn't follow them to Honolulu, Cody knew he would have a way of tracking him down.

So far Cody hadn't told Patrick anything of his real plans. He had wanted the boy to continue to act naturally for as long as possible. But now, as the man in line ahead of him was apparently finishing, Cody leaned over to Pat and spoke in what he knew the boy would recognize as a precise, no-nonsense manner. "Pay attention. . . . Listen to what I say . . . but don't interrupt. . . . Don't ask any questions. Understand?"

The boy nodded, and suddenly in this new confusion seemed more awake than any time since he had gotten up.

"Checking in, sir?"

She was chubby and quite pretty—shiny black hair with Hawaiian-Asian features. Her voice sounded tired, and it took him a moment to realize she was also quite pregnant. It caught him off guard. She was at least eight months, he guessed, and he remembered a photograph of Ann that he had always particularly liked. She had been almost full term with Damien . . . wearing a gingham shirt, smiling, and looking slightly embarrassed as the camera had caught her protruding stomach in full profile.

"Sir?"

"I'm sorry," Cody said. "Still a little sleepy. Actually, instead of turning in my car, I'm hoping to switch it . . . I'm getting a lot of gas fumes."

"Oh, that's no good," she said and meant it. She took the key he had offered and from the number on the tag found his file. "Mr. Cody?"

"That's right."

She picked up the phone and dialed three numbers. A child who didn't look more than a year old or so was playing in a sing-song voice in a well-worn playpen in the corner of the office. No one seemed to be answering on the other end of the phone.

"I've got a seven o'clock plane to catch," a short, stocky man in plaid shorts said loudly, half pleading, half belligerent. He was second in line behind Cody.

"I do, too," a tall elderly woman, even farther back in line, added in a trembling voice.

The young woman behind the counter looked apologetically at Cody, phone still in hand. "Gosh, I don't know what to tell you. . . . We're kind of in a rush right now. It'll probably be at least twenty or thirty minutes before I can get a replacement up here for you."

"Well, that's really not a problem," Cody said and tried to look like he wanted to help. "Actually, we have to go over to Honolulu this morning and won't be back for a couple of hours."

"Oh, we'd certainly have something by then."

"I'd like to be able to count on it. I'll be in kind of a hurry when I get back."

"I can't wait much longer," the man in the plaid shorts said loudly to no one in particular.

"I'll have it parked right out here for you," the

young woman behind the counter said. "I'll even have all your paperwork fixed up."

"That'll be great," Cody said and made a move as if to leave the counter, then he paused as if having an afterthought. "There are a couple of other things I'd like to ask . . . if it's possible."

"If I can," she answered, and the baby started crying.

"Oh for God's sake," whined the man in the plaid shorts. "I'm going to miss my goddamn plane."

"Hang on to this for me?" Cody asked and placed the parcel he'd been carrying on the counter. It was an over-sized manila envelope, folded over and taped together. From the outside, what was inside looked and felt to be sort of a soft brick. Actually, it was his Walther and spare clips, around which he had wrapped a roll of toilet paper to disguise their shape. He knew he could never get them through airport security carrying them on his person. The suitcase, of course, would be checked straight through to L.A. The parcel looked like something to be mailed. He had addressed it to Ann, using her maiden name and the address she had grown up at, and glancing at it now, for a flicker of a moment, he wanted to cry. "I had forgotten I'd left it in the car," he went on, "and with the post offices not being open today, I'd hate to have to carry it all the way to Honolulu and back."

"I'll have it with your papers and new keys," she said. The smile was strained now. The baby's crying was getting louder. The man in the plaid shorts was sighing with exaggeration.

"Thanks," Cody said. "One other thing—the car I'm turning in. I hate the color. . . . if you can, I'd like another color with the next car." There was no smile on her face this time, and he didn't wait for an answer. They had only a little more than twenty minutes before the flight.

"I thought we were going home," Patrick said as soon as they had moved away from the car-rental booth.

They had to wait for a tourist bus to pass. Cody draped his arm around the boy's shoulder and gave him a bit of a hug. "Only half right, I'm afraid . . . You're going home."

"I don't understand."

"You know I came over here looking for some people."

"Yes," the boy said.

The bus had passed. They dodged a car trying to back up to the terminal curb and kept going.

"Well, some things happened yesterday," Cody went on. "It could get dangerous here." How could he tell his twelve-year-old son his life had been threatened? "I'd just feel better if you were safe at home." While he talked he managed fleeting glimpses in the direction of the white-blond-haired man; they were passing within ten feet of him. Long, narrow nose . . . dirty, well-worn white trousers . . . Cody was careful not to look at him directly; he didn't want the man to know that he was aware of him. . . . He noted huaraches, the Mexican open-toed shoes. "And we won't talk anymore just now," Cody finished saying to the boy.

They moved quickly through the agricultural check, opening the suitcase for a brief inspection. The airline check-in line looked to be more of a problem. There were at least a dozen people ahead of them. *Christ, we should have started earlier*, Cody thought.

He wanted to look around to see if the white-blond-haired man was following them, but he didn't dare. *Christ, the line isn't moving. We'll have to do something or miss the plane.* But then, before he had a chance to act, a portly Hawaiian clerk opened up another window and called out, "Passengers for the seven o'clock flight only," and suddenly Cody and the boy were second in line.

"How much danger?" Patrick asked. His eyes were apprehensive now. The fun was gone. Ann's eyes.

Cody tried a smile and was aware he was lying. "Nothing more than when I used to be on the police force and would go to work every day."

The twelve-year-old tried not to, but after a couple of moments he was crying.

"Next please."

Cody had to go through the business of getting the tickets: first class, ten dollars more than regular fare. They had been the only seats available when he booked it three and a half hours ago.

Patrick had managed to dry his eyes by the time they moved away from the counter.

"Why were you crying?" Cody asked.

"Nothing," the boy said.

"Gotta be something." Cody paused and made the boy do so, too. People with suitcases and carry-ons were pushing around them. "Come on, tell me."

"It's just that I was always afraid when you went to work every day . . . I was always afraid someone would kill you." His voice was cracking, and he couldn't stop crying now. "And now there isn't even Mom."

Bastards. Cody wanted to turn around and find the

white-blond-haired son of a bitch and blast his goddamn face off . . . but he knew he couldn't. Not yet.

The boy stopped crying again, and as they passed
through the metal-detector Cody managed a glance
back down the corridor. Just behind the belligerent
man in the plaid shorts, the white-blond-haired man
had joined the short line for the seven o'clock
flight. . . . So the stupid son of a bitch was coming
to Honolulu with them.

Chapter Fifteen

It was raining softly when the plane touched down in Honolulu.

More madness.

The white-blond-haired man, having apparently bought the last fare-plus-ten-dollar first-class ticket had been placed in the seat just across the aisle from Cody.

Twenty minutes of not being able to turn his head in that direction. Twenty minutes of imagining the white-blond-haired man's eyes on him. Twenty minutes of nursing a terrible cup of coffee, orange juice, of looking at magazine pictures of Waikiki and volcanos with Patrick. He tried to make his mind work, to fit the pieces together, trying to make sense of all that had happened, and yet he knew he didn't have enough of the pieces yet. And a couple of times the cry of fear had come back to him . . . from the dark place . . . the fear and the little dog barking. Suddenly, the boy's words jarred him back to the present.

"Will someone meet me in Los Angeles?" Patrick asked.

The 737 was still taxiing, fat tires slicing through

the water on the concrete runways. Cody hadn't expected the question, at least not at that moment.

"I'll explain later, okay?" He said it quietly but with an inflection that discouraged any further conversation. He was concerned as to whether or not the white-blond-haired man had overheard the boy's words. And if he had, if he understood their implications . . . Cody knew he couldn't afford that. There was nothing else he could do. He had to take the chance. He turned and, for the first time, looked across the aisle. Christ, the man was staring at him. For one frozen moment neither knew what to do. Long, slender nose, white-blond hair, eyes and features dulled from years of drug use . . . Microseconds were slipping by, and then Cody pulled up and tourist-smiled. "Just another day in paradise, huh?"

"Yeah," the white-blond-haired man answered and relaxed and smiled, and both men broke the eye connection.

So he isn't just stupid, Cody mused. His brain had been fried, at great expense, over the years. Cody had seen it before; too many times. The sewers of society always turn up a sprinkling of drug burnouts like the white-blond-haired man. The problem was, he knew he couldn't count on him being that burned out, or that stupid. He couldn't count on him having missed the boy's words or their meaning . . . and perhaps most importantly, he couldn't count on him not being that dangerous. Sometimes the white-blond-haired man's type could be the most dangerous of all. Sometimes there was just enough working grey matter to know their lives had been wasted . . . and not enough to deal with the pressures that built up around them, and so, instead of coping, they exploded, mindlessly and savagely. Cody remembered a policewoman. Pretty and bright, she was going to set the world on fire, and then she had her face cut off with a meat cleaver because she had relaxed . . . because her suspect was a burnout. He had looked so simple and stupid . . . and then he had killed her.

"Please remain seated until the plane has come to a complete stop."

The stewardess's request over the intercom was mostly ignored. People were in a hurry: Open the overheads, pull together the carry-ons, crowd into the aisles. Make sure you don't let anyone in front of you. Outside, they were wheeling the stairway up, and they were ready to open the doors. Cody knew he had to think fast. On the trip over, his mind had been crowded with his own jumbled emotions and with the pieces of the case, and as the cobwebs of sleep and of his hangover had cleared, he had realized just how outgunned he was. So far, the other side had won every point. They were controlling the game with a strong hand. Something big was going down, something perhaps worth four million dollars, something that so far had been worth killing two people for. *Christ, four million dollars can buy a lot of death,* he thought. And if he guessed right, it was something that had been going on for a long time . . . something he had entered into late in the game. Even so, his appearance had become a nuisance, a dangerous nuisance, dangerous enough that they would threaten him through his son . . . but who were they? The man across the aisle from him was his best chance of finding out.

Madness.

The doors were opening. If the white-blond-haired man had overheard and understood what Patrick had said, he wouldn't follow them anymore. He'd slip away, warn the others. Cody knew he couldn't let that happen. There was nothing else to do; they'd have to reverse positions. They'd have to follow him, at least for a while.

"Just go along with whatever I say," Cody said quickly into the boy's ear, and then they pushed into the crowded aisle and started their shuffle for the front exit. So far no signs of alarm. The white-blond-haired man had waited for them to start their exit before he rose from his seat. He was three people behind them when they reached the door.

"Thank you for flying Aloha," the pretty stewardess said.

"Very nice flight," Cody replied with a pleasant smile . . . which then almost immediately turned odd, and he started to frantically check his pockets.

"Something wrong, sir?"

"I must have left my tickets to Los Angeles on our seats," Cody said, sounding somewhat frazzled. And with that, he and the boy started back up the aisle, against the crowded and shuffling traffic. "Excuse me, sorry . . . forgot something." The last statement he managed with a rather idiotic smile to an old Hawaiian woman as he slipped by her and the white-blond-haired man.

"Now I know what a salmon feels like swimming upstream," Patrick said, adding to the ruse and apparently enjoying it.

Cody waited a few moments after the white-blond-haired man had disappeared down the outside stairway, and then, with Patrick in tow, rejoined the shuffle for the exit.

About halfway back in the line, which stretched to the middle of the plane, someone broke wind loudly, which brought titters of laughter, a grin to Patrick's face . . . and a comment in a whining, belligerent voice that Cody recognized as belonging to the man in the plaid shorts.

"Oh shit."

"Not yet," replied a giggling, youthful if anxious voice. "But it will be soon if everyone doesn't hurry."

They reached the exit again. The stewardess smiled at them. "Find your ticket?"

But instead of answering, Cody stepped into the "ante-space" between the exit door and the cockpit. The boy followed automatically. Cody had to indicate for her to do so as well. Her name tag said her name was Maile, and he thought of Caleb's sister. Like this girl she was soft and pretty. She had taken care of Patrick, and he knew he'd been attracted to her, and he thought she had been attracted to him before the deaths. The car of deaths.

"Actually, I wasn't looking for tickets." He showed her his police identification and counted on her not noting he wasn't on active service. "I'm a policeman from Los Angeles. My son and I are here on vacation. The man who sat across from me, in 3B, is someone we've been looking for for a long time back in California."

"I see," she said, quite serious now. "What can I do?"

"I'd like to know the name he was traveling under."

She checked the boarding passes and after a half a minute showed him the one marked 3B: Mr. G. Davenport.

"Does that help?" she asked.

"Very much, thanks," Cody said, and he and Patrick rejoined the push and, moments later, stepped out into the soft rain.

It always helps to put a name to a face, he thought.

The face of a suspect. The face of a son of a bitch who threatened his twelve-year-old's life . . . Davenport, G. . . . George? Gregory? Gordon? It didn't matter; he'd find out in time, and when he did, white-blond G. Davenport would wish he hadn't. And then he couldn't help but smile, for there the dumb son of a bitch was, awkward as ever, on the edge of the tarmac near the terminal building, pretending to tie his shoe. So he hadn't overheard Patrick, or if he had, his dulled thought processes hadn't computed the words' meaning. But Cody's smile didn't last; his mind wouldn't let it. The image of the dead honeymooners, bloated and disfigured, was too fresh in his mind. Davenport might be dumb, might be burned out, but he was part of those murders. Christ, he was part of those murders . . . and now that he had spotted Cody and the boy coming down the stairs from the plane, he moved inside the terminal.

The rest of the way across the airport was no problem. Cody used the fact that neither he nor Pat had enjoyed the crowded jitney ride two days earlier, and that since the airport was even more jammed this Labor Day morning, it could only be worse, as an excuse to suggest they walk from the Inter-island terminal to the overseas one.

"Why not?" Pat agreed easily, with a smile that Cody didn't quite understand . . . but that wasn't important now. What was important was that white-blond G. Davenport wouldn't have a difficult time maintaining his clumsy tail on them.

It was a good ten-minute walk they had embarked on. Cody had managed to check on their white-blond tail once and was looking for a second opportunity when Patrick spoke up and took him by surprise. "Want me to look?"

"What?"

"Want me to see if he's still there?" the boy persisted.

"Who?" Cody managed and realized at once that the boy knew much more than he had assumed and that his own response had been less than brilliant.

"That blond guy, Davenport. He's following us, isn't he?" Patrick was smiling like that cat who had eaten the canary, and now Cody understood the smile he'd seen when he had suggested they walk across the airport.

"Well?" Patrick pushed.

A grin finally found its way onto Cody's face. "Can you do it without him knowing you're doing it?"

"Watch." Pat grinned back with determination and then sprinted through the moving crowd. About thirty feet ahead, he reached a drinking fountain, where he took a measured drink and then turned leisurely to wait for his father . . . his eyes now naturally looking back in the direction from which he had come. When his father passed he slipped back into pace with him.

"Well?" Cody asked.

Patrick couldn't control his grin. "Still there. Picking his nose. Right nostril, if you want that for your report."

And Cody found himself laughing. "All the world loves a smart ass, you know."

Patrick laughed back.

They waited in line for forty-five minutes to get their boarding passes. It was a huge open-air room. Outside, the soft rain came and went, only the heat and the humidity kept growing. Cody thought about Patrick and how he had just helped him check on the white-blond Davenport. Much of it was a child's game to him, not knowing the danger. But some of it wasn't. Some of it was him growing up, trying to take responsibility.

Christ, on top of the murders, the threats, the pieces of the case that didn't fit yet, the last hour had been filled with new realizations for Cody. Up until an hour ago in Lihue Airport he had never thought about the boys being left alone if something should happen to him. It had never come up when he was on the force. Oh yes, there had always been danger, the possibility of death, but there had also always been Ann. They had talked about that on a number of occasions . . . if something happened to him, she would always be there to hold the family together, to see the boys grow up straight and good . . . and now she wasn't there, and now he had to be afraid of dying because it would leave the boys alone, and yet even that was changing, because they were growing up . . . even little Pat.

There was a breeze on the open-air concourse to the planes. It helped. They stopped once at a news-stand, a souvenir shop. Davenport lingered out beyond the passing crowd of passengers. Cody bought souvenirs, among them a grotesque orange aloha shirt, a straw plantation hat, and some red-framed, mirrored sunglasses. Patrick settled for copies of *Mad* and *Cracked* magazines . . . though Cody did notice the boy's eyes scanning the covers of *Playboy* and *Penthouse,* etc. . . . time was marching on.

Davenport saw them all the way to the plane.

Madness.

Cody felt like waving.

''Why was he following us?'' Patrick finally asked

when they were in the enclosed boarding tunnel. He had been strangely quiet since their purchases.

"Some people didn't want me on the island," Cody said, trying to sound matter of fact. "Looking for who I was looking for."

"The honeymoon couple, you mean." The boy's words were more of a statement than a question.

"That's right," Cody answered.

"They're dead. It saw it on the front page of the newspaper when we were buying our stuff."

The fun was gone from the boy's voice. Cody had wanted to keep the news of the murders from him. In a-thousand-murders-a-year L.A. it would hardly get a mention in the press. Christ, how much did his growing-up son have to know?

"Yes, they're dead," he answered.

A middle-aged woman and her teenage daughter were staring at them oddly.

Cody began to worry. Five, six, seven minutes had passed since he'd last seen Davenport. It was crowded getting off of planes, crowded getting on. Finally they reached their seats. It wasn't a whole lot better, people pushing, trying to move past, others standing, stretching, trying to store carry-ons above and below. Two women were arguing over a block of seats.

"Either Grandma or Damien will meet you at the airport. You're not to go with anyone else, under-stand?" Cody asked as he stripped off first his jacket and then his shirt, much to the surprise of the other passengers around him.

"Yeah," Pat said, then hesitated before going on, "The people who wanted you off the island. Did they threaten to kill you?"

"You watch too much T.V."

"Don't lie to me." The boy was growing up . . . but he was also near tears.

Cody had the bright orange aloha shirt on and was buttoning it as he leaned over and tried to speak quietly.

"No. They didn't threaten to kill me." How could he tell the boy that he was the threatened victim? "Let's just say they wouldn't be too happy if I stayed."

The answer seemed to mollify the boy. "Did they say they were going to beat you up?"

"Something like that," Cody lied with a smile.

"I wish you didn't have to stay. . . . It's not like you're a policeman anymore."

"I know . . . but I can't walk away from this. . . . There's some really bad guys in this one, and I've got a feeling if I don't stop them, nobody else will. . . . I've gotta stop them." He wanted to say more. He wanted to talk about Ann and how much he loved her, and how, somehow, doing this was helping him cope with his madness. But he was afraid they'd just both end up in tears, and he couldn't take that right now . . . so he settled for leaning over and hugging the boy and saying, "I love you very much."

"I love you, Dad."

Cody smiled. "Tell Damien I said you guys could have pizza for dinner."

"Okay." Pat smiled.

They smiled at one another for several more seconds, and then Cody started away.

"Hey, Dad," the boy called.

"Yeah?" Cody called back. He was nearly at the front of the cabin, a forest of bobbing and shuffling passengers between him and his son.

"That shirt," Pat shouted. "It really stinks, you know."

And Cody found himself laughing again. *Christ, how many times has that been in the last couple of days?*

Eleven minutes after his last sighting of blond-haired Davenport, the man in the grotesque orange aloha shirt, straw Panama hat, and mirrored sunglasses emerged from the boarding tunnel.

There was no sign of him. Cody ran now, through the ever-growing crowds, sprinting most of the way down the concourse . . . still no sign of Davenport. Past the security checks, into the ticketing area . . . no Davenport. He stood still, slowly letting his eyes sweep the masses of people. The heat and humidity were almost unbearable. . . . And then he saw him, ambling his stupid way along, heading in the direction Cody had expected him to, back to the Inter-island terminal.

Cody closed the gap to twenty yards. He was fairly confident that Davenport wouldn't recognize him in his new attire, but no need to chance it. He kept his conservative distance.

According to a television screen, the next flight to Kauai was in fifty minutes. Luckily for both of them, the traffic to the outer islands was sparse this morning compared to that coming into Oahu. Cody waited until Davenport had bought his ticket and had disappeared down the walkway to the gates before he joined the ticket line. It took him twelve minutes, which left a little more than half an hour for some much-needed phone calls.

"Cunningham house, Molly speaking." Six-year-old Molly was out of breath as she answered the phone.

"Molly, this is Damien's dad. . . . Could I speak to Damien, please?"

The phone clattered, first to the table, then the floor. He could hear voices. Molly's oldest sister was almost seventeen. She and Damien had been dating for a couple of years. This was the second year in a row that her family had invited him along on their annual Labor Day weekend in Arrowhead.

"Dad?"

"Having fun?" Cody asked.

"Yeah, a great time. We're just about to go out waterskiing again. How about you guys? You're the ones in Hawaii."

"It's terrific." Cody tried, but couldn't hide the change in his voice. "Listen, I hate to break up your day, but I need you to do something."

"What's wrong?" Damien had known his father too long not to read the tenor of his voice.

"I've just put Patrick on a plane to L.A. . . . got a pencil?"

There were several moments of silence until finally Damien said, "Got one."

"He's on Continental flight 08, due to arrive in Los Angeles at five-forty this afternoon. I want you to meet him and take him back to the boat . . . and then stay with him."

"Is . . ." Damien paused. It took him a couple of seconds to frame his thought. "I don't understand; is he in some kind of danger?"

"Just stay with him. I think everything will be all right," Cody said, and he knew he sounded like a cop.

Silence.

"When will you be coming back?" Damien finally asked.

"I'll call you tonight," Cody said . . . then pressed. "Can you get to the plane?"

"I think so," the eighteen-year-old said.

"God damn it," Cody exploded. "You can't think; you have to know."

"I can get to the plane." The words were sullen.

"I'm sorry." Cody's response was almost automatic.

"It's all right." So was Damien's.

Silence.

How long will I keep yelling at my son? Cody wondered. *How long? Christ, they're all that's left.* Without them he was alone, maybe alone forever. Why couldn't he trust them? He had to trust them. He loved them. They weren't babies anymore, and he needed them.

"Christ," he said as he realized how much he needed them.

"What?" Damien asked.

Silence.

"I need your help, D," Cody said finally. "I can't do it alone anymore."

"I'll do whatever I can." The boy's voice had changed, too. He was being spoken to as an equal.

"You can't repeat any of this to your brother."

"All right."

"Last night I received a note threatening to kill Patrick if we didn't go back to Los Angeles."

"Oh my God." The words came out of the boy's throat a whisper.

"Two people have been murdered here already," Cody went on. "I have a feeling it could get a lot worse. I can't let them chase me off of this one." And then it all broke loose. He did his best to control the emotion in his voice, but he knew it was there. ". . . I don't know how to explain it, D, but somehow it's like Mom all over again. I haven't been able to do anything about her, to find her, to do any god damn thing . . . and it's driving me crazy. But on this one I think I can do something . . . for Christ's sake, I think I can finally accomplish something again. . . . The people who threatened me think I'm on that plane with Pat right now.''

Silence. The words had left Cody drained.

''Dad?'' Damien finally asked, and Cody thought he was crying.

''Yes?'' Cody answered.

''Get the sons of bitches. Get 'em for all of us. I'll take care of my little brother.''

And Cody knew he wasn't alone anymore. ''Do you know where my service .38 is?''

''Yes, sir,'' the boy answered, ''and I know how to use it if I have to.''

''I don't think anything will backfire on you, but just in case, check it, load it, and keep it ready.''

''I will. Anything else?''

''Yeah . . .'' Cody said, finding a smile again. ''I told Pat he could have pizza for dinner tonight.'' And the next thing he knew he was almost laughing again. *Christi,* he thought, *it's becoming a regular habit.*

Chapter Sixteen

Flames.

The conversation with Damien had left him feeling good, almost whole again. Then, in less than a minute, everything had changed.

Flames. Screaming.

He had tried calling Caleb. It was time; he could trust the young Hawaiian again. Any lingering doubt could be put aside . . . any possible concerns, he could keep an eye on. Patrick was safe on the plane, flying away from Hawaii. Until that had been accomplished, he had known he could only trust himself.

Flames. Pain. Searing white-hot pain.

The call hadn't gone through, and he'd tried the number again. He was feeling a little guilty about not having trusted his new friend. But too much had happened, too fast. He knew he couldn't have taken a chance, any chance, with Patrick at risk. But still there was the lingering feeling of betrayal. Caleb, his mother, his brother and sisters had made them feel comfortable in their home. He remembered how their fat, scratchy dog had even curled up and slept with Pat . . . and that was when he'd seen his first image of flames . . . heard the screaming . . . saw the dog again, teeth bared, leaping and snarling, and he knew then that the dog he'd seen on waking last night in the back of the police car had been Caleb's dog . . . not the Hannibals'. It had been fat, scratchy Bambi, who had snuggled up to his son.

He tried the operator, but she only confirmed that Caleb's line was out of order.

People were watching him, people who wanted to use the phone. Minutes passed; they seemed like forever. He stood, phone in hand, hand at his side. He dialed again, this time from a number on a small scrap of paper, soggy from the humidity.

"Kauai Police Department."

"I'd like to speak to Detective Caleb Ho, please," Cody said. His words echoed in his head. He knew he had to say them. He had to try. Maybe it was a mistake. Maybe the young Hawaiian's phone really was out of order, for a simple reason. Maybe he was too tired, still too hungover. . . . Maybe what he saw—the images, the flames, the pain, the screaming—was all something that could still be prevented.

"I'm sorry," the woman's voice said after a couple of moments, "Detective Ho isn't here right now. Could I take a message, or would you like to speak to another officer?"

"No. I have to speak to him. . . . It's important." His words were halting. He was aware that on the other end an extension had been picked up. Someone was listening, but he didn't care. "I've tried his home, but the line is out of order."

"Well, if you can hold, I'll try to get a location on him."

They've seen too many T.V. shows, too, Cody thought. *They're trying to trace the call.*

"That won't be necessary," Cody said. "Let me

speak to Detective Ho's immediate superior. My name is Cody.''

Silence. He heard muffled voices, and then someone was speaking, but Cody couldn't answer.

White, blinding, searing pain.

Cody's ribs were on fire.

"This is Lieutenant Rivera. Are you there?''

"I'm here," Cody answered. His words came in near gasps.

"Could you tell me where you are now, Mr. Cody?'' The lieutenant's voice was gentle. He sounded as if he were speaking to a child.

"They were shot, weren't they?'' The words came out of Cody's mouth unexpectedly. "They were shot, and then the house was set on fire.'' And he was conscious of knowing only part of the words. The others, the images, had a life of their own.

"We've been to your hotel, Mr. Cody.'' Tension was growing in the lieutenant's gentle voice. "They told us you'd checked out.''

"Compare the ballistics," Cody went on. "They'll match with the bullets found in the honeymoon couple.''

"Mr. Cody, it's important we talk to you. . . .''

Cody hung up in the middle of the gentle words.

The plane was already boarding when he reached the gate. He was one of the last ones on. He didn't care anymore if Davenport recognized him. *If he gives the slightest recognition that he does,* Cody thought, *I'll kill the son of a bitch where he sits. With my bare hands. I'll beat the son of a bitch to death.* . . . He felt half in a daze. He passed the white-blond man on the way to his own seat. Not even a glance. The son of a bitch was truly stupid, and Cody smiled in contempt.

He bought two of the little bottles of vodka to mix with his tonic on the way over. It wasn't enough.

. . . They weren't all dead. He sensed that. Maybe, though . . . he knew . . . he just hoped that . . . They weren't all dead. It kept coming back. *Christ, how long can hope keep coming back?* He had thought that hope was dead in him . . . nearly dead . . . only the flickering light for Ann . . . They weren't all dead. Then who was still alive? Who was dead? He thought of Derek, the husky Hawaiian-brown fourteen-year-old. He had taken Pat surfing. They had become friends. He wanted to be a fireman when he grew up. . . . Maile, beautiful Maile, and he knew now that he saw Ann in her. Not in her looks or even in her physique, but something in her being, a goodness, a patience . . . and then he saw her head ripped open by bullets, and he hated what he saw, and he hated what he was and the images that he sometimes got, ever jumbled with his own emotions, never quite knowing what parts were true . . . what parts were his own morbid fears.

White-blond G. Davenport never looked around. He was off the plane ahead of Cody, drifting through the clusters of passengers who had gathered to wait for their luggage, and then out of the main building and across to the parking lot.

The soft rain had been left behind in Oahu. Here the sky was still a rich, bright blue, with puffs of white clouds. The sun was hot, but a cooling sea breeze discounted the humidity and led the giant green cane fields to dance and sway over the red earth. *Beautiful Kauai*, Cody had thought as the plane swooped in low for its landing. *Beautiful Kauai. Murder and madness have opened a wound on you.*

Cody kept the numbers of people between himself

and the white-blond man, but hurried toward the car-rental booth, so that eventually the distance between them was parallel, as opposed to being ahead and behind.

The car-rental lady was good to her word. She smiled when she saw him approach and interrupted herself with a customer to hand him his new keys and the parcel he'd left with her. The baby was sleeping quietly in the playpen.

"Your car's just behind here," she said, "in space sixteen. A blue Toyota."

If it wasn't so monstrous he would have laughed. Was it a warning? An omen? Was he supposed to die in a blue Toyota, too? If so, it would be a bloody goddamn bath, he thought. He wouldn't go down as easily as the young couple had.

White-blond G. Davenport and his white convertible were easy to follow: left at the Kentucky Fried Chicken, left again at the McDonalds. *Christ,* he thought. They were following the same route he and Patrick had taken two days earlier to arrive at the police station. Suddenly he remembered the words in the note: "Tell the police and I will know." A bluff, maybe. He knew that. But then why was the white-blond G. Davenport going this way?

Then, on the street where he should have turned left if he was going to the police station, Davenport turned right.

Cody and the blue Toyota were eleven seconds behind, but by the time he turned the corner, the white convertible had disappeared. He kept driving. He passed an auto repair shop, some huge, overgrown oleander bushes . . . Then, there it was again, parked in the front yard of a 1920's-style white frame house. The front yard now served as a parking area. The house, at least the front of it, had been converted into the "Rainbow Health Food Store." And white-blond G. Davenport was heading around the side of the building.

The street dead-ended into a cane field a hundred yards down. Cody drove half the distance, made a U-turn, and parked. It was quiet, no traffic. A tiny old woman with Asian features watered her lawn and stared at him. Hers was one of the half dozen older homes left on the block. The other buildings on the street were now storefronts or housed light industries, and they, of course, were closed for the holiday.

Minutes ticked by.

The vapor of death was around him. He could sense it. And he remembered the policewoman again, her face cut off . . . He unpacked the Walther.

Ten minutes had passed from the time he parked until he got out of the blue Toyota and started walking back up the street. The Walther was in his waistband now, under his shirt—his grotesque orange shirt.

He paused on the sidewalk in front of the old house that was the Rainbow Health Food Store and made a show of looking up and down the street, as if searching for an elusive address. From his glances, the Rainbow Health Food Store looked quiet. Maybe it was supposed to look quiet, he thought. Maybe white-blond G. Davenport was waiting for him. Maybe it was a trap. Davenport could have spotted him, just like he had spotted Davenport . . . Maybe this was the place where he was to die. Maybe he was the one crying out in fear from the great blackness. He walked to the front porch, past the white convertible . . .

"Fresh herbs on Tuesday" the sign in the window announced. Next to it a larger sign said, "CLOSED." Quiet. Cody paused at the base of the porch. He stood there for a quarter of a minute. Still quiet. His hand touched his gun, then he moved around the side of the house. Overgrown hibiscus bushes leaned out at him, the flowers bright yellow and red. A hornet flew around his face. He heard music from inside, *The Flintstones* music. He ducked under the open window and kept moving for the back. The hornet lost interest. A grey-and-white cat looked at him from the top of the back-porch step. He paused, listened . . . no sounds from the room immediately above him. He looked around . . . no curious neighbors. He took the gun out of his waistband, moved up the concrete steps, and pulled open the weathered, filthy screen door. It creaked loudly. No turning back . . . he stepped inside the back porch. Grey, peeling paint hung like palm leaves from the ceiling. The room was filled with trash and bottles and beer cans. A cockroach the size of his thumb scurried across the worn and grimy wooden floor.

"Jackie, is that you?" a man's voice called. He assumed it belonged to the white-blond G. Davenport.

He opened the wooden door to the kitchen.

"Yabba dabba do," Fred Flintstone shouted, closer now.

Cody moved into the kitchen. It lived up to the promise of the back porch, cluttered with dirty dishes, half-eaten meals. Some looked to be several days old. More cockroaches . . . a trail of mouse droppings along the kitchen counter . . .

"Jackie . . . ?" The voice was louder, from the next room, as were the voices of Fred and Barney.

Cody crossed the kitchen and stepped into the next room without hesitation, the barrel of his Walther leading the way. Then he almost laughed . . . and that might have been what kept him from firing, for all the anger and rage had rushed back. All the frustration of Ann disappearing, of his twelve-year-old son being threatened, of murder and fire and pain . . . His raging urge wanted to fire and fire and fire until there was nothing left in the clip. . . . But there the stupid, white-blond-haired son of a bitch was, sitting naked, Indian style, in a shabby reclining chair, eating a bowl of Trix and watching *The Flintstones,* chuckling.

"Jackie." G. Davenport was getting impatient. "Will you get me . . ."

He never finished the sentence. Instead, as he turned his head toward the door, his eyes unexpectedly discovered Cody. For one frozen moment they stared at each other. The color drained from G. Davenport's face and Cody enjoyed the other man's terror.

"Just another day in paradise, huh, asshole?" Cody said. He grinned and took off his mirrored sunglasses and flipped them against the wall.

The naked Davenport seemed to go straight up as he lept to his feet in a race for the door, but Cody was too fast for him. At the door he grabbed him by the arm and spun him around, slamming him into a wall, and the naked, white-blond-haired G. Davenport shrieked like a trapped animal, and then he threw himself at Cody, pounding and swinging his fists. Cody kneed him hard in the naked groin, and a gasp that was almost comical came out of Davenport's body as he slumped to all fours with a stunned look of agony.

"What are you going to do now, Fred?" Barney Rubble asked.

And Cody knew he was out of control. He swung hard with his gun and hit the man high against his cheek, and he heard something break. The naked man yelped in pain as the blow knocked him sideways onto the floor. He tried to get up. Dark blood was pulsing out of his left eye socket. He struggled to his hands and knees, weaving back and forth like a dying horse. But Cody only felt the anguish of his missing wife and his threatened son, and he kicked white-blond-haired G. Davenport in the face. This time the cry of pain was like a child's. He tried to get up again, but then stopped, apparently thinking better of it, and tried to crawl into a corner.

Cody stood still for a few moments. He wanted the fear of what might come next to sink into the white-blond-haired man. Ten seconds passed. He moved to him, took the white-blond hair with his left hand and pulled the face up to look at his own. G. Davenport was whimpering.

"What you have to know," Cody said quietly, precisely, "is that you have only one chance of staying alive . . . and that's to answer all my questions."

"You broke my . . ." The white-blond-haired man broke off his garbled words. He looked confused. Blood was everywhere. In his mouth, on his lips . . . "My teeth . . . my cheekbone, I think."

But his words only brought back Cody's anger. "You think I give a goddamn?" he was shouting. The veins stood out on his neck. "You stole my wife . . ." And he knew immediately as he said the words that he wasn't making any sense.

Davenport was looking at him like a frightened child.

Madness.

Cody got up, moved across the room. He knew he had to regain control.

"Who told you to follow me?"

Family pictures on a long side-table . . . wedding pictures, when white-blond G. Davenport was younger, the all American young man . . . pretty wife, white veil and gown . . . pictures of an infant, growing into a pretty blond girl of four or five with an impish smile. Cody thought of the photos on Worden's wall in Canoga Park, Worden's awkward little daddy's girl . . . who had lived only to die in a brutal murder in the middle of a Hawaiian cane field.

Christ, there she was . . .

Madness.

The little girl, four or five . . . The little blond girl with the impish smile from the family photos . . . She was wearing a shiny blue swimsuit, and she knew that something was terribly wrong. Her father was bloodied, naked, and cowering in the corner, and a man in an orange shirt with a gun in his hand stood opposite him.

"Tell your little girl to back to her room and stay there," Cody ordered.

White-blond Davenport tried a couple of times to speak before the words struggled out. "Lynn, honey . . . go to your room."

She didn't move.

"Go to your room now," Cody exploded, "or your father will get hurt more.

Christ.

Madness.

He was as bad as they were.

She disappeared.

The two men stared at each other across the room. The two fathers.

"She's a pretty girl," Cody said, trying to apologize. "I'd never hurt her. I'd never hurt a child."

The anger was coming back. "Not like you, you son of a bitch." And he moved deliberately across to the cowering G. Davenport.

"Don't hurt me," the naked man pleaded.

"You don't understand," Cody said. "I'm going to fucking kill you if you don't tell me everything I want to know."

And the naked man began to whimper and shake and urinate. "Cuaresma. It was Cuaresma. He told me to follow you."

"Who's Cuaresma?"

"He's a dealer. My supplier."

"Drugs?" Cody asked, to be clear.

"Yeah," Davenport answered. His teeth were chattering so hard, it was difficult for him to speak. The blood flow from the eye had slowed. "He grows his own shit up in the hills, and some in cane fields. The hard stuff comes over by boat. This week, because of the holiday, it's not due until tomorrow."

"What does that have to do with me? With the dead people in the cane field? With threatening my son?" Cody's anger was boiling again; he wanted to hit him . . . but something wasn't right. The naked man looked astonished and frightened.

"I don't know anything about any dead people, or your son. . . . Shit, I wouldn't hurt anybody's kid. . . . I don't think I could hurt anybody. Cuaresma said you were a cop. Special detail from Oahu to bust us. He wanted to know where you were all the time."

The pieces weren't fitting again. These weren't the answers Cody had expected. Could the naked, bloodied, white-blond-haired son of a bitch be as burned out as he seemed? Why not? Here he was living on this beautiful island and he was living in a shit box in an industrial section of town.

"When did this Cuaresma tell you to start follow-ing me?"

"Saturday . . . ?" he said, but didn't seem sure. Then decided. "Saturday."

"What time?" Cody pressed. He wanted to know if it had been before or after he and Pat arrived on the island.

G. Davenport rolled his head. "Shit, I don't know . . . I was wasted on some good shit, and he came pounding on the door."

"I have to know what time."

The white-blond man couldn't seem to focus.

"Was it daytime . . . ?" Cody asked. "Nighttime?"

"It was dark," Davenport remembered. "Night-time. He was pounding on the door. Shit, I could hardly see. He made me get dressed and then wait in my car, and then I think he screwed Jackie." The memory made him pause. He looked pathetic.

"Who's Jackie?" Cody asked.

"My wife," Davenport replied. "That's her pic-ture over there."

Cody remembered the pretty woman in the white veil and dress with young, all American G. Daven-port beside her in a morning suit. "Charming. . . . So after Cuaresma screwed your wife, what happened?"

"He made me follow him out to the hotel where you were staying. . . . Shit, I could hardly stay on the road. . . . He showed me your car and said I had to stay there and follow you wherever you went and then call him and let him know."

"Did he tell you what I looked like, or show you a picture of me?"

"No. Not at first. Later on that night. . . . Shit, I was all cramped up in my car asleep. . . . He came back. He showed me a picture of your kid. I think he was sleeping. . . . And then he told me something of what you looked like.''

So it was Cuaresma who had taken the picture, who had broken into his room, who had stood over his sleeping child. The question, Cody knew, was who did Cuaresma work for? It had to be somebody else, if Cuaresma didn't even know what they looked like until late that first night on the island.

"Jackie doesn't want to screw him, you know," Davenport said. His words had an odd pleading and a helplessness to them. "He said he'd cut us off if she didn't let him. If we didn't . . . shit. He said he'd cut off all our shit, man. . . . How were we supposed to live?''

Christ. Madness. The man he'd come in hating, wanting to kill, to beat to a bloody pulp . . . he felt sorry for now. . . .

Chapter Seventeen

Cody heard the back-porch screen door creak open and then bang shut. He stepped to the wall near the open window so he could watch both the naked G. Davenport and the door to the kitchen at the same time.

"Geoff?" the woman's voice called . . . and a moment later she was coming into the room. She was Jackie, the bride in the photographs. Older now . . . Christ, older now: Her hair was dull, dirty blond, and done up in a ponytail. Her face, without makeup, was lined from the sun. But it was more . . . the promise, the happiness of the girl in the white dress and veil . . . it wasn't alive anymore.

"Oh shit," she said as she stopped several steps into the room, having discovered the situation. Cody's gun was leveled at her. Her dress was sleeveless, plain denim. She wore rubber thongs and didn't shave her armpits.

"Get him a pair of pants and a shirt," Cody ordered quietly.

"What are you going to do with him?" she asked in a voice that told Cody her first concern was her own safety.

"Nothing . . . if he does what I tell him to do . . . shows me where someone lives."

"Not Cuaresma?" the naked man whined in fear and then suddenly groaned in pain as he tried to move . . . and it all sounded to him like a voice from a warped recording. Blood began to trickle out of his mouth again.

"What have you done to him?" This time there was surprise in her voice, as if she hadn't fully realized how badly her husband had been hurt.

"I've beaten the shit out of him, that's what I've done to him," Cody said without emotion, "and I'm prepared to go on beating the shit out of him until the both of you do what I want. . . . Now, get him a pair of pants and a shirt."

Only nobody moved.

The girl in the shiny blue bathing suit was in the other doorway now.

Madness.

In her hands was a small black gun.

"Shoot him. Shoot him," the naked man wailed in his garbled voice.

The gun exploded with fire and shattered the window a foot from Cody's head. The noise and the kick of the gun frightened the girl, and she screamed and dropped the weapon and ran to her mother. For a moment, Cody thought the woman might make an attempt to retrieve the small pistol from the floor, but with her daughter in the way and Cody's gun pointed at her, she never moved. Naked, white-blond Geoff Davenport only groaned in disappointment and fear and tried to crawl farther into the corner. Cody moved across the room and picked up the gun. He thought of the policewoman who'd had her face cut off because she had relaxed, because she had felt sorry for a dull-eyed burnout. . . . and on television they were singing about a breakfast cereal.

The sun was hot. Turn right at McDonalds; keep going straight past the Kentucky Fried Chicken. They were heading back out the island's main road, the two-lane Kuhio Highway. It was a real family outing, Cody driving, white-blond, now dressed, Geoff Davenport in the passenger seat opposite him, and earth-mother Jackie and charming little Lynn in back.

Davenport's face had swollen into various distortions, and he rode with his head resting against the closed window, moaning occasionally. He couldn't stop shaking.

"He should see a doctor," Jackie tried as they passed the Wilcox Memorial Hospital. And a wave of anger passed through Cody, because he didn't care about this man . . . but he remembered Caleb talking about the missionaries who had stolen the islands . . . the Wilcox Museum . . . the Wilcox Hospital.

"Why did you stop following me yesterday?" Cody asked.

"He's hurt bad; you should take him to Emergency," Jackie said loudly. She was pushing hard, ugly, with a voice like a fishmonger's wife.

It was a voice she used, Cody reasoned, to get her own way. But this was the wrong man, the wrong time. "He can be hurt more if you don't shut up."

She did.

They drove in silence. Around some winding curves. Past an old church. The road finally straightened out again. Cody's anger hadn't gone away. He reached over and grabbed the white-blond man by the hair and turned his face to his. Davenport wailed in pain.

"Once again, why did you stop following me yesterday?"

"What?" Davenport seemed confused.

"His car broke down," Jackie said in her shrewish voice.

"I told you to shut up," Cody barked at her. He didn't want to let her get started. He knew if she did he'd never be able to stop her. He turned back to the white-blond man. "You followed us to church. What happened?"

Still only a blank stare. Cody hit the brakes and the blue Toyota slid to a jarring stop at the edge of a drainage ditch. He had startled them. He had meant to. And it only seemed right that giant sugarcane stalks swayed behind them.

"You listen to me carefully," he said. His voice was quiet and intense and told of death before the words did. "Two people were murdered in a cane field not far from here. They were shot in the head, and then their bodies were mutilated. I think your supplier, Cuaresma, was part of it. Hell, I think you were part of it."

"We didn't have anything to do with the killings," Jackie broke in with a certain desperation. "We didn't even know about them until we saw it on the T.V. this morning. If Cuaresma did that, that's not part of us."

"Then why did you stop following me?"

Davenport's lips only trembled.

"I have to pee pee," the child in the blue bathing suit said.

"My child has to go to the bathroom," Jackie said with belligerent authority.

Cody took the Walther from under his shirt. It lay sideways in his hand, pointed at white-blond Davenport's belly. "You don't understand, do you? Cuaresma got into my hotel room when my son was in there alone. Asleep. He took my twelve-year-old son's picture, which he then showed to you down in the parking lot. Later I got the picture in an envelope with a note threatening to kill my son. . . . No one threatens my children.'' His finger tightened around the trigger.

"It was like Jackie said," Davenport began. "The radiator hose busted; it's been bad for awhile. It happened right after I drove past the church. Shit, just all sorts of steam.'' The words were flowing out. White-blond Davenport was scared. He was afraid for his life, and the more he talked, the more Cody realized that he had been playing possum up to now. He wasn't as burned out as he appeared to be, but he used his burned-out appearance, at least part of it, as a mask. "The hose was split. Shit, I had to stop like three times to put water in before I got to a store and could buy some tape. By the time I got back to the church, everyone was gone. Shit, I was scared. Cuaresma would have killed me if I had let you get away. I didn't know what else to do, so I tried back at the hotel . . . and there was your car.''

He seemed relieved just remembering the relief of the day before.

"Then you started following us again," Cody said. "Only this time I pulled over in the cane fields. You kept going . . . but never appeared again.''

"Yeah, shit," Davenport said. He wore the frown of failure easily. "It busted again. Same hose, only this time I couldn't tape it up.''

"Bullshit," Cody overrode him. His voice was an angry hammer. But he remembered the smoke belching from the white convertible now, and doubt began to seep in.

"It's true," Davenport whined.

"I have to pee pee," four-year-old Lynn whined.

"She can go out there," Cody said.

The little girl got out with her mother, who helped her take down her shiny blue bathing suit.

"The place where I stopped," Cody went on, keeping one eye on Jackie in the side mirror, "was near where the bodies were. You kept going and disappeared because you knew they were there."

"No. I swear it," Davenport whined.

"You knew they were dead because you helped kill them. What else am I suppose to believe? What else are the cops going to believe?"

"It's not true," the white-blond man's voice was almost hysterical. "I didn't know anything about them then. . . . The hose . . . it had just crumbled into nothing down at the bottom. . . . Shit, I didn't know what to do. I called Jackie, and she walked around to some gas stations until she found a hose that would fit, and then she hitchiked out to where I was."

"And where was that?"

"The Hardwood Factory."

Cody knew the place. It was a big building, on the way to town, that stood alone on the edge of a cane field. It was advertised in the tourist magazines. He remembered thinking Ann would enjoy going there. "I didn't see your car there when I drove past."

The statement seemed to throw Davenport.

"He was parked around back," Jackie said.

"Yeah, that's right," Davenport agreed, seeming happy to have an acceptable answer.

"You can check the gas stations I went to," Jackie said. She and the girl were climbing back into the car.

Cody sensed they were telling the truth. More than

likely they didn't care about the difference anymore, but they were frightened now. Both sides were closing in on them. Cody represented the law; Cuaresma, pain and death. They'd do what they had to do to survive. Right now they were dancing for him, and he wanted to take advantage of it. He took out a photograph that the honeymoon couple had taken at Spouting Horn, the one with the Hannibals and all their assorted entourage, the enormous Carmel Beecher Van Kueren, Nelson Hobart, and Lillian Hannibal's sandy-haired stepson . . . and of course, the pixie-smiling Professor Polk. "You ever see Cuaresma with any of these people?" he asked as he handed the photo to Davenport.

White-blond Geoff tried to focus. Jackie leaned over the back seat for a look and gave a half-smile.

"Shit," Davenport said. "That's Dr. Jekyll."

"Who are you talking about?" Cody pressed.

"Him, of course," Davenport said and pointed to Lillian Hannibal's stepson, Stephen Auerbach.

Suddenly everything was out of balance again for Cody. He hadn't expected the answer. He had been hoping for a tie-up to the pixie-smiling Professor Polk.

"Do you know who that is?" Cody asked.

"Don't you?" Davenport answered and almost smiled.

Cody prodded the white-blond man's belly with his Walther. "You're too close to dying to get cute."

"His name's Auerbach." Davenport's flow was back on. "I think his first name is Steve. He's Cuaresma's best customer, has been for years, shit, since I came here. . . . He's a rich guy. His old man owned a big estate on the other end of the island, called Kamalani. . . . Only when his real mother died, a couple of years later, the old man married *her*." He pointed to Lillian Hannibal. "Then he died and left everything to her . . . or so they say. . . . Shit, bummer, huh . . . ? She's married to that old poet guy now, Hannibal something," he said, tapping the Great American Poet in the photograph.

Drugs, murder, four million dollars . . . it wasn't connecting for Cody. "Why do you call him Dr. Jekyll?"

"Shit, cause he's crazy, man," Davenport said, almost forgetting he wasn't supposed to smile. "He's the sort that gives druggies a bad name."

"They call him Dr. Jekyll because he'll take anything. Mix anything," Jackie stated. "And then he gets mean. He likes to beat women up. Girls. He likes to cut them. Some people say he even killed one a long time ago. . . . They say that's why he never leaves the island, that it was part of the deal that the cops made not to lock him up."

"Why would they make that kind of a deal?"

"Shit, because they're the money, man," Davenport chimed in. "The big money on the island . . . money, man, shit. The big brass even keep it quiet about him being on drugs. No one's allowed to investigate him. Money. That's the way of the world, ain't it?"

Davenport was almost grinning again, but Cody didn't care now. He was trying to sort the pieces out. The information on Lillian Hannibal's stepson refocused everything into a new equation. Heavy into drugs. Capable of violence. Perhaps murder. Could he have killed the honeymoon couple? Is that what the four million dollars was all about? A payoff? Blackmail? . . . No. No. It didn't make sense. It was a new equation, but it still didn't come together.

There were too many loose ends. If Auerbach never left the island, why would he need to steal photographs from the dead girl's room in Canoga Park? Why, if the family was so successful in covering up a previous murder, would they need to make a big payoff on this one? . . . For that matter, why would Evan Hannibal even care four million dollars' worth for his wife's stepson?

Cody started the car, and they rode in silence for some minutes. On the inland side of the highway, cattle grazed lazily on pastures that stretched until the dark green mountains rose above them. On the other side, a palm-tree-studded golf course rambled on until it reached the sea. In the back seat, Lynn began to sing to herself. . . . And Cody knew he couldn't be sure whether his adult passengers were lying. And if so, how much. He didn't care. He just knew he felt filthy, like he might have felt if he had been infested with lice, just being with them.

He followed Jackie's instructions. He turned onto the road just past the river. It took them past the huge coconut grove that was part of the hotel where he had stayed, past some pretty houses, climbed straight for almost a mile, and then gently the road began to bend, with the river now far below.

"Turn right here," Jackie instructed. She had taken the belligerency out of her voice and replaced it with a more businesslike tone.

The area was rural residential: plots of land, two and three acres, with small houses on them.

"This all used to be pineapple fields," she said, managing a hint of civility. And after another half-minute, "Better stop here."

He did.

"That's his place over there," she said, pointing to a two-story house set well back from the road.

The land was cleared for a half-acre in each direction around the house. *Landscaping for a drug dealer,* Cody thought.

"Who do the cars belong to?" Cody asked.

"The truck's his. . . . The station wagon, I don't know," Jackie answered. "What are you going to do with us now?"

"What do you think I should do with you?"

"Nothing. Let us go before Cuaresma sees that it was us that brought you here."

Cody considered, then handed her the photograph again. "Take another look . . . is there anyone else you ever saw with Cuaresma?"

They both looked. Both said no. Doubt was creeping back into Cody's mind. Either the pixie-smiling Professor Polk had been careful . . . or he had been dead wrong zeroing in on him.

"You can get out and start walking. I'll give you five minutes to get clear," Cody told them.

Davenport managed another groan. "Shit, I don't know if I can walk very far."

"Don't break my heart now," Cody said.

Jackie knew a good thing when she heard it. "Come on," she said and opened the door. Little Lynn scrambled out of the car after her. White-blond Davenport followed.

Cody watched them in the rearview mirror until they had disappeared. Five minutes finally ticked by. Christ, he wanted a drink. There had been no sign of movement from the house. With the land cleared in every direction, a clandestine approach to the house was impossible. He started the car, drove the hundred feet or so to the driveway, turned in, and continued toward the house. He parked just behind the station wagon. It was new, a red Ford. A minute went by, no movement from the house. The time for games was over. If someone was in the house, they knew he was there. They probably knew why. Walther in hand, he got out of the blue Toyota and headed for the front door. He kept first the station wagon and then the truck between himself and the house. At the end of the truck, he paused. There was no more possible cover between here and the house, which was still a good thirty feet away. But now caution gave way to curiosity. Something had caught his attention: stains . . . if he was right, blood stains. They were dry, and they led a large spotted pattern from the driver's side door of the truck to the front door of the house. He stepped back to the driver's side window and looked in. The seat was matted heavily with the dried blood, and bloody fingerprints smudged the door handle and steering wheel.

There was a sound from the house, a muffled sound of movement, then silence again. Crouched behind the truck, Cody studied the windows. There was no sign of life. Twenty, thirty seconds went by. Still only the quiet. He was out of options. Staying low, he ran for the front door.

He heard only the sound of his own footsteps. He reached the house, flattened against the wall. Silence. Carefully, he reached over and tried the door; there were more blood smudges on the handle. . . . It swung open easily. Still silence. He held his breath. Then, in a burst, he spun low through the doorway, gun ready . . . No one home. More silence. What passed for the living room was filled with arcade games: Grand Prix racing, Pac Man, Spacewars, Skeet

Bowling. Cuaresma must be a real fun guy. . . .
Again there were sounds . . . movement, feet running. Cody gave chase—through a door blindly. It
was a mistake. He had been suckered. He didn't see
the baseball bat until it had almost hit him. He tried
to duck and succeeded enough to make the blow a
glancing one, a foul tip instead of the line drive that
would have crushed his skull.

Everything went red and black. He was falling,
hitting first a chair, then the floor. Somehow the
Walther stayed in his hand. The Louisville Slugger
was coming down again. He did his best to roll. It hit
his left shoulder, which erupted in pain. He saw legs
and arms; he couldn't see a face. The images were
disjointed. The bat crashed against the corner of the
kitchen table, which was all that separated him from
death. Finally he managed to raise the gun and fire.
The man wielding the bat screamed and ran out the
outside kitchen door.

Cody couldn't stand. His body didn't know how to
make that movement anymore. He tried to sit up. It
was an experience from another dimension. Slowly,
slowly, yes, he managed it.

Outside, a car engine roared to life and then a
vehicle raced away. Cody assumed it was the red
Ford wagon, but he couldn't give chase. The world
was beginning to come back into focus, but he knew
it would still be several minutes before he could even
stand. And yet, battered and aching and desperately
in need of a drink, it wasn't so bad, he thought . . .
all things are truly relative. He was a hell of a lot
better off than Cuaresma, or at least the man who
matched the description the Davenports had given
him of Cuaresma. For he was dead, in a lake of his
own dried blood, half a dozen feet from Cody.

Chapter Eighteen

Cody could feel his heart pounding, echoing through his body. After some minutes, he managed to gain his feet and lurch across the kitchen. Thank God for small favors; there were two bottles of vodka in a cabinet that held a variety of liquor. Just as a precaution, he ignored the one that was almost empty, broke the seal on the full one, and made himself a drink, half and half with some orange juice he found in the refrigerator. . . .

It helped . . . a lot.

There would be no help for Cuaresma, though; he was still dead. Cody guessed he had been for six to eight hours. He pulled on the drink again and then moved over and lifted the dead man's wallet from his grimy pants pocket. It contained several pieces of confirming ID, the most conclusive being a Hawaiian driver's license with a photo . . . Thomas Edward Cuaresma. He would have been twenty-seven next month. . . . *Christ,* Cody wondered, *what happened to the boy, who was now a dead man? Didn't he have a loving mother? A father? Didn't he laugh and play? Have friends? Puppy loves? Hopes? Dreams? Ideals? How did the boy come to be the man who had stood over Cody's sleeping son? The man who was part of threatening the life of his son? The man who was probably part of two and maybe a lot more murders?*

Christ, what happened to all the promise of childhood? Where does it all go wrong? Or is it always a lie?

He knew he had to search the house, but he also knew he wasn't steady enough on his feet yet, so sitting at the kitchen table with the dead man's vodka and orange juice . . . he searched the rest of the wallet instead. In it he found a little over twelve hundred dollars in cash, some photographs, and three phone numbers, two on scraps of paper, one on a torn off matchbook cover. He tried the matchbook cover first and got lucky.

"Hannibal residence." It was the odd, manlike voice of Carmel Beecher Van Kueren. She sounded like she was eating something. "Hello, is someone there?" the enormous woman said after several moments.

Cody had been momentarily surprised with the result of his call and had almost hung up, but now, instead, decided to go fishing. "Yeah, is Steve there?"

"Stephen," she said in her baritone. "I'll have to see. . . . I'll have to put you on hold."

She did. He waited . . . finished his drink . . . made another. His head was down to a dull roar. His arm only screamed when he moved it.

"Hello?" The huge, redheaded woman was back on the phone. Over two minutes had passed.

"I'm here," Cody said.

"Stephen doesn't seem to be here right now. May I take a message?"

"Oh, don't bother. I'll catch up with him later,"

Cody said lightly with a laugh. "He's probably in town. I thought I saw him about half an hour ago . . . if he's driving a red Ford station wagon."

"That's quite possible," Carmel Beecher Van Kueren answered. "One of the estate cars is a red station wagon, though I'm afraid I couldn't tell you what brand it is."

"Right," Cody said with a smile in his voice. He knew the conversation was at an end . . . unless he jumped in feet first . . . and why not? He'd already been bashed over the head with a baseball bat, had his son's life threatened, had a dead man lying at his feet. "Tell me, if Stephen isn't there . . . could I speak to Professor Polk then?"

Several moments went by. "Who is this?" the enormous woman asked.

"Oh, just a friend," Cody said cheerfully. "I know one of the professor's students over in California, and he asked me to say hello."

Silence.

Then he was back on hold, this time without being told. Enough time passed so that he began to wonder if she had hung up on him. But then there was a click on the other end.

"Hello, this is Alex Polk."

It was a warm and friendly voice, more like a salesman's than a teacher's, Cody thought.

"Professor Polk?" Cody asked. He wanted to hear as much of this man's voice as possible.

"That's right. Who's this?"

"A friend."

"A friend of who's?" The professor's good humored tone was forced now.

Time to take the big plunge.

". . . Thomas Edward Cuaresma."

At first there was no answer. Then, when the voice finally came back, it was still friendly, but the air had been knocked out. "I'm afraid I don't know anyone by that name."

"Sure you do, Professor. He's the local drug dealer who helped you kill the honeymoon couple out in the cane fields."

Silence.

"Tell me, Polk," Cody pushed on, "what was in those photos back in California that was so important you had to fly back there and steal them out of her room?"

Again no answer.

A bad chill crept over Cody. He was almost sure he had his man, and yet he knew he didn't have any solid evidence, nothing that would convince the fat Dan Pynes of the world or the Lieutenant Riveras . . . nothing that would stand up in a court of law . . . yet he knew; he believed.

"I'm going to get you, you son of a bitch." Cody's words were almost a hiss. "I'm going to get you for everything you've done and everything you've planned to do."

Moments ticked by.

Finally the cheery voice was back. "Well, it was certainly nice of you to call. Thank you very much for alerting me."

He was playing for whoever was in the room with him, Cody thought. He wondered if it was the enormous fat woman, or maybe the cadaverous Nelson Hobart, planning another comeback, another group of boys.

"I'm going to kill you," Cody said.

"I wouldn't count on that," Polk said with a salesman's chuckle. "In fact, I'd be very careful myself if I were you. . . . Thanks again for calling. Good-bye."

He hung up.

Cody felt good. The adrenalin was pumping. He had been right. And he'd taken the offensive. He had tipped his hand, but just enough to trade whatever element of surprise he'd had for a chance to draw the other side out into the open, and he had succeeded . . . the man with the pixie smile. The son of a bitch.

He felt like calling Damien and telling him. But he knew his son wouldn't be home, and even if he was, it would be pointless without him understanding the overall complexities of the case. They had a victory, a hope, a chance of winning.

He wanted to finish his drink quickly and make another, but he knew he couldn't, not and still function. So he sipped and punched out the next number from memory. He needed help now. Information. He knew who his target was, but he still didn't know why. He had the bones, he needed the meat. After getting through the switchboard, the phone rang three more times before he heard the familiar voice.

"Pyne here."

"Cody."

"Cody, where the hell have you been?"

The anxious whine was what he had expected. But it had no edge. Cody could feel his fear, the fear of the man with blood in his urine, the fear of a man who thought he was going to die. "You haven't called the doctor yet, have you?" Cody asked.

"The captain's really angry. The Kauai Police aren't too happy, either. They want to talk to you."

"Tell me about the doctor."

"It's a holiday," the fat man stammered after some moments.

"Bullshit. The department always has a quack available." He used the old-fashioned slang to try and lighten the accusation.

"I can't talk about that right now. . . . Why didn't you call when you found the bodies?"

"I couldn't," Cody answered. "There were some things I needed to do first . . . and then there wasn't an opportunity."

"You always have an excuse." Pyne exploded with all his desperate frustration.

". . . They threatened to kill Patrick. . . . Is that a good enough excuse for you?"

". . . What?" Pyne said, sounding like he had been jarred out of a fog.

"You heard me. A slimy son of a bitch named Cuaresma got into my hotel room when Patrick was alone in there, asleep. He took his picture. . . . then later someone sent it to me with a note saying they'd kill Patrick if I didn't get off the island."

"Where's Patrick now?" Pyne asked with concern. The qualities that had earned him the nickname "Little Mother" had come to the fore.

"On a plane back to L.A. . . . Don't worry, Damien will meet him and take care of him."

"If Damien needs anything . . . anything, he's to call me."

"He knows that, Dan," Cody said and realized that at the bottom of it all they were friends. "At the moment, just for the record, I'm sitting in Cuaresma's kitchen, drinking his vodka. . . . He doesn't seem to mind; he's dead on the floor in front of me. And before you jump to any conclusions, I didn't kill him."

"Do you know who did?"

"I've got some notions, but nothing I can be

certain of yet. In any case, it's only a sideshow. The point is, something big is going down. . . . The honeymooners, Worden's little girl and her husband, somehow got caught up in the middle and paid for it with their lives. . . . I suppose in that way you could say I was lucky. When I wandered into the middle of it . . . they just threatened us.''

"Maybe they were afraid to do any more killing," Pyne suggested.

"I don't think so," Cody responded. "So far as I know, three people are dead already, but I have a feeling there's more. . . . The body count isn't over. . . . Whatever it is that's going down, I think, has to do with four million dollars, and maybe drugs, but I'm not sure about the drugs. . . . And whatever it is started in California, but now it's here and centers around, of all people, the poet Evan Hannibal.''

"Evan Hannibal?" Pyne interjected. "I didn't even know he was still alive."

"He was as of yesterday. He has a big estate here," Cody said. "The four million dollars we're talking about is his. What the money is for, I'm not sure. . . . I've got someone trying to find that out. . . . Frankly, I wouldn't take bets that Hannibal even knows himself; he's pretty old and his wife seems to call most of the shots. . . . Her name is Lillian Hannibal. Write that down."

"What? Why?"

"God damn it," Cody flared. He was feeling hot, his head dizzy again. "Just write it down. I need to know everything you can find out about her and a couple of other names I'm going to give you. . . . Lillian Hannibal, she's been married at least once before that I'm aware of." He waited, then went on. "Also a woman named Carmel Beecher Van Kueren."

"How do you spell the last name?" Pyne asked.

"I'm not sure. But she runs some sort of a church in L.A. that has to do with cosmic forces. She's a looney tune of the first water, maybe the kind that can be dangerous. She's a houseguest of the Hannibals . . . as is the next guy to check . . . Nelson Hobart. He used to be famous for running boys' choirs. In the last few years, I have the impression that he's been living off of Hannibal."

"I remember him," Pyne said. "His boys sang at a jamboree one year. He seemed like quite a good guy. . . . You really think these people have something to do with Worden's girl being killed?"

"Oh, they're all involved, whether they know it or not. They're part of a fabric, along with some others. . . . For instance, Lillian Hannibal has a stepson by an earlier marriage who apparently never leaves the island. If my guess is right, he's the guy who just tried to knock my head off with a Louisville Slugger . . . and almost made it."

"Cody, are you all right?" Little Mother had snuck back in.

"I'm mending. . . . The point is, the stepson is into drugs, and possibly a murder in the past. . . . I'll sort that out from here. The other key player is the guy I asked you to check out yesterday."

"Polk?" Pyne seemed surprised.

"He's another houseguest of the Hannibals. Believe me, he's involved. He's the spider. I don't think he's alone, but he's the deadly one."

"I'm afraid we didn't get much on him," Pyne said clumsily. "I mean, we ran a check, but it came up clean. . . . Neither the girl nor her husband ever took a class from him."

"How long has he lived in California?" Cody asked, not knowing quite why.

There was a rustling of papers on the other end.

"Came out of Tennessee less than a year ago. . . . Over the years he's taught at several colleges down there. . . . I'm telling you, everything's clean."

"Then everything you have on him is a lie," Cody said bluntly after some moments. "The man I'm talking about is the center of this. I can't prove it yet, but I'm telling you, he killed Worden's daughter; he killed her husband . . . then he mutilated their bodies. . . . A man who's capable of what he did . . . didn't get to this point in his life with a squeaky clean record. . . ."

"If you can't prove it, then you're shooting from the hip again," Pyne complained, whining with departmental caution.

"Pyne, think. . . . The fact that he's been in California less then a year would fit. . . . Check the schools in Tennessee; if I guess right this guy has got to be someone else. . . . It wouldn't be the first time someone's faked school records." He stopped short. He'd been thinking aloud. It was the first time that the possibility that Polk was an inpostor had occurred to him . . . but right now it was the only answer that made any sense.

"I can't run with it. Not this time," the fat man said. His attention was drifting. He sounded on the verge of tears.

"You have to," Cody pressed. He knew he couldn't let Pyne slip away. "Get a photograph of Polk; the college in Pasadena must have one. . . . Then get it to the schools where he was suppose to have taught in Tennessee. If they can't identify him, then you'll know I'm right."

Nothing was said for several moments.

"Pyne?"

Still silence.

"Pyne?"

Cody began to think that he had lost him. Then there was a deep gasp.

"I'm scared," Pyne blurted out.

Cody knew what his friend was scared of . . . of the doctors and what they would tell him. Of dying. . . . He had no imagery or sense of what the fat man's medical condition was . . . but he knew what Pyne wanted to hear, what would spur him into taking the actions that Cody wanted him to. "You don't have to be," Cody said.

"What do you mean?" Pyne's voice was almost pleading.

". . . You know sometimes I sense things."

"Yes," Pyne responded eagerly.

". . . You're going to be all right."

"I am? You're not just saying that?"

"If you see a doctor in the next day or so, everything will be all right. It won't be like your father."

". . . Boy . . . I hope you're right," Pyne laughed. "I mean, I know you are. . . . I should go see the quack. I'd be crazy not to." The fat man was almost giddy. "I'll put out that request for you, to the colleges in Tennessee . . . with the photo. If you're right, we'll trap that spider of yours. . . . It would be a help, though, if you calmed the Kauai cops down."

"They're my next call," Cody stated. He felt a little guilty for manipulating his friend, but not much. He was too tired. His head and shoulder hurt too much. And he had a dawning awareness that he was on the outside now . . . outside both the police and the bad guys: in his own private war, his own private crusade . . . he alone . . . alone with the boys, D and P.

Pyne was talking again.

"You did mean it, about me and the quack?"

"Trust me," Cody said, knowing he was lying. A moment later, they both hung up.

Christ.

He finished the drink and stared at the wall.

After some minutes, he got up to search the house and discovered somebody else already had. Drawers were turned out, furniture and mattresses slit open. It took almost an hour of careful sifting to decide that there was nothing left that interested him.

Back to the kitchen, the vodka, the phone. It was the call he had been avoiding . . . the information he didn't want to know, but knew he must find out.

"Kauai Police."

"Lieutenant Rivera. . . . This is Cody."

"Just a minute, please," the operator said with a sudden urgency.

An atmosphere of dread had settled on him during his fruitless search, dread centered on Patrick. He was worried now that he shouldn't have tipped his hand so soon to Polk. What if he went after Patrick in California? Christ. He must be mad. A war? A crusade? Against what? Where would it start? Where would it end? Depression engulfed him like a blanket. He wanted to hang up, to go away and hide and sleep and just be left alone. He knew he couldn't, and he thought of Ann and the times she had battled to bring him out of his great depressions. It seemed so pointless for him to go on. The wave of evil and ignorance was always so overwhelming. Why did he fight? Why did he care? "You never should have been a policeman," she used to say. "You care too much; you hope too much . . ." And then she'd add, with her soft smile, "And because of it you have to end up in despair . . . because you believe too much that there really is good out there, and no matter how much you're able to do, there's always another drug pusher, another rapist, another child molester, another judge who slaps their hands, another parole board who lets them go free . . . another crooked cop who betrays his trust . . . and yet, what would the rest of us do if there weren't people like you out there to fight the battles . . . ?" It always sounded good . . . but then she had always believed more then he had, Cody knew. She had always believed in his basic goodness. He doubted it, as he supposed he doubted his faith . . . not openly, just never fully facing it. But he hoped. She was always right about that. He hoped he was right. He hoped he was good . . . and yet he wondered how much was just habit, from a job he liked, a job he did well . . . from an attic of childhood beliefs.

"This is Rivera."

"Tell me about the ballistics check."

". . . There hasn't been enough time," Rivera said cautiously.

"There's been enough time to tell if they're the same caliber." Cody didn't try to hide his irritation.

"They're the same caliber," Rivera answered and then tried to take charge of the conversation. "I want to know where you are."

"Soon enough," Cody answered. "First I want . . ."

Rivera overrode him. "No, now. I want to know now where you are, or I'll put out a warrant for your arrest."

"Don't do anything that will make you look stupid, lieutenant. You tell me what I want to know and I'll tell you where I'll meet you in an hour. . . . What happened at Caleb's house?"

There was a long pause before Rivera spoke, and when he did, it was with biting sarcasm. "I thought you knew everything. I thought you were a psychic."

Cody's instinct was to be angry. Christ, how many times had he gone through this before? He didn't like this man, but he also knew that he needed him. He spoke his words calmly. "No. I don't know everything. Sometimes I sense things . . . or see fragments of events. . . . They aren't always correct, but many times they can be helpful. Please, tell me what happened; I may be able to help you."

"An unknown assailant . . . ," Rivera started and then paused, his voice becoming unsteady. After several moments, he seemed to regain control and then went on, ". . . entered the Ho residence at about 3 A.M. . . . shot and killed the family dog. Shot and killed female victims . . ." His voice broke again, but he didn't seem to care anymore, and he went on, ". . . Mrs. Eunice Ho, aged fifty-eight . . . Miss Maile Ho, aged twenty-seven. . . . Shot and killed male victim Rodney Ho, aged eleven. . . . Shot and wounded male victim Detective Caleb Ho, aged twenty-five . . ."

No one spoke for some moments.

"And the others?" Cody asked finally.

"Young Derek and his thirteen-year-old sister escaped. The boy says Detective Ho made them go out a window and run for the cane field where they could hide."

"How bad is Caleb?"

"He's in Intensive Care at Wilcox Memorial. . . . He's not expected to live."

Christ.

"What about the fire?"

"There was no fire," Rivera said too matter of factly.

"I thought I felt fire . . . gunshots and flames."

Silence.

"You're not telling me something," Cody said.

". . . It's possible that the assailant meant to start a fire," the Hawaiian lieutenant said reluctantly. "There was a five-gallon can of gasoline left near the front door."

Christ. Six people dead and one dying. Madness. Fucking madness, and he knew who was at the core of it. He also knew he had no way of proving it, not to police minds, not to this asshole on the other end of the line. He'd seen and had to deal with people like him too many times in the past.

"Had Caleb's gun been fired?" Cody asked.

"Four times."

"I think I can account for three of the bullets. Does the name Thomas Cuaresma mean anything to you?"

"He's a drug dealer," Rivera said. "We've never been able to pin anything on him."

"Why, because you've been too busy protecting his best customer, Stephen Auerbach?" Cody tried.

Silence.

"Well, it won't matter anymore. Cuaresma's dead. I'm sitting with him in his kitchen."

Chapter Nineteen

"Just another day in paradise, huh, Joe?"

It was old Mr. Jackson, who Cody had seen on his first visit to the poolside bar, and Cody was reminded now how kind the soft light of evening could be. Here in the glaring midday sun, the old man looked almost transparent, with ugly blue veins showing through and brown age-spots clearly highlighted.

"You're down early today, Mr. Jackson," Joe said with his friendly smile.

"Only to say aloha and mahalo for all your kindness." The old man spoke with a forced emphasis of sincerity on the Hawaiian words. Cody also saw in the daylight that the old man's toothy smile was the half-smile of someone who has had a stroke in the past and has never fully recovered from it.

"We're going home today."

"It seems like you just got here," Joe said with disappointment, and he moved down to the old man to finish the ritual.

Cody waited and got lost in his own thoughts, in his fatigue, and in the double vodka-tonic in front of him, which he knew he shouldn't have ordered. Which faults and "uglies" did the bright glare of the sunlight reveal about him, he wondered? Semi-alcoholic? The failed cop? The great detective who couldn't even find his own lost wife? Semi-alcoholic. *Alcoholic.* The word disturbed him. Was he? He didn't know. He only knew that the drink stopped the pain, the overriding sense of anxiety that was always with him since Ann had disappeared. Anxiety . . . "protect us from all anxiety" . . . the words were mouthed by priests every day, every Mass. "Protect us from all anxiety" . . . How long was he suppose to wait in hope? How long before the anxiety was lifted from him, before he would be set free?

"Sorry about that," Joe said. "The Jacksons are regulars. They've been coming back here every year for twenty-two years. There are a lot of folks who do; that's what makes it great . . . anyhow, about the Greens. . . . You remember we talked that night, and I thought there was something in the back of my head . . . but I didn't remember it until the next morning when I had to go out for milk for my kids. . . . See, once when I went to Pono's—that's a little market up in Kapaa—Well, I saw them. They were across and down the street."

"The Greens?" Cody asked.

"Yeah, they were laughing and talking to this guy, and then they all got into their car. And I remembered wondering who the guy was because I had never seen him before."

"Did they drive off?"

Joe frowned a moment. "I don't know. They could have. I got in my car and drove back home. I waved to them, but I don't think they saw me."

Cody considered telling him that their not seeing him might be a contributing factor to why he was still alive. Instead he asked, "Do you know what day that was?"

Joe frowned again. "I've been trying to work that out. Especially since I read in the papers about them being found dead and all . . . jeez, it's so awful . . . anyhow, I was off that week for four days and had to fly over to the big island. That's where I'm from. My dad's been pretty sick . . . so I can't be exactly sure, but it was either the day they disappeared or the day before."

"The man you saw them with," Cody said, "would you recognize him again if you saw him?"

"Jeez, I don't know. I might. I know he wasn't a guest here."

Cody showed him a photo from Spouting Horn.

"The Greens took this."

Joe looked at it and grinned. "That's Evan Hannibal. So they did get to meet him."

Once again, showing the photo, he had been looking for an identification of the professor with a pixie smile . . . a piece of solid evidence, something he could show to the fat Dan Pynes and Lieutenant Riveras of the world. . . . But once again he'd been taken by surprise. "What do you mean . . . 'they did get to meet him'?"

Joe had to interrupt himself to make a Mai Tai and a Blue Hawaiian for a pair of new customers.

"Mrs. Green," he started when he came back, "was really bubbling over one day. She'd had four glasses of white wine and was really in a giggly mood . . . jeez." He suddenly frowned. "I keep thinking about them being dead. . . . Anyhow, I asked her what she was so happy about—you gotta remember her husband was at the other end of the bar talking to a couple of other guys about baseball. . . . So she says she's happy because her husband—I told you he was a writer . . . anyway, he's maybe going to get to meet Evan Hannibal and interview him. It's like Hannibal and Hemingway and some other name she said, they were her husband's idols . . . and to get a chance to interview him was really something, because Hannibal supposedly doesn't give interviews anymore. . . . And of course, it would give her husband a real great article to sell to some magazine. 'It's a big break,' she kept saying . . . 'A real big break.' Only they had to keep it quiet. . . . Anyhow, right about then Mr. Green comes back, and he was really kind of upset about her telling me . . . but he tried to laugh it off and said something about never talking about a no-hitter when it was in progress. He made me promise I wouldn't tell anyone . . . because if he did get to see Hannibal it would be as a special favor. . . . So nobody could know what they were doing for the couple of days he'd be doing the interview.''

"Did he say who was arranging the special favor?'' Cody asked.

"No,'' Joe answered after some thought. "He just kept asking me not to say anything to anybody. I promised I wouldn't . . . and then I forgot about it until you showed me that picture. . . . Do you think it means anything?''

"It could answer the question of why they told everyone they were going on an overnight hike into the mountains,'' Cody said and then thought that it could also be the reason why they would have lied to her father. If the interview with Hannibal was such a big break, a coup for the fledgling writer, it wouldn't do to tell her father and risk having the news announced on late-night phone-in shows. . . . But was Hannibal really going to give him an interview? If so, who was arranging it? Lillian Hannibal seemed to

control the old man's life. Then, of course, there was
pixie-smiling Polk. But why would an interview end
in double death?

Joe had to make several more drinks for customers before they could go on talking.

"Other than the Hannibals, is there anyone else in
that picture that you recognize?"

Joe looked again. "Is that Stephen Auerbach?"

"Yes," Cody answered. "What do you know about
him?"

Joe shrugged. "Not much, really. I hear he's kinda
weird. Supposed to have spent a couple of years in
the booby hatch over on Oahu when he was a kid."

"Any idea why?"

"No," Joe said after thinking. "It's just one of
those rumors you hear. You know, people like to tell
rumors about rich people."

"Anybody else in the picture?" Cody asked.

Joe looked puzzled.

"The man you saw with the Greens that day you
went to the market, is he there?"

"I was just wondering that," Joe said. "Maybe
this guy," he said pointing to Polk.

This was as close as Cody had come to getting
something solid. . . .

"Can you be sure? Would you testify that it was
him?"

Joe frowned. "Jeez, I can't be sure. I mean it
could be . . . then again, I'd hate to get a guy in
trouble . . ."

More customers arrived. Joe slipped away. . . . So
had Polk, once again. A "maybe" identification of
him with the Greens wouldn't convince anyone. Cody
felt frustrated. It would be so much easier if he could
get the army of law enforcement behind him. It

would relieve the pressure. But he knew he didn't have a case, not even one that would stand up against the lowest of criminals . . . let alone against people as respected as Evan Hannibal and his group. He had a case of missing photos in California . . . sought-after photos in Kauai . . . a snapshot taken at Spouting Horn that any tourist might have taken . . . and a pixie-smiling Professor Polk, direct descendant of the eleventh President of the United States, who got very nervous when accused of double murder over the phone and then pretended in a charming voice that nothing had happened. His case was a house of cards, and half the cards were invisible.

He finished his drink and didn't dare another. He said good-bye and thanks to Joe and then walked around the long way to the dining room so he could walk along the lagoon, walk through the dreamlike setting he wished he could bring Ann to. But the walk through paradise didn't help. His left arm still hummed with pain, and he felt like a shell, haunted and empty inside. . . . The carrier of death.

A little girl, about five, and her blond brother, who couldn't have been more than three, suddenly burst out noisily with happy excitement. The girl, with her five-foot bamboo pole, had just caught a fish from the lagoon. It was four or five inches long, wriggling and bouncing on her line. But then, in a matter of moments, the happiness had turned to fear and upset. Four different cats appeared, bobbing and jumping and trying to pull the fish off her line.

"Let me help," Cody said.

He moved over and took the wiggling prize off the hook. The cats weren't pleased.

"What do we do with him now?" Cody asked with a rescuer's smile.

"Throw him back, of course," the little girl said.
He did.

The children stared at him.

He went away.

Cody was halfway through a hamburger and fries
when Lieutenant Rivera arrived in the dining room.
He turned out to be the Hawaiian J. Edgar Hoover
from the night before. He had a sidekick with him, a
short, youngish reedy-looking man with dull, thinning red hair.

"That search up at Cuaresma's your handiwork?"
the reedy man asked as he and the stocky Rivera
arrived at the table.

Cody wanted to tell him to go to hell or punch him
in the face. "No," he said simply.

"Oh, really," the reedy man said. He seemed to
take Cody's mild response as a sign of weakness.
"Then if you didn't do it maybe you could have a
vision or something and tell us who did."

"I take it you're Rivera," Cody said to J. Edgar
Hoover.

"That's right," the lieutenant answered tightly.

"Who's he?" Cody asked pleasantly, meaning the
reedy redheaded man.

"His name is Detective Harry Smith," Rivera said,
showing his impatience. "He's my personal assistant."

"Now that's who I thought he might be," Cody
said, squinting over in Smith's direction, as if for a
better look. "Funny, but from here his nose didn't
look quite brown enough."

"I don't know who you think you are . . ." Rivera was angry.

"I'll tell you who I am," Cody interrupted, showing his own anger. "I'm someone who was asked to

do a favor. To help a man find his missing daughter.
I did it and uncovered a whole nest of ugly and
growing snakes on this island . . . but get this straight.
I uncovered it. I didn't invent it . . . or overlook it
. . . or ignore it."

"Are you saying we did overlook or ignore it?"
Rivera was at the exploding point. *He has been a
lieutenant too long,* Cody thought. *He isn't used to
having people speak to him like this.* He thought of
bringing up Stephen Auerbach's protected position,
but it would be off the point. All the murders had to
be connected to something much bigger than some
poor bastard's drug problem.

"You're better equipped to answer that than I
am," Cody said, finally backing off.

A waitress came. Cody ate some more of his
hamburger and ordered a light beer. Rivera and Smith
ordered coffee.

"How did you know to look in the cane field for
the bodies?" Rivera asked. The waitress was gone.
His tone was more civil.

"Something I saw . . . an image, a feeling of fear
. . . of nothingness." Cody's words were soft. His
listeners didn't move. "I felt it in the morning, about
ten thirty, when we were driving by. It was very
strong. I ran into the cane field. . . ."

Nothing was said for some moments. The same
distress he'd felt then was back upon him now.

"You didn't report the bodies until late afternoon,"
Rivera said.

"We didn't find them until late afternoon," Cody
answered. The feeling of distress was ebbing. "I was
confused in the morning. The image I had seen was
very brief. . . . I took it to mean something else. I
knew somebody was dead. . . . I took it to be my

wife, an image of my wife. She's been missing for almost four months now.''

"Yes, I know," Rivera said. "I'm sorry."

Cody went on. "It wasn't until late afternoon that I thought of trying that spot again.''

Rivera and his reedy sidekick exchanged a look.

"Mr. Cody," Rivera said after some moments, "I want to ask you a question, and I want you to think about it carefully before you give me an answer. . . . Your wanting to look in the cane field, is there any way that Detective Ho might have suggested that to you?''

"No," Cody responded immediately.

"I asked you to think about it."

"I don't have to," Cody said. "I saw an image of the Greens dead. . . . Later I confused it, thinking it was my wife. . . . Caleb had nothing to do with any of that.''

Rivera and his man Smith exchanged another glance. Cody sensed he wasn't following their line of thought. If he guessed right, he hadn't given them the answer they were looking for. What the hell were they looking for?

"Tell me how you got to Cuaresma's?''

Cody told them . . . about being followed the previous morning, about the photo with the note telling him to leave the island . . . then how he was followed again this morning, all the way to Honolulu. He told how he had followed the white-blond Davenport back to his house and . . . persuaded Davenport to tell him about Cuaresma and the fact that Cuaresma was the one who had ordered him followed in the first place.

This time, from the exchange of looks between Rivera and Smith, Cody reasoned that what he had told them had answered a lot of questions.

"Now, if you want to know who was giving Cuaresma's orders, I'm prepared to tell you that, too . . . only I don't have any evidence yet that can back it up, and you won't like what I tell you."

"Try me," Rivera said. But Cody had the feeling he was being indulged.

He tried anyway. He talked about the photos, the ones missing in California, the ones looked for in Hawaii . . . about pixie-smiling Alex Polk and four million dollars . . . about Lillian Hannibal and the strange group of hangers-on out at Kamalani. He talked about Stephen Auerbach and Cody's suspicion that Auerbach had been the one who had searched Cuaresma's house, probably in search of drugs, and then, when surprised, had tried to bash Cody's brains out with a baseball bat.

They listened until he stopped. Cody sensed that Rivera was embarrassed; Smith, cynically amused.

"Yes, Mrs. Hannibal told us you had forced your way into Kamalani yesterday," Rivera said with carefully chosen words. "It was very upsetting for both her and Mr. Hannibal."

"I bet it was," Cody said. He knew he'd lost.

"Mr. Cody . . ." Rivera said, biting his words and yet trying to be civil, "I've talked to your people back in Los Angeles at some length."

Here it was again.

"Right. They tell you I was crazy, or only half-crazy?"

"They told me that you were under a lot of stress because of the disappearance of your wife. . . . I lost my own wife to cancer last year. I know how devastating that can be."

"My wife's not dead. God damn it, she's not dead," he shouted and realized how desperate he sounded, how much he had overreacted, how impotent he felt. He got up from the table abruptly and walked to the bar. He wanted a drink, but then changed his mind and moved outside into the covered walkway between the hotel buildings and the lagoon. But there was nowhere to go. Children were fishing on the banks of the lagoon. Old women were selling handmade jewelry on rows of card tables. He went back inside and ordered a double vodka and orange juice. Polk was clever. Christ, he was clever. He had left nothing that could link him to the murders in the mind of any rational cop.

"If what I told you about Polk and the Hannibals and the four million dollars isn't it . . . what is the answer?" Cody asked as he sat back down at the table with his drink.

"Sometimes, as you would know . . ." Rivera started in a fatherly tone, "the truth can be so obvious that we don't see it . . . like missing the forest for the trees."

"What is the truth then?" Cody asked.

"You referred to a growing nest of snakes that you uncovered. . . . You're right. It was here. We were aware of it, but we could never track it down. I told you on the phone that Cuaresma was a thorn in our side for a long time . . . and just for the record, I'll tell you something that most of our police officers don't even know: Yes, we were aware that Cuaresma was supplying drugs to Stephen Auerbach. He's a very troubled young man. Mrs. Hannibal has made some enormous efforts to try and help him. . . . But the point is, we've never been able to catch Cuaresma red-handed. Every time we thought we had him, he came up clean. . . . Because of that . . . unfortunately, in the last few months we have come to the reluctant conclusion that Cuaresma was being tipped off . . . by someone inside the force.''

''This morning,'' Smith continued for his boss, ''the newspaper got a call. Anonymous, of course. The caller said that the reason Detective Ho and his family had been hit was because he was a dirty cop, that he was mixed up in the big-time drug trade on the island.''

So this was what they were going after. Cody felt numb, as if the accusation had been made about him. ''You don't believe that?''

''Believe me,'' Rivera said, and the pain in his words showed, ''I've known young Ho since he was a boy. His father and I were friends.''

''Then tell me you don't believe it,'' Cody repeated angrily.

''We found ten thousand dollars worth of cocaine in the trunk of his car,'' Smith added.

''Then it was planted,'' Cody insisted.

''I wish I could believe you,'' Rivera said, ''but the truth of the matter is that there is no fanciful scheme, which I understand you've been known to come up with in the past. Even Hannibal and his family and friends have nothing to do with any murders. The facts are, we're dealing with the ugly nest of snakes you talked about, and it's drug dealers, falling out with one another.''

No one spoke for some time.

''I want to see Caleb,'' Cody said finally. He knew there was no point in arguing with them or trying to change their minds. They thought he was mad. Fine. It wasn't the first time.

''He's in a coma,'' Rivera said. ''I told you, he's not expected to live.''

''What you mean is, it would be better if he didn't.''

Cody didn't try to disguise his anger. "Better for you. Better for the department. If he dies, he can't deny the charges. You could close the books. I want to see him."

"All right," Rivera said crisply. "We'll drive you."

"I'll drive myself."

"Then I'm sure you won't mind if Detective Smith goes along with you."

"I'd mind a lot," Cody said and got up.

"We want you off our island," Rivera said as he bounced to his feet.

"Oh, does the island belong exclusively to the police department now?" Cody responded.

"Don't make it hard on yourself, Cody," Rivera said with a tight smile. "I have enough on you to put you in jail and keep you there for at least several days."

"You said you knew Caleb when he was a boy . . . then he became a cop." Cody's words were soft but pointed. "Where's your sense of loyalty? Is it so shallow it goes out the window with some planted drugs, an anonymous phone call . . . ? I'll leave your god damn island . . . after I see my friend."

Cody walked out. Smith started to object, but the man who looked like the Hawaiian J. Edgar Hoover stopped him.

Chapter Twenty

He was getting to be a regular on the shuttle planes to Oahu. Smith had made sure he was booked on a four o'clock connecting flight to Los Angeles. Cody, of course, had no more intention of taking that flight than he had had of taking the one earlier with Patrick. He'd return to Kauai . . . tonight. He had to. His case was there. Polk was there. The Hannibals were there. Somewhere in that rambling house at Kamalani were the answers to why so many people had had to die. He knew he had to get in there.

He had seen Caleb. There wasn't much to see . . . tubes and wires. The young Hawaiian had seemed more dead than alive. . . . Why?

Victor's little boy, with the rolling limp, had been playing on the lawn out in front of the hospital as Cody had driven in. Victor himself, with his naturally smiling face, was in the waiting room, along with three fat Hawaiian women who Cody guessed were also relatives.

"What do you want?" Victor had finally asked when he realized that Cody would not be ignored.

"You know what they're saying about him?" Cody asked in return. "Why he and his family were shot?"

"It's a lie," Victor said, trembling.

"I know it is, too." Cody nodded. "But we're outnumbered. Myself, I'm going to try and prove them wrong. . . . I could use some help."

It was almost three thirty when the plane touched down at Oahu. The soft rain had disappeared, and it was hot and blue-sky balmy. Cody moved through the terminal toward the Overseas side long enough to determine that he wasn't being followed, then took a cab to Waikiki. Why not? He'd always heard about the place.

He liked it. It was quite different from Kauai, which now seemed to him untouched by comparison. There was a certain excitement and charm in the mix of high-rise hotels and swaying palm trees, in the giant white stretch of beach and the crush of people . . . the tanned bodies and bikinis, the bicycle rickshaws along the boulevard, the outriggers and sailboats just beyond the waves.

As he strolled along the sidewalk, an old man proclaiming that ". . . an eighty-four-year-old man has been to and lived on the planet of Heaven for five days . . ." thrust a leaflet into his hand. He almost laughed. Who was mad? A dozen Hari Krishnas danced and chanted in front of a huge open-air collection of shops and stalls called the International Marketplace. Thirty feet away, a man with blond pigtails shouted passages from the Bible.

Cody found what he was looking for, a store where he could buy some more clothes and an overnight bag at reasonable prices. Next, he found and checked into a small hotel. Once in his room, he called home.

"Patrick Cody speaking." The boy's words burst

into the phone with typical sincere energy after several rings.

"I see you made it."

"Dad?"

"It's me." Cody smiled. "Flight okay?"

"Yeah, it was great, except the lady next to me kept snoring," Pat giggled. The twelve-year-old seemed to have forgotten his concern. "Damien met me at the airport. We're just going out for pizza. . . . You want to talk to him?"

"Sure."

"Dad," Damien said.

"I'm here. Everything all right?"

"Everything's fine here. How about you?" The eighteen-year-old was referring to the case.

"I'll know more after tonight," Cody said.

"Dan Pyne called. He said he needs to talk to you, but that he won't be home until ten thirty . . ."

"What time is it there now?" Cody asked.

"Quarter to eight," Damien answered and seemed a little surprised. "What time is it there?"

"Quarter to five . . . I'll call Pyne after ten thirty." Neither spoke for some moments.

"Get 'em, Dad," Damien finally said softly. Cody guessed it was so Patrick wouldn't hear.

"I'm going to do my best. . . . I'll talk to you tomorrow."

The last plane back to Kauai left at nine. Cody slept until a quarter of eight. He took a shower, letting the hot water pour down on his sore left shoulder for several minutes, then dressed in fresh clothes and called Pyne.

The fat man was feeling better about life. He'd actually called a doctor at home and had an appointment to see him at noon the next day. His enthusiasm had spread to the case, as well.

"I have to admit, I thought you were a little off when you asked me to check out Hannibal's wife . . . but, oh boy, I found some interesting stuff. . . . As far as I can find out, her first marriage was to a guy named Alan Bushells. He owned a big insurance company here about twenty-five years ago. . . . This guy Bushells was in his sixties when he met her. . . . His first wife had died about a year before, and he wanted to try and put it all behind him by traveling. . . . That's how he met her, Lillian; she was a travel agent. . . . They were married a month later. But Bushells had a couple of grown daughters . . . and that's where all of our information came from. They made some complaints after he died, which was less than a year after the wedding. It seems that at first they thought it was great for their father to remarry. They liked Lillian. . . . But then, as time went by, all the old friends were gradually cut out, and a whole bunch of new ones, 'weirdos' the daughters called them, were brought in: a lot of spiritualists. They started having seances so Bushells could contact his first wife. . . . Guess who used to run the seances?"

"Carmel Beecher Van Kueren," Cody tried.

"You got it," Pyne said. "Then, like I said, within a year Bushells was dead. And when they went to probate the will, several million dollars seemed to be missing, and what was left went to Lillian. The daughters were cut out. The daughters raised hell for a while, but nobody could prove anything. . . . Then Lillian left the state."

"Beginning to build an interesting pattern," Cody said. "From what I picked up here, she married a very wealthy man from Kauai. . . . When he died, everything was left to her again.''

''And now she's married to Evan Hannibal, and he's about to pay somebody four million dollars. Sounds kinda fishy, doesn't it?'' Pyne surmised. ''Any more on what the four million is for?''

''Not yet,'' Cody answered. ''How about Polk?''

''Nothing yet. I sent the requests out with an 'urgent' on them once I picked up the information on Lillian Hannibal . . . but everybody's closed today because of the holiday,'' Pyne said. ''So now we sit and wait.''

''Afraid there's not time for that,'' Cody said.

''What do you mean?'' Pyne asked, starting to sound worried again.

''Just that whatever is going down is going down fast. The body count has doubled since the last time we talked, and a young cop in intensive care is liable to become number seven. . . . We haven't got time to sit on our hands.''

Victor was waiting in the parking lot at Lihue Airport. Cody had reasoned that there were too many people on the island who might connect him to Caleb. He wouldn't risk a more public meeting. The man with the naturally smiling face got out of his black pickup truck as Cody approached.

''How's Caleb?''

''Still alive,'' Victor said. ''The machines are still keeping him breathing.''

A car door opened thirty feet away, and one of the fat women Cody had seen at the hospital got out and started toward them.

Cody turned his attention back to Victor. ''What about the telephone company?''

"It was like I thought," Victor said. "Caleb had called his cousin Dwight. Dwight says that the phone numbers of the shops that Caleb gave him had been called two times from the phones out at Kamalani . . . once on the sixteenth, then again on the eighteenth."

Cody smiled and sighed.

"Does that help?" Victor wanted to know.

"The honeymoon couple were last seen alive on the fourteenth," Cody said, and for the moment he couldn't stop grinning.

"Then we should tell the police. Whatever they're saying now . . . Lieutenant Rivera is a good man. His wife used to sing at our church."

Victor wants desperately to set the world back up straight, Cody thought. *Christ, don't we all.*

"Not just yet," Cody said. "Those phone calls are like everything else I have, circumstantial. Right now, the cops don't want to hear about it."

"Then why did you smile when I told you?" Victor asked.

"Because it means the son of a bitch that I'm after is capable of making a mistake," Cody explained. "He doesn't always cover his tracks completely. I smiled because you gave me hope."

The fat Hawaiian lady had arrived some moments before, but had waited patiently a couple of yards away. "You must be Caleb's aunt who works on the newspaper," Cody said, trying to sound friendly.

She stepped closer, and he saw that she appeared to be in her forties. She seemed overdressed in a white silk muumuu with Japanese overtones. A cloud of floral scent moved with her. "Yes, I'm Lelani Makalua," she said nervously. She had a large file folder under her arm. "But you have to understand, I'm not a full-time reporter. I sell real estate." She offered him a card as she spoke the last few words. "My number is on there if you ever need me."

"I'm sure whatever information you have will be of help," he said, trying to relax her.

"I've dug out everything I could on Lillian Hannibal, going back to when she was Lillian Auerbach, of course," she said, indicating the file folder. "There's some on Mrs. Van Kueren, too, but not much on the others, I'm afraid."

"You seem to have quite a bit there," Cody said. "Maybe we could talk as we ride. I do want to go to the hospital."

"Whatever you like," Victor said after an awkward look to Lelani. "I'll meet you there, if it's okay with you? That way I won't have to come back for my truck."

"No pilikia," she answered in pidgin, and then, realizing it, said to Cody with a smile, "I'm sorry, just Hawaiian talk . . . 'No pilikia' just means no problem. . . . Come on, we'll go in my car."

Victor with the naturally smiling face rumbled off in his pickup as they settled into her three-year-old Oldsmobile. "Do you mind if I smoke?" she asked.

"Not at all."

Her whole body seemed to shudder with relief. "Victor is a very nice man, but he doesn't like smoking . . . let alone when I might have an occasional drink. He can make me very nervous," she said. She laughed and lit a Salem, inhaling deeply. "Oh, that's much better."

Cody smiled, and she saw it, and, for the first time, did fully relax.

Across the parking lot, the man with the pixie smile lit an unfiltered Camel. He, too, inhaled deeply.

But he felt anything but relaxed. He felt ready to explode.

"Everything I have is in the files," Lelani said.

"What I'm looking for probably isn't there," Cody responded. "What I'm looking for is something that you, as a reporter, would have become aware of, might even have researched . . . but would never be able to print in the papers."

She took another drag on her cigarette and smiled. "You want the dirt?"

"You've got it." Cody nodded. "Especially anything about Lillian after Auerbach died and apparently left everything to her."

She thought for several moments, brought the memory up. "He did leave everything to her, you know. A lot of people found that *pulule* . . . you know, crazy. They had hardly been married a year and yet, except for a trust fund for the boy, she got everything."

She started the car.

"What about Carmel Beecher Van Kueren?" Cody asked.

"Oh, she's been there forever." Lelani laughed. "I like that woman. With more people like her around, I could feel thin."

"What do you mean she's been there forever?"

She backed out of the parking space and then started forward as she talked. "It's all in the clippings. She and Lillian were on a cruise together to Egypt to finish research on a book about the secrets of the Great Pyramid. Mr. Auerbach was on the same cruise. He met Lillian, and they got married when they got back."

"You're saving something." Cody smiled. "I can tell."

She grinned and turned onto the two-lane road to town. It was empty now. "I'd wash my keikis' mouths out if I heard them saying this, but the rumor going around after Mr. Auerbach's death . . . I mean, no one could prove it . . . but the rumor was . . . you know . . . she was sleeping with Auerbach's son, Stephen. Her stepson. He was all of fifteen then. The rumor was, Mr. Auerbach caught them and they killed him . . . which is why the boy ended up in the sanitarium for a couple of years. He's supposed to have had everything, electric shock . . ."

It was her last word. The back of her head exploded in blood a microsecond before Cody heard the shot. The next one shattered the passenger-side window behind his head. The next, the windshield.

He hadn't even seen the red station wagon until the shots started. It had come alongside, headlights on. Cody had had an uneasy feeling back in the parking lot: the distant sense of fear, the crying out for help from the nothingness. But he had put that aside as just being part of being back on the island, of closing in on the Hannibals, on Polk. The fourth bullet found the top of his left arm, ripping out skin and flesh, and his head snapped back and banged hard against the headrest. He was operating on instinct now. He yanked hard on the wheel and ran the car off the road into the cane field that banked the airport. He turned the key off, opened the door, and rolled out as the car was still moving. Keeping low to the ground, he ran through the whipping stalks of sugar cane.

The crop in this field wasn't as far along as the crop where they had found the honeymoon couple. The top of the plants only reached four to five feet high. He knew he had to stay below that, and, he also knew that perhaps more dangerously, any movement he made against the stalks could be seen from the top. He ran for what he guessed to be a minute, zigzagging through the field, and then went to the ground.

He remained motionless.

Then, all at once there was the darkness. It threatened to flood his mind, and he realized that his left arm was on fire with throbbing pain and that it hadn't stopped bleeding. Maybe he had been wrong. Maybe it was more than a flesh wound. He was slipping into the darkness. Maybe he was bleeding to death. Then he realized that they must have known he was going to be there . . . at the airport. They had known. How? His mind was spinning. Couldn't he ever get ahead of them? Spinning . . . He tried to grab hold, but it was too late. He was falling and it was icy cold and the desperate cry of fear was all around him.

He didn't know how long his blackout had lasted . . . maybe a minute, maybe two or three. He could hear them coming, at least two of them, legs thrashing through the stalks. Then they'd stop and wait, listening. Cody knew that in the past he would have gone after them, even weak and unarmed as he was now. But he couldn't anymore. All that had changed, as he had realized that morning. Ann wasn't there anymore. He had to take caution. He had to try and stay alive for the boys.

Moments ticked by. His arm throbbed . . . not as badly as before, but enough to make him want to yell out. Silence. Then footsteps. Then silence again. Sweat rolled off him. Now he could see the pant legs of one of them. He didn't breathe. A giant cane-spider crawled up his body, across his neck.

Madness. How long was the man going to stand there? Madness. He thought of Ann and Waikiki and the beaches and the hotels. Why hadn't he ever taken her there? Why had they never been able to have a vacation more than several days long? Why had he never learned to relax? *If the son of a bitch moves three feet this way he'll see me,* Cody thought. *He'll blow my brains out . . . Christ.*

Then suddenly they were going away. Running. Then the sound of their movement gave way to the sound of a jet taking off three hundred yards away.

He waited a full ten minutes and then stood up. The red station wagon was gone. He started back through the cane for Lelani's car. His legs were wobbly underneath him, and three hundred yards away another jet thundered into the sky . . . and he knew then why they had left without killing him.

Chapter Twenty-One

Cody swerved Lelani's car into the hospital driveway and banged into the low lava-rock wall that bordered the entrance. With a scraping and tearing noise, he managed to back up and then maneuver the car into the driveway and, eventually, into a parking space.

His head had cleared enough for him to reason that the other side couldn't have known he was coming back to the island. It was impossible. Only he, Victor, and Lelani had known. The other side, Polk and whoever was with him, couldn't have been waiting for him. He must have surprised them, startled them into action. . . . And he realized that earlier, when he had tipped his hand to Polk on the phone to draw him out, to prove to himself that Polk was the one . . . he had frightened the beast. He had set him loose, rampaging, racing to the end of whatever it was that was going down. Christ, he still didn't know what . . . and Lelani, a harmless fat woman who liked to smoke and have an occasional drink, was dead. He should have waited . . . waited for the reports to come back from Pyne, waited to have heard from Bobby Cormier, to have broken into the

Hannibals' house. Christ. . . . And he knew he couldn't have waited. He'd had to strike out at Polk when he did. He had to flush the son of a bitch out when he did or it might have gone on and on until it was over, and the son of a bitch would have slipped away clean, leaving only a trail of murder and misery behind. . . . And he knew he was rationalizing. He knew that Lelani's children wouldn't have cared about all the bodies before . . . wouldn't have cared if the killer had gotten away, if only their mother had, too.

The hospital was only dimly lit. A sign directed after-hours visitors or patients to follow the red line down the corridor.

But Victor was in the lobby . . . in the shadows.

"What took you so long?" he asked. Then he saw the blood on Cody's shirt.

"Lelani's dead," Cody said. "She's back in the cane field a couple of hundred yards from the airport. I couldn't push her over into the passenger seat, so I had to just pull her out onto the ground."

Victor sank to the floor.

"They were trying to kill me. The same people who killed Caleb's family. . . ." Cody stopped. He knew he had to gain control. He couldn't let Victor slip into shock. "Get up . . . God damn it, get up before someone sees you," he said angrily.

Victor struggled to his feet. Cody helped him across the lobby into the men's room and then helped him sit down again on the floor. Cody got what he had come for, his Walther and clips that he had taped under the third wash basin from the wall. He slipped a clip in.

He felt better with the loaded gun.

Carefully, he unbuttoned his shirt and managed to slip it off. The arm had stopped bleeding. With some wet paper towels he cleaned up the wound as best he could. It had been a bad day for the left arm.

"It's a nightmare," Victor said.

"I'll need your help getting this shirt on," Cody said. He had brought one of the new ones with him from the car. Victor didn't move, and Cody suddenly roared in a rage, "Get off the god damn floor!"

Victor did . . . helped him with his shirt.

"I want you to drive me," Cody said. He was beginning to feel whole again.

"What about Lelani?"

"There's nothing we can do for her," Cody said, starting to button the shirt.

"We should call the police," Victor said.

"Not yet."

"I can't leave her lying in a field."

"Don't you understand, we're beyond the police . . . beyond the law," Cody flared. "We're talking about the man who's behind the killing of the honeymoon couple, behind the killing of Caleb's family, the attempt to kill Caleb . . . the killing of Lelani. . . . If I'm not mistaken, the only reason I'm alive right now is that he's getting away. He's on his way back to California. . . . I'm alive because he had to catch the last plane out to Honolulu. . . . I know who he is, but I can't prove it . . . not yet. God dammit, I need your help."

Victor's black pickup truck pulled to a stop near the end of the public road. Beyond, guarded by iron gates, lay the entrance to the half-mile of winding driveway that led to Kamalani.

"It'll be safer if you don't wait here," Cody said.

Too much had happened for the Hawaiian with the naturally smiling face to cope, to think on his own. "What do you want me to do?" he asked.

"Do you have a watch?"

Victor looked at his wrist as if the answer would be a surprise one way or the other. "Yes."

"It's a quarter of eleven now," Cody said. "Come back in two hours. A quarter to one. Better have your lights out. If I'm not here, don't wait . . . find a phone and call Lieutenant Rivera. Tell him what happened to Lelani, and then tell him where I am and that I'm either dead or being held captive."

"I don't think I can do it," Victor said weakly.

"You have to do it. Do it for Caleb. Do it for Lelani and her kids," Cody said, and after several moments the Hawaiian nodded.

Cody got out of the cab of the truck.

"One thing I don't understand. You said that the man behind the killings is getting away. . . . I don't understand. Why are we here?"

"Because the man behind the killings wasn't alone. He had help, I think from someone in that house. . . . There're answers in there. There have to be. I want to find them before somebody else has to die."

Cody waited until the pickup truck had turned around and driven away. There were no streetlights. He had only the moon to guide him, and he regretted not having a flashlight as he studied the gate. There was a two-way speaker mounted on an iron pipe for visitors to communicate with the house. Other electrical equipment indicated both the remote control of the gate and the fact that there was a security system. The question was, how much of the perimeter did it cover?

He left the road and started making his way through the high grass. Within a matter of a dozen feet, he was under cover of trees, and it became almost pitch dark. He moved carefully, but not carefully enough.

Suddenly the ground gave way, and he tumbled down the side of a gorge eight or ten feet deep and landed hard on his shoulder again. He rocked silently back and forth with the pain for a number of minutes before he was able to go on. And then he realized he was sitting in a stream and that his pants were soaking wet. He decided to follow the stream, and it wasn't more than another dozen paces before, because of the dark, he almost walked into a low-hanging branch. It was in ducking under the branch that he saw the trip-wire strung a few inches off the ground. It was at a height that most animals, depending on their size, would either go over or under . . . but just the right height for a man's foot to catch on it and set an alarm off. He stepped over it and started working his way back through the landscape toward the driveway.

It was four minutes past eleven when the house came into view. While several rooms blazed with light, most of the house was in darkness. It would have to do. He would have preferred the whole house to be asleep before he entered, but he didn't have that luxury anymore. Not if he was right. Not if Polk, the deadly one, was on a plane heading back to Los Angeles. He had to try and stop him. If he was lucky, he'd find evidence solid enough to have him arrested as he got off the plane. . . . He also knew there was a possibility he could be wrong. Polk could have returned to the estate. . . . If he had, he'd be waiting for him.

As his eyes adjusted, he could see the silhouettes of several cars. Staying in the shadows, he moved toward them. The red station wagon was there, the white Rolls, and a bronze BMW. The hood of the station wagon was still faintly warm.

Someone was shouting inside the house. Then there was the sound of breaking glass. The shouting stopped. Doors slammed. Then someone was coming outside, heading straight for Cody, for the cars. He retreated deeper into the shadows and slipped the Walther into his hand.

Closer, closer . . . it was Stephen Auerbach. He looked angry and stoned. He lurched for the door of the red station wagon, finally managed to open it, got in, and just sat there. What was he waiting for? Had he spotted Cody? Cody considered rushing the wagon. Auerbach himself could have a lot of answers. Auerbach was likely the one who had attacked him with a baseball bat. He could also have been one of those in the cane field tonight, one of those who had killed Lelani. But then the engine roared to life, and a moment later the wagon peeled out, cutting a wide circle across the lawn before finding the driveway and racing for the gates.

"In times of stress, I often find it helpful to reflect on the Great Pyramid," Carmel Beecher Van Kueren was saying in her husky baritone, "for it is truly what it was meant to be, a sermon in stone."

"I know. I know," Lillian Hannibal replied with anxiety, "but we're in such great danger of it all being destroyed."

They were packing in what appeared to be the master bedroom. It was the best guess that Cody could make, having had only a quick glance in. He had entered the house a minute earlier, through the kitchen.

"You can't let Stephen upset you . . ." the enormous woman said. "I truly believe, despite our trials, despite the . . . horrid things that have happened, I feel that destiny is upon us. We are to succeed, to help lead the way to the new dawning.''

''I know,'' Lillian said again in a voice that desperately wanted to believe. ''It's just sometimes . . .'' She broke off, and her voice took a more matter of fact tone. ''Do you want to take your color notes?''

''Absolutely,'' the woman with the man's voice said, suddenly booming with enthusiasm. ''I had a dream last night about how to finish it . . . in fact, I'll be right back.''

Cody ducked into the shadows. The enormous woman glided out of the room and down the corridor, moving away from him and into the next room. Several moments later she was out again with a stack of papers several inches thick. ''I took the manuscript out and was working on it this afternoon,'' her voice called as she moved back into the room with Lillian Hannibal.

Cody decided to move to the dark side of the rambling house.

He found the writing room where he had rested the other day. He wanted to have a look through the desk drawers, but a toilet flushed nearby, and he reasoned it would keep. He kept moving down the darkened corridors until he found the far wing. He went all the way to the end of the hall and listened outside the door there. Hearing nothing, he turned the knob. The door opened silently; he stepped inside.

The room reeked of brandy. Nelson Hobart lay across a bed, asleep. He was wearing a Hawaiian shirt and nothing else. His chestnut toupee had flipped over, the adhesive on the front being all that kept it from falling off.

Cody searched the room. The contents were spare: two more bottles of brandy in a drawer; clothes, mostly worn, and few; prescriptions, lots of medicines—and then Cody recognized the other odor in the room, the one of corrupting flesh, of dying, of cancer. He had smelled it before, in the last weeks that his mother had been alive. She had been trying to go on, trying to wear clothes that were much too large . . . and he remembered the photograph taken at Spouting Horn and how he had thought Hobart looked like he was wearing the shirt of the much bigger Evan Hannibal.

Hobart interrupted his snoring to begin a hacking cough. Cody froze. Then the sleeping man rolled over and revealed a magazine on the bed with him. Cody stepped closer and saw that the well-worn pages were filled with photos of naked pre-teen boys.

In a suitcase, Cody found some more clothes and several more magazines of the kind on the bed, mixed in with publicity pictures of Hobart and his boys' choirs. He felt like throwing up and wondered why he felt no sense of rage, just weariness. He had turned over a rock and found an old and dying child molester.

He slipped out of the room and across the darkened corridor to another door. He listened again. Nothing. He turned the handle and stepped in. No one was home. He turned on a desk lamp. Whoever had been there had left recently. The doors to the empty closet were open. The bed was still mussed from a night's sleep. There was nothing in the drawers. Cody tried the wastebasket. There were several balled-up pieces of paper. He straightened them out to discover they were note papers: "From the Desk of Abraham Crocker." *So Hannibal's Boston attorney has gone home,* Cody thought. Had he been one of those in the cane field tonight? No. It didn't fit. But then, what did?

He moved back into the corridor and down to the next door. He was obviously in the guest wing, which meant probably somewhere along here would be Polk's room. Again he opened the door silently, and as he did it hit him, the same chilling sense of fear he had first felt when entering the girl's room in Canoga Park . . . and he was falling into the darkness . . . and there was the cry of fear and for help . . . and suddenly he was ice cold again.

Moments went by. The initial surge passed, but the anxiety remained. The evil had been here. Polk had been here, he was sure, and he remembered having the same sense of fear and dread when they had first arrived at the hotel. Polk had been there. He had followed them. Christ, he had been that close. But how had he known Cody was coming in the first place? There were still more questions than answers, but one answer for sure. Polk was gone.

The drawers and closet revealed a shirt, some socks and handkerchiefs, and a pair of shoes. He had left in a hurry. There was nothing in the wastebasket. There were stubbed out Camels in the ashtrays. Nothing. Christ, still nothing to tie him to the murders, to even prove this was his room. Depression overtook Cody, and he realized how much he had hoped to find answers here. How empty his evidence was. . . . Then hope returned. There were three books on the nightstand.

Cody tried the first one, *The Complete Works of Evan Hannibal*. He flipped the pages, looking for anything hidden inside. There was nothing. He turned on the desk lamp and read the inscription: "To my good friend Alex . . . Evan Hannibal." . . . The *Favorite Poems of Evan Hannibal* had much the same inscription, and similarly, nothing hidden in the pages. The depression was creeping back. Maybe he was mad. What was he doing? He had broken into the house of America's best-loved poet to try and prove he was somehow involved in a string of brutal killings. . . . Madness.

Unlike the first two, the third book was old and a bit battered, but it too was written by Hannibal. *Discovering the real William Shakespeare . . . Francis Bacon* was the title . . . and Cody noted that, while the book was old, the date of publication being 1959, the inscription was as recent as the ones on the other books . . . and perhaps much more interesting. "To my good friend, Alex, I hope this humble book and myself can be of some small assistance in your noble work . . . Evan."

Noble work?

He flipped through the book. Passages were highlighted in bright yellow on almost every page.

"*Mark Twain, Nathanial Hawthorn, R. W. Emerson, all believed that* Shakespeare was not the writer of the plays."

On another page:

" '*I am haunted by the conviction that the divine William is the biggest and most successful fraud ever practiced on a patient world'—Henry James.*"

Yet another . . .

"*Sir Francis Bacon is the only man of his time who could have written the plays. William Shakespeare, the boor from Stratford, certainly couldn't have, for it's been proved that the man couldn't read or write.*"

And . . .

"*Sir Francis Bacon's cipher number was 33. In the first part of* Henry IV, *the word 'Francis' appears thirty-three times on the page.*"

"If this was the noble cause, proving Bacon was really Shakespeare . . . what the hell does it have to do with murder," Cody wondered. ". . . Christ, not just murder, seven murders and four million dollars."

"Where did Shakespeare gain his knowledge of numerous languages, law, history? How could he write of so many foreign countries in detail when it is known that he never left England."

And then Cody began to sense a pattern. This Shakespeare-Bacon theory was obviously a pet cause of Hannibal's . . . after all, he had written the book. This would have been how Polk ingratiated himself with the Hannibals, embracing their pet cause. And that pattern would fit with the honeymoon couple, the young man who had wanted to be a writer. If Cody guessed right, Polk had promised him an interview with Hannibal in order to ingratiate himself with the couple. . . . But to what end? Where and why did murder and four million dollars come in?

He looked at his watch. Christ, an hour had gone by. He should have given himself more time. He had to return to Hannibal's writing room. He had to risk it. If a man was going to pay out four million dollars, there would have to be some record of where and why.

Chapter Twenty-Two

"Well, sir, good evening to you."

The old man's voice startled Cody. He was sitting at the desk in the darkened writing room, having just started to go through the drawers of the desk, when Evan Hannibal spoke. The Great American Poet was sitting across the room, in a large wicker chair.

"How exciting," Hannibal chuckled. "I believe this is called burglary," he added, rolling the word, "burglary" melodically. "But then, you being a policeman, I don't know what you might call it."

"Burglary is a pretty good term," Cody said. "Not quite as strong as murder, of course. And murder is why I'm here . . . what I'm investigating."

". . . You truly baffle me, sir," Hannibal said after some moments, in a voice that now sounded troubled. Then he quivered and strained and managed to rise out of his chair and snap on a floor lamp, the light of which cut across the top of his desk and revealed Cody's Walther lying there.

"Perhaps if you told me what you are looking for, I might be of some assistance," the old man said and stepped toward him. He was wearing gold silk pajamas and a sweeping black-velvet robe.

"For starters, I'd like to know why the honeymoon couple was murdered."

The old man frowned, seeming to remember, and lowered himself into another wicker chair, closer to Cody. "In fact, I thought of you when I heard they were found dead. I knew you'd be deeply troubled. . . ." He broke off for several moments. "Your eyes pretend to be those of a hunter," he said with a gentle smile. ". . . But the secret known only to the heart . . . was that the hunt was to help the wounded, not to wound . . ."

Cody realized the old man was reciting a line from a poem he had written long ago. His eyes looked as if he was drifting back into time and space. Cody tried to pull him back.

"Mr. Hannibal?"

The old man focused on him again and seemed surprised.

"The honeymoon couple. Did you agree to give the young man an interview? An interview that would take two days and that he could publish in a magazine?"

"You keep coming back to them." Hannibal laughed, but it was a laugh to cover confusion, to cover the fear that he might have forgotten. "I don't know the young people. I never knew them."

"Did you agree to give anyone an interview?" Cody pursued the matter.

"You'll have to ask my wife, Lillian," he said after some moments. "I don't think so, but she arranges all that . . . I . . . The human child is a delicate creature, don't you know." He smiled. "Especially when he gets to be as old as I am. . . . Lillian thinks it best if I don't give interviews anymore." He paused and frowned, then his lips moved for a few moments without any words. "When we appear at a banquet or a luncheon, Lillian is always there next to me, ready with a glass of water to spill in my lap in case it becomes necessary.'' His eyes twinkled with a certain mischievousness and sadness. ''You see, my bladder sometimes forgets to ask me if it's alright to release its contents. On such occasions, Lillian becomes a very clumsy wife and spills the water on me, thus explaining the sudden flood . . . . Of course, we can only pull that trick once at each location.'' He paused again, and the smile left his face for the moment. ''I'm afraid . . . Indeed, my deepest fear is that on occasion my thought processes have the same sort of lapse. . . . And as you can see, in such cases where I might make myself sound like a babbling idiot . . .'' He chuckled at his choice of words. ''. . . Lillian's water trick would be of no use at all. So, I don't do interviews anymore . . . not for several years I believe.''

''Then why would Professor Polk promise the honeymoon couple one?'' Cody asked.

''Alex? He would never do such a thing,'' Hannibal said and seemed truly surprised. ''Unless, of course, Lillian . . .''

Cody didn't let him finish. He wanted to see the old man's reactions without giving him time to think.

''Oh, that would be the least of his sins. . . . You see, if I'm not mistaken, your Professor Polk murdered the honeymoon couple.''

The Great American Poet gasped. ''That's preposterous. Alex Polk is a fine young man.''

''Is he?'' Cody said. ''I'm not sure the young policeman who was with me yesterday would share that opinion. . . . You see, half his family is dead now too. He's in Intensive Care. . . . And then there was a nice fat lady I met tonight. She too was shot, if I'm not mistaken, by your Professor Polk.''

Evan Hannibal looked stricken. ''There must be some terrible mistake.''

''Evan?'' Lillian Hannibal's voice carried into the room as she approached. ''Who are you talking to?''

Then she gave a little scream when she reached the door and saw Cody. ''What are you doing here?'' Her voice was almost a shriek.

''He thinks young Alex killed someone tonight,'' Evan Hannibal said. He seemed badly confused.

''Oh, that's a laugh, isn't it?'' Her voice was vitriolic. ''You accusing someone else of murder.''

''What the hell is that supposed to mean?'' Cody asked.

''I'm afraid you know all too well,'' she retorted.

''Lillian, what's wrong?'' called Carmel Beecher Van Kueren's husky voice.

''Don't come here; call the police,'' Lillian ordered.

''I don't think that's a smart idea,'' Cody said, putting his hand on his Walther.

''Oh my God,'' said the Great American Poet as he suddenly sensed he was in mortal danger.

As it turned out, the enormous woman with red hair was too curious to obey Lillian's command. ''What is wrong?'' she demanded as she glided through the doorway. ''Oh, I see,'' she said when she spotted Cody. Then a smile of triumph fixed on her face. ''So this is how desperate you are. . . . Well, I'm afraid you'll have to tell your employers you've failed. The Lunaeburg is not here. It will be nowhere you could possibly know. . . .You've risked exposure for nothing.''

''The Lunaeburg,'' Cody repeated to fix the word in his mind, having no idea what it meant.

"It's not here," Lillian Hannibal said in a shrill voice.

"Do you know where the Lunaeburg is?" Cody asked Hannibal.

"The money hasn't been paid yet, of course we don't have it," the old man said in a mix of fear and confusion.

"Don't tell him anything," Lillian implored.

"The four million? Is that the money to be paid?" Cody pressed.

"Tell him nothing," Lillian was shrieking now.

"Then you tell me," Cody said suddenly and harshly to Lillian, rising out of his chair. "Why did the honeymoon couple have to die?"

"You can't bluff us, Sergeant Cody, or whatever your real name is," Lillian said. "We are all too aware that the brave young man and young woman were killed by, if not you personally, at least your people."

Madness.

"He's going to kill us, too," Evan Hannibal said weeping.

"I'm not going to kill anyone," Cody said.

"Don't you recall?" Carmel Beecher Van Kueren said smugly. "Alex warned us he might come back here, that he might be dangerous. . . . But he also said he wouldn't dare hurt us." This last part she said in a comforting voice as she glided to console the old man.

"He said Alex killed someone tonight," Hannibal said again, sounding lost.

"Yes." The enormous woman chuckled with her man's voice. "Alex also said he would come and tell the most horrible lies about him. . . . Don't you see? It only shows you how desperate they are."

"Alex Polk, he's arranging for the Lunaeburg, isn't he?" Cody asked.

"Say nothing," Lillian said. "He's looking for information. Perhaps his people don't know as much as we thought."

"Oh, but if you would only join us Sergeant Cody, or whoever you are," Carmel Beecher Van Kueren intoned, sounding like an evangelist. "You may not know what your masters do, but we are on the verge of the greatest dawn in the history of man . . . or the greatest and forever darkness."

"He knows what he wants to know," Lillian said cynically.

Cody studied their faces, half in shadow, half in light. What mad world were they living in?

"My name is Cody. I was a policeman in Los Angeles. That's easily checked. And to tell you the truth, I haven't the faintest idea what a Lunaeburg is. . . . But I'll find out, just like I'm going to find out who your Professor Alex Polk is . . . because I'd bet my last dollar he isn't who he says he is. . . . I'd bet my last dollar he's responsible for at least seven deaths, and that he's conned you somehow into giving him four million dollars . . . no doubt for the Lunaeberg."

No one said anything for several moments, and then Hannibal chuckled. "Then, sir, you would lose your last dollar. Alex Polk didn't even believe the Lunaeburg existed. It was the boy who told us how to get it, the boy who gave us the proof." He chuckled warmly again and was crying with tears of happiness.

"What boy?" Cody asked.

"You've said too much," Lillian told her husband.

"The boy of gold," Hannibal said. "The boy of our dawn, our future."

"Evan," Lillian warned.

"Did Polk bring the boy?"

Hannibal laughed. "Could the Baptist bring Christ . . . ? The boy appeared on his own. . . . He only used Alex as his guide . . . and then he told Alex what to do."

"Evan, I don't want you to say any more," Lillian was sounding like the head nurse again.

"And you saw this boy . . . touched him?"

"Of course. We all did."

"Then why did he need a guide?"

"Because he is only a small tyke," Carmel Beecher Van Kueren boomed. "When he was tired, he only liked to speak in French."

"We're telling him too much," Lillian shrieked. "Don't you see, we're placing the child in danger. He's the one they want the most. The boy is the one they have to kill."

Madness. And Cody realized that she was as desperate as he was.

Madness.

Four mad people, and he was in the center, gun in hand.

"Where did Polk go to?" Cody asked.

No answer.

"When will you give him the four million for the Lunaeburg?"

"This week," the old man answered with a certain innocence.

"Where?"

Hannibal started to answer, but Lillian overrode him. "We'll say no more. Do to us what you will."

Cody considered. His arm ached. His body ached. His soul ached. "Where's your bar?"

"What?" Lillian asked, surprised.

"I'd like a drink, and then I'll leave you alone."

Actually, he had two.

They had all trooped to a sun-room where a bamboo bar was located. They were stiff drinks, half and half, maybe a little more. Evan Hannibal had decided to join him and sipped an Amaretto. The two women just stared.

"You're having your doubts, aren't you, sergeant?" the enormous Van Kueren woman finally said. "We could use Saint Paul . . . a strong and brave defender of truth."

Chapter Twenty-Three

An hour before dawn, Lieutenant Rivera stood alone in the middle of the road that led to the airport and watched the coroner's wagon take Lelani Makalua's body away. He was not happy. He had been even less happy an hour and a half before, when a call from the sergeant on duty had awakened him at his home in Hanapepe to tell him that Cody was back on the island, and that there was yet another dead body.

While Rivera had dressed and fumed and planned miserable events for Cody's future, Cody was, in fact, sitting at Caleb Ho's desk and running up the police department's long-distance phone bill.

His first call was home. Damien was already awake. Bobby Cormier, calling from Boston, had seen to that. Cormier thought he had the information that Cody wanted and had left a number where he could be reached. Cody wrote it down and then asked the boy for a number out of their own phone book . . . that of Malcolm Trapper. Damien gave him both the home and UCLA numbers.

"Is everything all right?" Damien asked.

"Yeah. . . . It feels like it's all coming together. If I can get a couple of breaks fast enough, I think we'll run the son of a bitch to ground. Either that or I'm liable to end up in the Kauai jail as the island's biggest pain in the ass in history . . .''

Both Codys smiled.

"Damien?" Cody said after some moments.

"Yes?"

"I love you," the father said. "You and Pat."

"We love you."

And Cody knew, for the first time since Ann had disappeared, that they could make it. They could survive.

Bobby Cormier sounded mush-mouthed. He excused himself to splash cold water on his face. He had been up all night drinking with an old P.D. friend who was now a private investigator. One of the friend's clients was the Legal Offices of Abraham Crocker . . . Hannibal's attorney. According to Cormier's friend, Crocker was really pissed off. Hannibal had been a client for years. He had done his contracts, investments, everything. What he was pissed off about was that the old man now wanted four million dollars cash to buy something. At first Hannibal wouldn't even give him an idea what it was . . . but the best Crocker could figure out . . . it was some old book, maybe three, four hundred years old.

"Did it have a name?" Cody asked.

"Yeah . . ." Cormier said. "I've got notes here somewhere."

"Was it called . . . the Lunaeburg?" Cody tried.

"Yeah, I think so," Cormier answered. "Anyhow, what my friend was asked to investigate was a certain college professor named . . ." He paused, obviously looking for his notes.

"Polk," Cody said. "Alex Polk."

"Cody, can I ask you a question?"

"Sure."

"What the fuck am I doing in a cheap motel in Boston with the worst fucking hangover I've ever had in my life, or at least in two or three months, and you know every fucking answer before I give it to you?"

"What did your friend find out about Polk?" Cody asked with a smile.

"Nothing really. He made some phone calls down South. The guy checked out okay. He told Crocker he'd like to go down and check the guy out in person . . . but Crocker said there was no point. The old man's wife had told him to gather the money and butt out. As near as he could figure, the four mil was being paid off tomorrow, in L.A. . . . and—are you ready for this?—in used twenties and fifties. . . . What kind of a whacko case are you on?"

He caught Trapper just going out the front door for his morning jog. The parapsychologist was happy to hear from him. He asked about Ann, and Cody had to tell him that there was nothing new. Nothing yet. Then Cody told him why he had called, that he needed help. He had some information, but he didn't know what it meant. He needed someone to translate it for him . . . and in a hurry. Trapper had helped before when Cody had needed specialized information. UCLA was a huge university. There always seemed to be someone there who knew the answers.

Cody told him about the Hannibals and Carmel Beecher Van Kueren and her talk of cosmic forces . . . about the spirituality she found in the Great Pyramid. . . . But most importantly, he told what he had learned just a few hours before: their belief that they were on the edge of either the "greatest dawn in the history of man," or the "greatest darkness, which would last forever," . . . and that this fate seemed to have something to do with aquiring an old book called a Lunaeburg, something they were willing to pay four million dollars for in used bills. He told Trapper that they talked of a boy . . . the boy of gold they called him . . . an apparently magical boy who had appeared to them and had told them about the Lunaeburg and had instructed them how to get it. Also that the boy liked to speak only in French . . . and that a college professor, who Cody believed was a con man, was the "guide" for the boy.

"My God," Trapper said and laughed darkly. Then he excused himself long enough to set up a tape recorder and had Cody repeat everything. The second time through, Cody remembered to mention the book about the Shakespeare-Bacon debate. "Though," he added, "I'm not sure if that has anything to do with anything . . . it was probably just the way Polk wormed his way into the Hannibals' good graces."

Trapper said he thought he knew someone who could help, but that, in any case, he'd have some answers for him by that evening.

It was the next call Cody made that finally broke the dam and probably kept him out of the Kauai jail. Pyne had heard back from two of the universities in Tennessee. Professor Alex Polk was a well-respected and much-loved man. . . . Folks were real disappointed when he decided to move to California to accept a lucrative position at a small school in Pasadena. . . . The problem was, the Professor Alex Polk they knew, wasn't the man in the photograph Pyne had sent them.

Christ, he'd been right. The son of a bitch was an impostor.

Who the man really was, the people in Tennessee didn't know, but one of the staff thought she might have remembered his face from a prison/university program. Obviously, they were checking. Cody told Pyne to also check and see if Evan Hannibal had ever appeared down there, either at the school or at the prison . . . and also to see if the man called Polk was on any of the red-eye flights from Honolulu to L.A., though he doubted if the man would be dumb enough to still be using that name.

Lieutenant Rivera and his reedy-looking sidekick, Smith, came in during the last of this. Cody had the call switched over to a speaker box and asked Pyne to repeat everything for the Hawaiian J. Edgar Hoover. The fat man did . . . and as Cody knew he would, also built up his own as well as the L.A.P.D.'s involvement and importance in the unfolding case.

Rivera thanked Pyne, but had no questions to ask.

Cody told him he'd call again in a couple of hours and then hung up.

The three men stood in silence for some moments.

"Well, if you ask me," Smith finally said, "this still doesn't clear Caleb Ho."

Cody hit him, breaking his nose and sending him crashing back into the partition, shattering a piece of rippled glass . . . and the man who looked like the Hawaiian J. Edgar Hoover turned and left the cubicle as if nothing had happened.

Cody and Rivera rode out to the latest murder scene together. On the way, Cody tried to bring the lieutenant up to date on everything he knew or was guessing at. Rivera didn't speak until he had brought the car to a stop.

"In the last thirty-six hours I have seen more murder and brutality then I have known in thirty-one years on the police force."

Cody nodded. "The hell of it is, it's business as usual in any of the major cities on the mainland."

Using the lieutenant's flashlight, they found her body. Other vehicles arrived. Cody gave statements to uniformed officers and showed them where Lelani's car and the station wagon had come off the road, then where he had run to.

And so it was, an hour before dawn, that Lieutenant Rivera stood alone in the middle of the road and watched the coroner's wagon drive off with Lelani Makalua's body, and he knew he'd have to face her children; he'd have to tell them.

Back at the police station, Cody made a reservation for a flight to Los Angeles later in the morning that he actually planned to keep.

Then he bummed a ride to the hospital with a young uniformed cop who was going off duty. A doctor in Emergency cleaned out the wound in his shoulder and redressed it. Afterwards, he walked down to Intensive Care. Caleb looked the same. But the nurse in charge said he was slightly better. More reason for hope. Maybe it was going to be a good day.

He decided to walk back to the police station. The sky was growing light and the cool, balmy breeze relaxed him.

Smith was almost past him when he hit the brakes and made a U-turn, pulling up alongside. The reedy-looking policeman had a strip of white tape across his nose. "The lieutenant wants you to know that the

Hannibals, the Van Kueren woman, and that Nelson Hobart are at the airport. They're booked to fly back to Los Angeles.''

''It figures,'' Cody said. ''They have an appointment with four million dollars there.''

''Well, what do you want us to do? The lieutenant wants to know,'' Smith half-whined and half-demanded.

''Nothing,'' Cody said. ''Let 'em go.''

Smith considered. ''I think that's what he was going to do anyway,'' he said and then drove off and left Cody standing alone on the street, and Cody laughed out loud.

Seven hours later, a brown layer of smog reached out beyond the Santa Barbara Islands to seemingly welcome Cody home. He had had two drinks on the flight back and had actually managed an hour's sleep. The sleep was difficult; his mind was racing. He felt good. The case was coming together. It was like old times. The world was coming back into place for him. He even managed hope for Ann. He remembered cases of amnesia, real ones. . . . Not many, but how many did he need? Christ, he loved her. Please, she had to be all right. He knew she was. And he knew he was fueled by a euphoria from the case, but he didn't care. It felt so damn good to feel good again.

As the jumbo jet crossed the California coastline twenty-thousand feet above and started its descent into LAX, the man capable of the pixie smile pulled to a stop in front of the house in Canoga Park. His nerves were frayed. He had been so careful. He had planned and executed every move with such precision. He had played all the people so well, and even when they had first resisted paying the money, he had been ready, with the back-up plan with the honeymooners. And now, because of Cody, everything was coming apart . . . and quickly. It had started, of course, with that one string coming loose. The unexpected factor that he had always been afraid of . . . the girl and her damn camera, the pictures at Spouting Horn, the pictures with him. . . . the pictures he couldn't find. . . . The pictures that sooner or later could be matched up with the pictures in her room. What the hell had she done with the film? How had Cody gotten ahold of it? . . . He had tried to control the situation by coming here, getting into the girl's room and taking whatever photos of himself that he could find. . . . Then the pictures at Spouting Horn would be meaningless. . . . How had Cody known? He had eliminated the only connection that could have linked him to the dead couple when he took those pictures from her room . . . and yet Cody had known.

A red-and-silver Ford van loaded with kids rumbled by, and then the street was clear. He put the rental car in gear and pulled into the worn-out asphalt driveway. He had rented the car with his back-up ID, which he hadn't wanted to use yet. It was the ID he had planned to disappear with. Cody was pushing him to the brink. Past the rusted-out swing set, the shell of the old Studebaker, the haphazard pile of lumber, he pulled to a stop again.

He had considered torching the place the first time, but had decided against it, because he felt it might draw too much attention if first the girl and her husband were missing and then her blind and crippled father's house burned to the ground. Now he had no choice. With the string pulled, the whole project being ripped open, questions would start to be asked. The girl's father might remember too much too soon from conversations with his daughter. He still felt confident that he could pull the project off. He just wished he knew how much Cody and the police knew. . . . But first things first. He had to cover his bases as best he could. He was flying by the seat of his pants and knew in a way he was enjoying it. He got out of the car and smiled, for he also knew that, even if worse came to worst and he was exposed, he still had a plan that would bring final success. And it was that thought that made him smile, because that would involve Cody, and he would enjoy twisting the knife in him.

Chapter Twenty-Four

Cody was still in a good mood as he got off the plane. As he came out of the boarding tunnel, he looked for Pyne but found Shepard instead. Shepard was a likable man in his thirties who had partnered for a while with Pyne, before Pyne had become too fat to work in the field. And now Cody remembered that Pyne had a doctor's appointment. But that should have been hours ago.

"Where's Dan?"

"In the hospital. They're going to operate on him in the morning," Shepard said.

"Christ, that fast," Cody said, and a wave of depression went through him as he remembered the feeling he had had when he talked to the fat man from Cuaresma's house the day before.

"Apparently he had had a lot of symptoms he had been ignoring," Shepard added. "Beth's scared shitless. . . . How about a drink?"

"Aren't you on duty?" Cody asked, knowing he now needed one himself.

"Yeah," Shepard said, "but that doesn't mean I don't want a drink."

* * *

"Ground ball up the middle and the Tigers take the lead."

Back in the real world, Cody thought, *with chrome bars and baseball games at every turn.* They had settled at the open cocktail lounge in the arrival/departure area. *Not a great spot to commiserate over a sick friend,* Cody thought. *Thousands of strangers milling around, loudspeakers blaring announcements . . .* But somehow it seemed to fit with the real world they lived in.

Shepard avoided his eyes.

"Christ, the way you look, he must be bad," Cody said.

Shepard started to say something, but then didn't.

"Get a make on Polk yet?" Cody finally asked.

"Yeah, he's a real sweetheart, too. His real name is John Barton Davis," Shepard recited, seemingly happy to talk about anything other than his ex-partner. "Did his first hard time when he was just eighteen, for a string of rapes and aggravated assaults. He was the all-American boy, president of his high school student body, cheerleader. He was named his hometown Young Achiever of the Year three days before he was arrested. Seems several of his victims spotted his smiling face in the newspaper."

"Could explain why these days he doesn't like to have his picture taken . . . or left lying around," Cody thought out loud.

"He got an education in prison," Shepard went on. "The next time he was busted it was for counterfeiting . . . good quality; he was working with a top old pro. He did nine years in Leavenworth for that one. The last time he went in was in Tennessee . . . pulled off a computer swindle on an insurance company. Took them for almost a million before he was caught. . . . He's apparently quite intelligent. Prison tests put his I.Q. in the 160's. . . ."

". . . I'll tell you what else he is,' Cody said suddenly, feeling tired and angry. "He's a god damn maniac is what he is . . . a total fucking sociopath, who doesn't give a damn about anyone else in the world except himself. . . . Why didn't the great brains in the prisons tell us that . . . ? Why the hell did they have to let him loose on the god damn streets? So far we've got seven people dead, maybe eight if we ever find out what happened to the real Professor Polk. . . ." He paused. He knew it wasn't Shepard's fault, but Christ, you had to be angry at somebody sometime, all cops did, and they usually took it out on their own. "Any idea where Davis is now?"

"No. He wasn't on any of the red-eyes that we could check. We're waiting on a warrant to go through a house he rents in Eagle Rock."

It was then that Cody felt it—the fear again . . . the darkness closing in . . . the desperate cries for help.

"I've got to talk to you," Shepard was saying.

"Not now," Cody said. "Take me there. To Davis's house."

"Cody." Shepard was upset.

But Cody was on his feet. "God damn it, take me there."

They were on the freeway for forty-five minutes. It was hot and smoggy, the traffic stop-and-go. Neither man spoke. But all the way the cries of fear and for help grew inside of Cody. He wanted to cry. He wanted to reach out and try to help, but he knew he couldn't.

The captain was already there when they arrived,

along with three other department cars and two television news teams. It was becoming a sideshow.

The house was wooden and painted red. Roses of several different colors grew in the front. And Cody knew death lay inside.

"Open the door," he said.

"We're waiting for the landlord; he has a set of keys," the captain answered, looking uncomfortable.

Cody was in no mood to talk. He advanced on the front door and kicked it in.

The living room looked like it had come out of a magazine: neat and perfect. He had no use for the room . . . or for the first bedroom he tried. It was the back-bedroom door where he stopped.

"Oh Christ," Cody said, and he was crying.

He opened the door. The inside of the room was dark. The windows had been covered over with pieces of cardboard. A bed with a filthy sheet and a battered teddy bear was the only piece of furniture. The bed had chains with manacles that were fitted for a small wrist.

"Tell me about the boy," Cody said. "Any idea where Davis picked him up?"

"How did you know about the boy?" the captain demanded.

Cody realized he hadn't told Pyne about his most recent conversation with the Hannibals. But that didn't matter now. This was no time or place to explain, and his deep feeling became anger. "God damn it, just tell me what I want to know."

And it was then that he heard the little dog begin to bark.

"As near as it can be pieced together, the last time he was released from prison he jumped parole and moved to Louisiana," the captain said, but the horror of the room was beginning to affect his words. "He got a job in an air conditioning factory there, joined a local church . . . and a widow and widower's club. His story was that his own family, wife and children, were killed in a car crash in Michigan, and that he had come to Louisiana to build a new life. After a few months, he married a woman with three small children. He managed to convince her to sell the house she owned outright, thanks to her first husband's insurance, so they could move out West and start a new life. . . . They got sixty-one thousand dollars for the house. . . . Two days later, Davis disappeared with the money and the youngest boy, who was almost six then."

"Did the boy speak French?" Cody asked.

"The whole family did," the captain answered.

"Davis learn his French in prison?"

The captain nodded. "The last two years he was there. Very bright student. The people connected with the prison/university program were quite impressed with him. . . . That's how they happened to remember his picture."

"How long before Davis started taking French did Hannibal appear at the prison?" Cody asked and moved to the filthy bed and sat down.

"A few months," the captain answered.

Cody held the battered teddy bear, held it like it was a child and stroked it and protected it, knowing that this was where the cries of fear had come from . . . the darkness, the falling. So afraid. The small boy had shared the common strand with the young woman dying in the sugarcane field so many miles away.

Cody led him to the backyard. The little dog next door kept barking and barking.

You can stop now, my friend, Cody thought. *We've found him; we'll take him home. He won't have to be afraid anymore.*

They dug in the area Cody showed them. In less than half an hour, one of the shovels cut through a buried plastic garbage bag.

And the coroner's wagon came and took what was left of the small body away.

And down the street, the man who was capable of the pixie smile watched. He knew what he had to do now, his one last card to play. He knew he'd still win.

"I need to talk to you," the captain said.

Cody was sitting on the front steps of the red wooden house. It was almost dark now. He had used the phone inside to call home and tell the boys he'd be home later. But he hadn't been able to find any liquor in the house . . . Christ, wouldn't you know you can't trust a man who doesn't drink. . . . so he had sent a uniformed cop for a pint of vodka and some orange juice. Only Shepard didn't care to drink anymore, so he drank alone.

"I'm going to get this son of a bitch," Cody said.

"Oh, we'll get him. It might not be easy. He'll have run for cover by now," the captain said.

"You're wrong," Cody said. "He has too much at stake: four million dollars and, from what you've told me, over three years of planning."

"How would he expect to get the money now that we know who he is?" the captain asked.

"Because the people who want to pay the money think that we're the bad guys. The more we tell them about Davis and who he really is, the more they're going to believe we're lying."

"I can't believe that."

Shepard lurched in front of them; he looked stricken. "Captain, we've just heard from the Valley. . . . Worden's dead. Someone splashed his house with gasoline and set it on fire."

"Someone?" Cody said sarcastically. "You want to play twenty questions? Don't you understand? It was Davis. . . . I'm telling you, the son of a bitch isn't going to quit." And as he said the words, he knew the boat wasn't safe anymore. Nothing was safe anymore. He had to move the boys. He was getting to his feet when the captain spoke.

"Cody, I need to talk to you."

"I have to call home first," Cody said.

"Cody," the captain said forcefully, "it's about Ann . . . Shepard was supposed to tell you, but I guess . . ." The captain paused a moment before he could plunge ahead. "The Long Beach Police have a guy who says he killed her. . . . He took them out to the Angeles Forest, showed them where her car was at the bottom of a three hundred foot cliff. There were parts of a skeleton nearby."

Chapter Twenty-Five

He sat in the coroner's outer office for almost two hours. For awhile, somewhere nearby, someone was listening to a baseball game, but it wasn't loud enough for him to know who was playing or what the score was.

"The guy's confessed to killing eleven women in this area and another six in Houston," Shepard had told him on the ride over. "He just sat in shopping center parking lots and watched for women driving in. When they'd park and go into the stores, he'd just hide in the back of their cars."

Someone going down the hall was laughing. He wanted a drink, but he was afraid to leave. The tiles on the floor were grey and pale yellow, and Shepard avoided his eyes. Christ, he wanted a drink, but he was afraid he'd miss the announcement, afraid he'd miss the information.

"Dead bodies float with the stream, live ones fight against it." He didn't know why, but the words kept coming into his head. She used to say them. Ann. She used to tell the boys. "Dead bodies float with the stream, live ones fight against it." They had heard the words first in Kernville. They were on one of their three-day vacations, hiking, fishing. He didn't drink as much in those days. The boys were six and twelve. It was the priest at Sunday morning Mass who had used the phrase in his sermon. She had never forgotten it and had used it when she tried to give the boys a sense of purpose, of reason, when they were going to have to be different, when they weren't going to be allowed to go along with the crowd, to do something just because everyone else was doing it . . . and he knew over the years it had helped give the boys a sense of independence and confidence to make their own decisions.

"Dead bodies float with the stream, live ones fight against it."

"What?" Shepard asked.

And Cody realized that he had spoken out loud. Shepard looked embarrassed. An olive-skinned woman in a white work coat had appeared and was looking at Cody.

"Mr. Cody?"

"Yes," he said, and he knew his voice was hollow. He knew this was the end.

Madness. She was smiling.

A piece of food was caught between two of her upper front teeth. "Your wife's dental charts don't match with the skeletal remains."

"What?" he asked and sat down again because he couldn't stand any longer.

She repeated her first statement and then added, as if talking to a child, "It isn't your wife."

Cody felt disoriented.

"That's great," Shepard said with an enthusiastic smile.

"You said it was her car," he said accusingly to Shepard, and he knew he felt cheated. She had al-

most been dead and now she wasn't. The anxiety of
not knowing had almost been over and now it wasn't,
and he felt guilty for feeling cheated, and yet he
knew he couldn't stop it.

"Shit," Shepard said angrily. "That's what they
told me." Then he turned on the woman in the white
work coat who had a piece of food in her teeth and
demanded to know where a phone was that he could
use.

She told him, and he disappeared. It was the woman
in the white work coat who now felt cheated. "I
thought you'd be happy."

"We weren't even notified about this thing until
this morning," Shepard told him as they drove the
late-night freeway back from Long Beach. "Even
then everything was kinda confused. The guy named
the wrong shopping center for where he said he
picked up Ann. . . . We thought it was best to let
them check it all out before telling you. Then, of
course, this afternoon they had found the car." The
traffic had thinned out by the time they turned off the
Marina. Christ, he wished Shepard would shut up.
". . . or at least the right license. They said it was
too far to pull the car up, but they're going to send a
team down tomorrow to double check if it's Ann's or
not. . . . But, I mean, even if it is, it could have
been stolen, or the license plate stolen. . . . I mean
the important thing is that it isn't Ann."

Shepard was trying so hard to be cheerful. Cody
wanted to smile or nod or give him some indication
that everything was all right.

"Thanks for the ride," is what he managed as they
pulled to a stop in the Marina parking lot. They were
the first words he had said on the thirty-minute trip.

"I can pick you up tomorrow," Shepard said eagerly.

"And go where?" Cody asked.

Apparently Shepard hadn't thought that far ahead. "Anywhere you like," he said after some moments and then added, "I'll stay on top of those Long Beach guys, too, up in the Angeles Forest."

Cody stepped into the night, watched Shepard drive away, and then started down for his boat.

Less than fifty feet away, the man who was capable of a pixie smile sat in his darkened car and watched.

It was a few minutes past eleven, and the world was beginning to come back into focus for Cody as he made his way through the gate and down the jetty. A stabbing sense of regret and fear was overtaking him as he remembered the boys and remembered that he was going to have moved them . . . was going to have had Damien drive himself and Patrick out to their grandmother's. Christ, the sense of Davis, the pixie-smiling maniac, was flooding his mind. Everything about him, the Hannibals, the dead honeymooners, the little boy buried in the plastic garbage bag, had been blocked out for the last several hours and now. . . . He was running when he reached the boat. Then he slowed himself deliberately as he went aboard.

The door was locked the way it should be. Relief. His heart slowed to almost normal. He unlocked the door and climbed down into the main cabin.

"Cincinnati three, Atlanta two. . . . In the Astrodome, the Astros climbed all over the visiting Giants . . ."

Down the passageway he could see Damien asleep with the flickering light of the television playing off his face, and Cody smiled . . . and smiled again when he saw Pat's sleeping silhouette in his cabin.

". . . In the American League, the Angels played host to the Royals . . ."

Funny, Cody thought as he closed the door to the passageway. In an odd sort of way, the case these last few days, the danger, was bringing his little family closer together, like it used to be. And he couldn't remember the last time Damien had curled up on his mother and father's bed to watch T.V.

There were four telephone messages: one from Beth Pyne, three from Trapper. He didn't want to talk to Beth, not tonight. He had had enough depression and anxiety for one day. He didn't really want to talk to Trapper either, but the last message said, "Important—will be up until midnight." So he made a drink without ice, more out of habit than need, he was mildly surprised to note, and dialed his friend.

"Hello." Trapper answered on the first ring, sounding as fresh as he had seventeen hours earlier when Cody had interrupted him on his way to his early-morning jog.

"It's me, Cody."

"I'm glad you could call. I have a woman I think you should talk to. The trouble is, she's leaving town tomorrow morning. She said she'd wait for your call until midnight. I have to tell you, she lit up like a Christmas tree when I played the tape I made of our phone conversation this morning."

"What does she do?" Cody asked. "I mean, what does she specialize in?"

"Philosophy," Trapper answered. "She's an associate professor right now, but believe me, she's very bright; she's going far. She's spent the last several years doing research that apparently's right down your current alley. . . . It's for a book about, are you ready? . . . 'Secret societies and mysteries of the ancient world.' "

"Christ."

Eleanor Murphy answered only after eleven rings and sounded out of breath. Cody had to remind her who he was and that Trapper had told him to call.

"Oh yes yes, yes, you're my Lunaeburg man."

"You make it sound like I'm selling vacuums."

She laughed. "You'll have to excuse me, I'm a little demented tonight. We're supposed to leave on a vacation tomorrow, and I'm still packing. Let me change phones."

She did.

"Yes, here we are, Carmel Beecher Van Kueren . . . I must tell you she's one of my favorites." She said the last part liltingly, as if she knew she was talking about someone from outer space. . . . "Hold on . . ." She broke off, and he heard the rustling of papers. "Trying to explain to your three school-age children's teachers that they are going to miss the first two weeks of school is not something you want to know about. . . . Ah, here we are. I've got it all now," she said finally and then paused as if refreshing herself with the materials. "Okay, what exactly is it you want to know?"

"Everything you can tell me . . . what any or all of it means."

She laughed again. "I wouldn't ask Carmel Beecher Van Kueren that question. She'd talk for days and then tell you she'd only scratched the surface. . . . I've made some notes on this; let me see if I can put it in some perspective for you . . . at least the way I'm reading it. . . . Do you have any idea of what the great mysteries or the secret teachings of the ancient world are?''

''I'm not sure.''

''I think you might. . . . At least I think some of them will sound familiar to you when I mention them. . . . And I should tell you, there are a good number of people, including groups as large as the Masons, who embrace all or at least part of the beliefs we're going to talk about. Anyway, let's start with the Great Pyramid, which you said Mrs. Van Kueren was expressing her belief about.''

''She called it a sermon in stone,'' Cody remembered aloud.

''Yes, I've heard her say that at her seminars. You see, to many of those who believe in the great mysteries and secret teachings of the world, the Great Pyramid of Gizeh is unmatched as the ancient world's most important achievement. It stands alone, almost as a cornerstone to all the other great pagan religions.''

''Pagan?'' Cody repeated with some surprise.

Once again, she laughed. ''Yes, I know what you mean. When I was a little girl in Catholic school, we used to bring our nickels and dimes every day to buy pagan babies . . . but technically, the word 'pagan' refers to any religion outside the religious mainstream of Christianity, Judaism, Buddhism, Islam, and so on . . .''

''I hate to stop you,'' Cody said, interrupting. ''But how does this all translate into a Lunaeburg and four million dollars?''

''Oh, I think I can show you,'' she said. ''You see, as preached by Carmel Beecher Van Kueren and others, the great pagan religions all have one common thread, stretching from the Great Pyramid, which they believe was built by an advanced civilization seventy thousand years ago. That common thread continues on, through the worship of the Sun itself as a deity, to astrology, tarot cards, magic, sorcery, on and on and on, all the way down to the subject of the book you talked about on the tape . . . the belief that Francis Bacon was really Shakespeare.''

She paused for effect.

''That's a hell of a long thread,'' Cody said.

''Not when you realize,'' she went on, ''that these people believe that there are messengers who have traveled across time to keep the secret mysteries and teachings alive . . . all, of course, in preparation for the time when the world will be ready to receive them . . . or another way of phrasing it . . . when the world will be ready for the great dawn of mankind.''

''And that great dawn is tied to the Lunaeburg?'' Cody asked after several moments.

''In this case, apparently so, and it makes a lot of sense if you come at it from their point of view. . . . You see, Francis Bacon was considered to be one of those messengers across time, and in the plays he wrote, known as Shakespeare's plays, he hid, in cipher, the clues to the discovery of the location of the ancient mysteries and secret teachings . . . teachings that must be revealed before the great dawn of mankind can take place.''

''I don't understand,'' Cody said. ''Why would they have to be hidden?''

''As Carmel Beecher Van Kueren will tell you,'' she answered, ''because the powerbrokers and the churches had done their best to destroy the pagan religion and its truths. . . . To save them, they had to be hidden until the time was right . . . until man had progressed enough for his great dawn.''

"Right," Cody nodded. "Sorry for the interruption."

"You see," she went on, "Mrs. Van Kueren, and people like her, trace Francis Bacon all the way from ancient Egypt, through history, all the way to the Declaration of Independence."

"He's had a busy career," Cody commented.

"Do you have a dollar bill on you, Mr. Cody?" she asked.

He looked and found one in his pocket. "Yes," he said and realized he had barely sipped his drink.

"Turn it to the back," she instructed. "Do you see the pyramid?"

"Yes."

"The unfinished Pyramid of Gizeh is widely recognized as a Masonic emblem. And you have to remember, Francis Bacon is credited with establishing the Free Masons . . . and with writing a book, a hundred and fifty years before the Declaration of Independence, called *The New Atlantis,* which many people credit as the foundation of our United States . . . which also isn't surprising, because most of the founding fathers, such as Washington and Jefferson and many more, were Masons." She paused to catch her breath; she was enjoying this. "Now the bird across from the pyramid, you see him?"

"He's there," Cody said.

"What kind of bird is he?"

"An American Eagle?" Cody tried.

"Ah, that's what most of us think," she said.

"How did I know I was going to be wrong," Cody sighed. "Let me guess, it's really Francis Bacon's mother?"

Eleanor Murphy laughed. "No, according to Carmel Beecher Van Kueren and others, it's actually a phoenix . . . and, I believe, the final piece to your puzzle. . . . You see, the phoenix can be traced back through ancient mythology. It's a bird of which only one lives at a time . . . and each lives for about five hundred years. . . . When the time comes for it to die, it builds itself a nest of frankincense and myrrh, which it then enters and dies in. . . . Let me ask you, when was America discovered? Not by the Vikings, but for real, when the Europeans started to colonize.''

"In 1492, just about five hundred years ago," Cody said, following her line.

"Right," she said. "Now back to the phoenix. After it dies, from its decomposing body, a worm emerges . . . and from this worm are born two other creatures . . . another phoenix and a Boy of Gold, and together they can bring the dawn of a new age of man. . . . You don't have to think long before you see the symbolic connection of the frankincense and myrrh and the birth of the Boy of Gold . . . and the birth of Christ, two thousand years ago. . . . For despite Mrs. Van Kueren's displeasure with the Christian churches for trying to stamp out the ancient mysteries . . . Jesus Christ is accepted as one of the messengers of a universal consciousness. . . . Of course, she also believes that Christ's true story is one of the mysteries yet to be revealed.''

"But if the Boy of Gold is already here . . . " Cody was puzzled, ". . . then we must already be in the dawn.''

"No. The dawn can only come with the final revelation of the secret mysteries and teachings. That's where I think your Lunaeburg comes in. Remember, Bacon, using cipher, has hidden the directions to where the secrets are in the Shakespearean plays.''

"Is the Lunaeburg one of the original editions?" Cody tried.

"Close, but not quite," she answered. "In 1622, the first folio of the Shakespeare plays was published. . . . A year later, in Lunaeburg, a curious book on cryptography was published. Carmel Beecher Van Kueren and many others have maintained for years that the obscure little book, published in Lunaeburg, contains the cryptographic key to the original Shakespeare folio . . . only no one has ever been able to turn up a full and authentic copy."

"So if somebody could," Cody mused, "especially someone who was being helped by the Boy of Gold . . . they would hold the key to the future of the world?"

"Yes," Eleanor Murphy said. "And if I were a believer, under those circumstances, that Lunaeburg would be worth a lot more to me than a paltry four million dollars."

Madness, Cody thought. The whole world was mad . . . and yet it was so ingenious.

"On the other hand," she went on, "if I were a con artist, which Trapper says is what you are after, I couldn't pick a sweeter piece of bait than a Lunaeburg . . . or a target more ripe for picking than Carmel Beecher Van Kueren and her followers, who have been searching for and believing in this for forty years."

It's so goddamn ingenious, he thought. The man with the pixie smile had really built a piece of work.

He thanked her for all her information, and she laughed again and said that it had been fun and asked if he would let her know how it all turned out. He promised he would.

The phone was back in its cradle less than ten seconds when it rang again.

"Cody," he said, and as he did a sickening chill gripped his body.

"I warned you to stay out of it . . . and now I have your son."

It was *his* voice, the man with the pixie smile. Davis. Polk. The maniac.

"No," Cody said. But the word came out like a wail of pain.

"Really? Better count heads."

Cody dropped the phone, moved to the passage-way door and opened it. Damien still lay on the bed where Cody had seen him earlier.

"D," he called out.

The eighteen-year-old stirred and groaned, and now Cody saw the dried trickle of blood coming from behind his ear. Christ, he knew the worst. He snapped on the light in Patrick's cabin. What he had thought before was the silhouette of the sleeping boy was only a pair of pillows and a blanket.

His twelve-year-old son was gone. Patrick. Christ. The maniac had Patrick.

Chapter Twenty-Six

The phone was dead when he returned to it. For a panicky few moments, he thought maybe he had disconnected it or had actually broken the phone when he had dropped it. He hung up and waited for it to ring, and at the same time was torn, wanting to go to Damien. But now Damien was coming to him, down the passageway, unsteady on his feet.

"Dad?"

He braced himself in the passageway door. Cody helped him into a chair and quickly examined the wound behind his son's ear. It was split open and would need stitches. He no doubt had a concussion, but Cody knew he'd be all right.

"Do you remember anything about what happened?"

"I'm not . . ." Damien started and then stopped and tried to pull his thoughts together. "This man came. Sergeant. He said he was a sergeant and that he had information on Dan Pyne, and then Pat came out and looked at him sort of funny . . . that's all I remember . . . Dad?"

"Pat's gone," Cody said. "He took him."

Damien began to cry.

* * *

They waited.

An hour passed. Cody, afraid to use the phone and afraid not to test it, finally picked it up and hurriedly called the "time lady."

It was twelve thirty-one and twenty seconds.

"It's my fault," Damien said.

"It's no one's fault," his father said.

"I was supposed to protect him," the eighteen-year-old insisted vehemently.

"So was I," Cody blurted out. "Christ, I was supposed to protect your mother." And suddenly he felt drained.

Another forty minutes passed before the phone rang again.

"Cody."

"It was all going so well until you got involved . . ." the man who was capable of a pixie smile said, still with a trace of the smooth salesman's voice. "You've really stirred everything up."

"What do you want from me, Davis?"

"So you know who I am." There was no smoothness left. Cody had just answered one of his questions.

"We know everything," Cody said, trying hard to keep his voice matter-of-fact. "Even about the little dead boy in your backyard in Eagle Rock."

"Want to try for two dead boys?" Davis shot the words back like a counterpunch. And Cody sensed he enjoyed making the threat.

"Listen to me carefully," Cody said in words that were almost a hiss. "You win . . . got it? Game's over. You win . . . and I'm prepared to do whatever you ask me to do to get my boy back safe and sound. He's more important to me than the police, more important to me than the Hannibals' four million dollars. He's more important to me than the law. . . .

I repeat, I will do whatever you ask for his safe return. . . . On the other hand, if you harm my son, if you don't return him . . . you'll have to spend the rest of your life looking over your shoulder . . . and sooner or later, I'll be there. And I won't be the law, and there won't be any jails for you . . . only a lot of pain and then more pain and more pain, until you'll think you can't stand it anymore, until you think you're going to die. But I'll make sure you don't. . . . I'll make your pain my life's work. . . . Do you understand?''

Silence.

And then the line went dead.

''He hung up on me.''

''Oh, no,'' Damien said, afraid.

''No,'' Cody said. ''It's a good sign. At least the son of a bitch scares.''

Seven minutes went by. The phone rang again.

''Do we understand each other?'' Cody asked.

''Just like you said, you do what I want you to do and you get the boy back safe and sound,'' Davis answered. ''On the other hand, you cross me and you'll get him back in pieces, and we'll start with his blond peach-fuzzy little balls . . . do you understand?''

Cody thought he might pass out. It was like Ann disappearing again . . . the anger. Only this time he could talk to the one responsible, and he knew that even if he got Patrick back safely, he was going to track this man down. He was going to kill him.

''We understand each other,'' Cody said quietly.

''All right,'' Davis said. ''From now on it's nothing personal, strictly business . . . agreed?''

''Agreed,'' Cody answered.

''How much do the Hannibals know?'' Davis asked.

''The last time I talked to them you were John the

Baptist, and I was a bad guy who was working for some dark forces who had killed the honeymoon couple. . . . I was also doing my best to keep them from getting their hands on the Lunaeburg and the world from a bright and shiny new dawn.''

Davis sighed. ''Good. As you may or may not have figured out, one of my built-in safety devices was that if things did start going wrong, that the more negative things people said about me, the more it would prove to the Hannibals that I was really who I appeared to be. . . . But like all good things, that can only go on for so long. . . . Have the police talked to the Hannibals since they found out who I am?''

''I don't know,'' Cody answered. ''I would doubt if they had. Things were still breaking pretty late last night. . . . Worden dying in the fire, I presume that was your doing?''

Davis didn't answer.

''Then, of course, there was the discovery of the boy's body,'' Cody went on. ''Different things happening in different divisions. . . . The division commanders would have to get together and compare notes, decide what to do. And, of course, Evan Hannibal is a respected citizen, not the sort of guy you bust in his house and start asking a lot of questions of . . . no, I doubt if they would have gotten around to talking to him yet.''

''For your son's sake, you better hope that's true,'' Davis said. ''Because it's going to be your job to keep the cops from damaging my character too much.''

''For how long?'' Cody asked.

''At least until the Hannibals have the four million dollars,'' Davis said. ''And at least until they turn it over to you so you can deliver it to me.''

"Me? They'd never trust me to give me the money."

"You let me take care of the Hannibals," Davis commanded. "You just do what I tell you to do . . . as far as I'm concerned, you have to be the one . . . there's no one else I can trust as much as you. You have your boy's peach-fuzzy little balls on the line. . . . I'll call again, noon . . . be there."

At six A.M. Cody found the captain in the surgery waiting room at St. Joseph's Hospital. Betty Pyne was there. She looked like she hadn't slept in a couple of days. She and Cody hugged, and he said the words she wanted to hear, about how Dan was strong and that he was sure he'd come out of this okay, and he knew as he said them that they were lies.

When the ritual was over, he moved to the captain. "What has anyone done with the Hannibals?"

"Nothing yet," the captain answered. "I called last night. Made an appointment to go over today. It's rather a sensitive area . . . did you know Evan Hannibal is going to the White House next month to receive a Medal of Freedom? They're having a dinner in his honor, for God's sake. What the hell am I going to tell these people? They think this Davis character is a wonderful human being."

"It could work out nicely if they could go on thinking that for a couple more days," Cody said.

The captain studied him for several moments. "You still think Davis is going to go after the four million dollars?"

"I know he is. He's kidnapped my twelve-year-old son to make sure I deliver the money to him."

Cody was back at the boat by eight thirty. He knew he had to sleep. He had to try.

"No calls," Damien reported. The eighteen-year-old was pale, with dark circles under his eyes. A doctor friend from down the jetty had come by and taken care of his wound.

Cody scrambled some eggs, and they both tried to eat, tried to hold on.

Alone in his cabin, he closed his eyes and tried to find the nothingness. His mind spun like a nightmare wheel. Patrick. He kept seeing Patrick, and then the smiling, olive-skinned woman with the piece of food in her teeth, saying, "It's not your wife. It's not your wife." And then he saw the honeymoon couple, their bodies naked and bloated in the baking sun, and Caleb in the bed in Intensive Care, and he was falling and falling, deeper and deeper. And then he was back in the room again, the one with the filthy bed and the little manacles, and Patrick was there. He was the prisoner. And then they were digging up the plastic garbage bag. Patrick was calling him, "Dad . . . Dad . . ."

"Dad?"

Damien was in the passageway door. Cody had been asleep for almost three hours.

"He's on the phone. The man who has Patrick."

It was one of the old, elegant Spanish-style homes, the kind that movie stars built in the 1920's and 1930's. There were only a couple dozen of them left in this section of Hollywood. They stood like fortresses, with their iron gates and ten-foot walls, trying to hold out the creeping poverty and sleaze that the surrounding area had become.

"My name's Cody. I'm here to see the Hannibals," he told the security man.

He was flabby and in his thirties. His grey uniform

was ill-fitting, and he seemed to resent the interruption of his reading. He pulled the gates open for Cody without a word.

The same Filipino houseman who had helped him to his feet in Kauai ushered him into the house.

"Feeling better today, sir?"

"Yeah, just grand," Cody answered.

The houseman led him to and left him in an atrium crammed with hanging ferns and exotic flowers. A fountain bubbled, and white doves, from inside their black wrought-iron cages, cooed, and he felt like he had stepped back in time.

"Sergeant Cody." Lillian Hannibal's voice echoed across the polished Mexican-tiled floor as she approached. She was wearing a sweeping lavender cocktail gown, and the tone in her voice said she was the head nurse again, in charge. "I must admit, I found it quite remarkable when Alex phoned this morning and said that you were now with us."

"We live in remarkable times," Cody said.

She was unsure of him.

"Do you know what the police are saying about him?" she asked.

"Yes. That's one of the reasons I became convinced that you must be right," Cody said, repeating the line he had practiced on his drive over . . . his drive from the Hollywood Division Police Station where they had taped the monitoring devices to his body. "I know that the police are fabricating evidence against Professor Polk."

"I knew it," Lillian said with a burst of enthusiasm, which revealed there had been doubt.

"What I don't know, is why," Cody added.

"The why is not important for you to understand now. Perhaps you will later," she said and then seemed to consider. "But then, perhaps not. It's not given to all of us to understand everything . . ." She managed what passed for a warm smile. "You'd better come with me."

She led him back through the entry hall and then through the living room, talking as they went. Everywhere there were photographs of Evan Hannibal. *It's another living shrine, another museum,* Cody thought. He saw Hannibal with F.D.R., Hannibal with Clark Gable, with Will Rogers, Joe Dimaggio, Harry Truman, Eisenhower, John Kennedy, Robert Kennedy, Pope John XXIII, on and on.

"I will tell you this," Lillian Hannibal said as they walked. "In the late 1930's, a brilliant woman named Maria Hall came very close to unearthing exactly what we are looking for, Francis Bacon's secret tomb." Her voice was that of the true believer again.

"But Maria didn't have the Lunaeburg," boomed Carmel Beecher Van Kueren, startling both of them as she spoke. She emerged from the shadows ahead like a hidden truck and glided toward them. "She never would have found the vault."

"All the same, she's a brilliant woman," Lillian Hannibal said in her defense.

Carmel Beecher Van Kueren snorted in apparent contempt. "I will say this, she came pretty close, close enough that she scared the powerbrokers into action to stop her."

The three of them had come to a standstill by a concert grand piano. On it was a photo of Hannibal and Gandhi.

"Who were the powerbrokers?" Cody asked.

"The same ones we face today," Lillian stated. "The Rockefellers, the courts, the politicians, and of course, the church."

"Don't forget the Jews, dear," the enormous woman added ominously. "Never forget the Jews."

"One of the things I don't understand . . ." Cody said, doing his best to sound like a pure, if ignorant, convert, ". . . is, since the revealing of the secrets will be so good for mankind, why do these people want to stop us?"

"Be good for mankind," Lillian almost smirked. "That's like saying the gift of sight would be good for the blind man, or the breath of life good for the newborn baby."

"They try to stop us," Carmel Beecher Van Kueren interjected dogmatically, "because once the secrets are revealed, they know they will be thrown from power."

"Lillian?" Evan Hannibal's voice called from the lighted room ahead of them.

"Coming, dear," she answered.

And the trio proceeded into what turned out to be a study. Hannibal was seated at a game table, looking again as if he had been posed. He was apparently playing checkers with Nelson Hobart, who sat across from him.

"You forgot to say about the boy," the old man said, seeming distressed. "Maria couldn't succeed because she didn't have the boy with her. We do . . ."

"Yes, dear, we do."

The old man hiccupped.

"That's why we have the money," Hannibal said as if he had just remembered it, and then, with surprising ease for his age, he bounced up and tottled over to a pair of brown leather suitcases.

"Show him, Lillian," Hannibal insisted.

And she did, unsnapping first one and then the

other suitcase, revealing bundles and bundles of twenties and fifties.

"Four million dollars, sergeant," she said finally. "It seems so much and yet so little for what's at stake."

"Are you sure you can get it to Professor Polk?" The Van Kueren woman wanted to know.

The question seemed to both surprise and frighten the Great American Poet. "He must get the money to him . . . why wouldn't he get it to him?"

"It's all right, dear," Lillian said, trying to calm him down. "I told you what lies the police were telling about Alex, how desperate they were getting. We have to be very careful."

"If they had any real proof, they would have been here today," insisted Carmel Beecher Van Kueren. "They made that sniveling phone call last night, but they didn't dare keep their appointment today, did they?"

"You have to get him the money." The old man was almost crying. "How can I be a boy again if you don't get him the money?"

"Are you sure you won't be followed?" Lillian asked.

"I was a policeman for twenty years," Cody said. "I know how they maintain surveillance. I also know how to lose it."

Cody's words seemed to reassure them. Lillian closed the suitcases and then rang for the Filipino houseman and asked him to take them to the front door. Nelson Hobart began his hacking cough.

"We wish you God's speed, sir," Evan Hannibal said, having recovered from his earlier emotion. He shook Cody's hand and then held it for several moments, as if he was almost afraid to let go. "You take the hopes of mankind with you."

"I know," Cody said.

And so it was with dreams and desperate hopes that they parted.

Cody carried the two suitcases to his station wagon and put them in the back. The flabby guard opened the iron gates for him, and he drove into the Hollywood night.

Chapter Twenty-Seven

Cody arrived at the gas station on Pico eleven minutes early. He used the time to go to the men's room, strip off his jacket and shirt, and untape the monitoring device from his body. It was meant to keep him in contact with the police, who were following. He knew they wouldn't be happy, but he didn't care. He had taken them into his confidence only to keep them away from the Hannibals. He had. Now he had to go after his son and as he had told Davis, that didn't involve the police anymore, or the law . . .

The call to the phone booth came exactly on time. Davis gave him his instructions. Cody left the phone booth, dropped the listening devices in a trash can, got back in the wagon, and pulled out into traffic. He turned left on La Brea. He knew the police would be nearby, watching, waiting. Three, four, five blocks, and suddenly he made a right turn into a residential street and stomped on the gas. Three blocks down, he pulled a left, then a left again into an alley. He turned his lights off and raced the length of the alley to the next street, turned right, two more blocks, right again, and stopped. A minute passed. No cars approached. He was almost safe. Lights still out, he drove down another half a block and parked.

Damien was there with his grandmother's car. They transferred the suitcases and exchanged keys.

"Stay here for ten minutes, then you can drive home," Cody told him.

"What if the police stop me?"

"Don't say anything. There's nothing they can do to you."

They looked at one another for several moments and then embraced.

"Your grandmother would flip her wig if she knew she had four million dollars in the backseat of her car," Cody joked, and they both smiled . . . and then Cody drove off with the car and the money.

And as he drove away, he wondered if he would ever see Damien again, for he knew that tonight would end in death for either himself or Davis

The phone booth he had been sent to was in a small parking lot across from the Forum. He parked next to it and waited. It was nearing nine o'clock, and the temperature was still in the nineties. Twenty minutes passed. A group of boys, mostly black, sauntered by, laughing, talking. Three fire engines raced to a rescue. And then, all at once, the sense of fear and cold and the crying from eternity were back . . . and then he heard a tapping on the glass, and he turned to see the man with the pixie smile looking in at him. It was as if he had appeared from thin air. Cody hadn't expected this. He felt unbalanced, and then an angry rage exploded inside of him and he wanted to rip through the steel and glass of the car and kill the son of a bitch who was standing there. And in the same moment he knew he couldn't . . . not while the madman had Patrick. His adrenalin racing, he knew he had to appear calm as he climbed out of the driver's side door.

"I think it's best if we keep the car between us," Davis said.

"I was expecting a phone call," Cody said, and he knew his words sounded odd. But he had to play the game. He had to convince Davis he was playing the game, the game that Davis had won. These were only the formalities . . . money for the boy and no repercussions. . . . And he knew again that before it was done he would kill the little son of a bitch who stood across from him.

"I thought this would be simpler. From all appearances, no one has followed you."

"The money's there, in the backseat," Cody said. "Where's my son?"

"Be patient. You fulfill your part of the bargain and your son will be returned as promised, safe and sound."

"I've brought the money," Cody pressed.

"You haven't brought the money where I want it . . . believe me, I have no desire to have you hunting me for the rest of my life. As I said on the phone, this is nothing personal, strictly business."

"Where do you want the money?" Cody asked after some moments. His words were becoming tense.

The cries from the darkness filled Cody's head. Anger and rage. Davis was growing uneasy.

"Believe me, I did come armed, just in case you tried anything stupid. But even if you were to some-how overpower me . . . I think you know enough about me now to know I'd never tell you where your son was . . . no matter what you did to me . . . not until he was dead . . . and every minute of it you'd have to live with the fact that he was slowly and painfully dying because you tried to be some kind of an heroic asshole. . . . Like it or not, you're going to have to trust me . . . agreed?"

". . . Agreed," Cody managed, and his ears were ringing.

"You have one more leg on your journey . . ." Davis started. "The airport. There's a Continental flight leaving for Denver in an hour. You have a reservation on it. I want you to take the suitcases, check them onto the flight, pick up your ticket, and then go to the closest bar to the departure gate and wait."

"For how long?"

"One thirty A.M. That will give me plenty of time to arrive in Denver . . . and fade into the landscape, as they say."

"What about Patrick?"

"You do what I say and you'll have him back before morning, safe and sound . . . you don't have a choice," Davis said, and then after a moment turned and started away.

"Davis . . ."

The man who was capable of a pixie smile turned back.

"Since this is strictly business . . ." Cody began, "and since I will probably never see you again, you mind answering a few questions?"

Davis seemed amused. "One professional to another? What do you want to know?"

Cody said nothing for a few moments as if considering what he should ask. There were, of course, questions he'd like the answers to, but it was more important to him now to observe this man. His voice, his mannerisms. The things one can't change like hair color or an added mustache or beard. "Let's start at the beginning . . . The whole idea of the con—it came out of Hannibal making an appearance in your prison, didn't it?''

''That's right, at least the beginnings of it . . . though it took almost a year of research before I knew enough to figure out how to play it,'' he said and smiled. ''The old man came to read poetry to a classroom of con-writers. His wife and the blimp were with him.''

''Mrs. Van Kueren?''

''That's right. In the discussion that followed, somehow it got onto Bacon and Shakespeare, and the two women especially started to come on with all that shit . . . and you could tell just by watching them that they really believed in it. I started thinking then, this is it, this is the gold mine I've been looking for. . . . You see, I had gotten tired of people putting me in prison for my work, and I had decided my next score was going to be perfect, so perfect that, even when it was over, even after the walkaway, no one would know a crime had taken place. I almost pulled it off, too, until you showed up.'' A sense of resentment had crept into his voice during the last of his words.

''Well, the best laid plans . . .'' Cody tried with a smile. And the smile came easily, because he knew that every word Davis said would help him find him later . . . trap him . . . kill him.

After a moment, Davis relaxed and the pixie smile returned. ''And actually, when it's all over, the Hannibals and the blimp will be happy. I'll send them their Lunaeburg, and it's a damn good piece of work, too. I paid good money for it, to a great artist.''

''Same guy you went to Leavenworth with?'' Cody asked.

''You do know a lot about me . . . yeah, same

guy,'' Davis said and laughed, and his laugh was like a toy machine gun. He was opening up; he was enjoying bragging about his work. ''When things were getting to the critical stage, you know, whether or not the old guy was going to come up with the money, I had the kid bring him a page from the Lunaeburg. . . . I pretended I was skeptical. But the blimp and Hannibal's old lady got working on it, you know, breaking the cipher, and guess what the secret message was . . . 'E Hannibal save' . . . To make it really look good I had him spell Hannibal with only one '*n*' and had the '*e*' dropped off of 'save' . . . I thought they were going to bust a gut, they were so excited. And it was all I could do to keep from laughing.''

''You enjoy your work, don't you?'' Cody asked.

''Why shouldn't I?''

''Even with all those people dead along the way? The little boy in the garbage bag?''

The smile left Davis's face for a moment and then returned, even bigger. He was laughing at Cody now. ''You think I'm some kind of evil bastard, don't you?''

''Either that,'' Cody smiled, ''or totally fucking insane.''

The smile was gone. ''You like living dangerously, don't you?''

''You won't do anything to my son,'' Cody said. ''This is strictly business, remember? And you know if you do hurt him . . . I'll become as insane as you are until I find you.''

Davis glared at him for several moments, and then the glare gave way to the pixie smile. ''You think I'm insane, my friend. I'm not. I'm just a man of my times. The people's hero. The one they love . . .

don't you know who I am? I'm the great American dream maker.'' Davis laughed. ''I am, just look at the Van Kueren woman, the blimp . . . and Lillian Hannibal. They wanted everything, all that shit they believed in, to be true . . . so I'm making it true for them. The old man, he's afraid of dying; he wants to live forever . . . so presto, I'm giving it to him.''

''You really told him he could be a boy again?'' Cody asked with a hint of a smile of admiration.

''The kid told him,'' Davis giggled. ''The Boy of Gold promised Hannibal. Of course, I did the interpreting . . . . The boy told the old man that if he helped get the Lunaeburg . . . that when the new dawn came, he could be a boy with the Boy of Gold.''

''Christ,'' Cody uttered.

''The Boy of Gold was the key to everything. When I realized they had been believing in him and hoping for him for years, I knew I had the answer. All I had to do was come up with a kid.''

''So you married the widow in Louisiana?''

''The woman wanted a husband . . . and all that goes with it . . . and the kid wanted a father.''

''And when you were through with him, you just threw him away.''

''I didn't cheat him. He wanted a father. I was a very loving father to him,'' Davis said. ''For a lot of the time, I was very good to him.'' The words were coming harder now. *If he feels any remorse,* Cody thought, *it is for the child.*

''Even with the boy,'' Cody said quickly, not wanting to lose him, ''you must have had help inside the Hannibal house, someone who would help sell the boy as the Boy of Gold.''

''Don't you know who?'' Davis asked almost coyly.

"My best guess is the choirmaster. Hobart."

"You see, there's another dream I filled. A life-long dream at that. I gave him the boy. . . . He had been lusting after little boys all of his life. I waited one night until he had drunk his bottle of brandy and had passed out in his room, then I slipped in and put the pretty little naked boy into his bed. I thought the old faggot was going to have a heart attack. He couldn't control himself, and then he couldn't do anything except fondle the little shit. . . . You know what he told me later, the stupid asshole? He said that in all the years he had had the boys' choir, he had never touched one of those kids. He had always wanted to . . . but he hadn't wanted to ruin their lives, he said. He was crying. He said he was dying and now I had ruined his life . . . that's because I had told the old asshole I'd ruin him in public if he didn't help me. See, I had pictures of him and the kid. . . . I gave him his dream . . . he just had to pay his price. It was his job after that, that whenever I told him . . . the nights that the boy was to appear, he had to make sure the wine they drank at the dinner table was properly doctored."

"You drugged them?"

"Just enough to help them step into the twilight zone and not know it." Davis grinned and then glanced at his watch. "You have a plane to catch."

"One more question," Cody requested.

"All right."

"The honeymoon couple, why did they die?"

"They were part of a back-up plan that I had to use," Davis answered with a sigh. He glanced at his watch again and decided to go on. "I met them a few months ago at a campus party. Somebody told them I knew Evan Hannibal, and they wouldn't let me go.

The guy especially was really after me to get him an introduction. I decided to use them as a hedge against any wavering resistance. . . . As it turned out, it was good I had them. . . . See, what happened was, the blimp, the Van Kueren woman, was sold hook, line, and sinker. The old man was ready because he wanted to be a kid again. . . . It was his wife, Lillian, who was the roadblock. Not that she didn't want to believe, she was just tight with a buck. I had to shock her into action.''

''By killing the honeymoon couple?''

''Almost. . . . I had told them that the honeymooners were really emissaries for the Boy of Gold, that they had come with a message that time was running short and the money had to be paid soon. That day at Spouting Horn, where the asshole girl took the pictures—I still don't know how you got your hands on those when I couldn't.''

''She put them in to be developed under her maiden name,'' Cody answered.

''Shit,'' Davis said. ''. . . Anyway, the day she took those pictures, I walked over to them, and as I had arranged, the guy gave me his resume and a list of questions he wanted to ask in the interview with the old man. . . . See, there I was again, fulfilling people's dreams. The guy was going to be famous for interviewing Evan Hannibal. . . . The resume and the questions, of course, were in an envelope, which I switched before we got back into the house. . . . The envelope I gave Lillian Hannibal had a second page of the Lunaeburg in it . . .''

''But why kill them?'' Cody pressed.

''Very simple. Because the Hannibal woman was still wavering, and believe me, I was nervous as hell about it. . . . It was, in effect, my last card. If it didn't work, the whole scam could fall apart. . . . So the next morning, I told her I had received a message from the couple, saying that they had to see us . . . the situation had become dangerous . . . the forces that were trying to stop us were on the island. Both Hannibal's wife and the blimp went with me. . . . The meeting was in a cane field. I think you've been to the spot," he added with a hint of a smile. "The couple, of course, were dead. Both of the women became ill . . . but both then realized they had to act, now or never. For the other side to go this far, to commit murder, they felt we had to be very close to the truth. . . . She started making phone calls to pull the four million together that afternoon."

"So they died just to be part of the setup?"

"Such is life, huh?" he said with a shrug.

"You kill them alone, or did Cuaresma help?"

"He helped. I made him do the cutting afterward, too."

"And the Hannibal woman's stepson?"

"Now he's the one who ought to have his head checked . . . but he has nothing to do with us . . . just a dope-head." He looked at his watch again. "We really shouldn't wait any longer."

Davis started away, then paused and looked back with a pixie smile. "You know, Cody, in a way I'm giving you your dream. . . . I'm giving you your kid back."

Cody picked up his ticket and checked the suitcases in forty minutes before the flight.

The bar wasn't hard to find. Chrome and glass. The Dodger postgame show was on the T.V. He ordered a drink and suddenly felt terribly alone and defeated. This wasn't the way he had expected it. He had thought there would have been some kind of an exchange, Pat for the suitcases. And after he had gotten Pat, he would have found some way to get at Davis. But it wasn't to be. He had been out-planned. He had been out-thought. He had been beaten. Pat was still out there. His little boy's life was hanging on the whim of a madman. And why? Why? Because he had become involved on a case, because he thought he had been going mad because of Ann disappearing. He had thought that somehow working through it would help . . . and it had, but at what cost? Christ, less than thirty minutes had passed since he had left Davis . . . hours to go before the plane would arrive in Denver. Hours to go before morning, when he had been promised Patrick would return, and he didn't know how he could fill the hours . . . and then he saw him. In the bar mirror. His blond hair first, his face, looking . . .

"Pat?"

The boy saw him and started to run, first with a smile and then with tears, and Cody caught him up in his arms.

Chapter Twenty-Eight

Davis was not on the plane to Denver. And when the suitcases that Cody had checked in were opened, they were found to contain newspapers. Later, Lillian Hannibal would admit that the switch had been made when her Filipino houseman had carried the bags from the study to the entry hall, and that Carmel Beecher Van Kueren had herself delivered the money to Professor Polk/Davis.

Cody realized that his whole visit to the Hannibal house, at least on the women's part had been a performance. All the time he thought he had been playing them, they had been playing him . . . so anxious to give away the four million dollars . . . so anxious to fool him, because they knew he was still connected to the other side, the evil force trying to stop the dawn. *Madness,* Cody thought and laughed, because right now he didn't care. Right now he had Patrick back, and that was all that mattered.

From talking to Patrick, he realized that once Davis had been satisfied that Cody was faithfully carrying out his misdirection, he waited just long enough for Cody to do his business at the airport and then dropped the boy off there, telling him where he could find his father.

So simple. So clever.

Chapter Twenty-Nine

Then, with the morning, came the phone call that Cody had been afraid of. It had been a mistake. Everyone was very sorry. It had been a mistake. Someone had mixed up dental charts. The skeletal remains found in the Angeles Forest were Ann's. Everyone was so sorry. Were they sure now? Yes. Could there be no mistake? No. So sorry.

And so Cody told his sons, and they cried together and felt relieved, and then they felt guilty for feeling relieved. But they talked about it and realized what terrible pressure they had all been under, and they knew Ann wouldn't want them to feel badly. Not now, not when she had had to leave them alone.

Old Father Concannon said the funeral Mass. All the children from the school were there. Cody felt good about that. Ann had always loved the children. She had spent every Wednesday and Friday working with some of the under privileged ones. And the children sang the new Mass songs, the ones he didn't like, but somehow they sounded beautiful coming from the mouths of children.

And then the freeway ride. . . . They buried her in San Fernando Mission Cemetery, near his mother.

Beth Pyne was there. Dan would be coming home from the hospital in a few days. The surgeons, on opening him up, had decided that there was nothing they could do for him, and they had just closed him again.

Later, a lot of the mourners had gathered at Ann's parents' house. It was big and wooden and had been built in 1911. Cody wandered from room to room and heard pieces of conversations:

"I suppose they'll sell the boat now."

"I wish the boys would come and stay here for a while. It would be the best thing for them."

"He drinks."

"Imagine, they had this crazy idea they were going to sail around the world . . . just goes to show you."

"He doesn't even have a job."

"The poor boys, how are they going to get along?"

Chapter Thirty

It was snowing when the Jet Liner that Cody was on touched down in Salt Lake City. Three weeks had passed since the funeral. When he and the boys had gone back to the boat, and when the fact that she was never coming home again had sunk in, they had cried again.

He rented a car and, following directions, headed for Park City. The roads were slick. The snow continued to fall gently. In a little over an hour, he pulled into the Holiday Inn.

"The money's starting to show up," the captain had told him on the phone. At Cody's suggestion, they had pressed the bank officials to let them photograph as many of the fifty-dollar bills as they could before turning the money over to the Hannibals.

His clothes weren't warm enough. He bought a couple of ski sweaters and a down jacket.

"How long can you give me?" Cody had asked.

"I'm going to be sick for the next three days," the captain answered. "I can't stall acting on the information much longer than that."

"With luck . . ." Cody didn't finish the sentence. He knew what he would do with luck. With luck he'd find Davis and execute him. Shoot and shoot and shoot until there were no bullets left. Until there was no Davis left.

"I never made this phone call," the captain said.

"I know."

To his surprise, he found that the town of Park City itself wasn't anything like the sprawl of modern condos that surrounded the hotel. It was, in fact, an old mining town refurnished. It had a sense of character and fun to it that made Cody feel comfortable. And the whole town only stretched three blocks.

The photographed fifty-dollar bills had been turning up at the local banks, suggesting that they had trickled in from various stores and restaurants. *Everyone has to eat,* Cody reasoned, so he settled on a restaurant just up and across from what passed for the town's supermarket. He chose a table by the window that looked out onto the street, and then he told the proprietors that he was a writer and would like to sit here for maybe a couple of days, absorbing local color. He offered to pay twenty dollars an hour for the privilege, and they accepted.

He watched the foot traffic and sipped coffee, and then he realized that he was being watched. He had been there for two hours. He was suppose to be a writer, but he wasn't writing. He had brought a notebook and a handful of pens as props. He decided that he'd better use them.

But what to write? He stared at the blank paper. How could he pretend? Then he knew what he wanted to write.

Dear Dearest Ann,
I love you so much and now you're gone. I don't

*know how I'll go on without you. I know I will. I
have to. I have to for the boys. For us. For you
and me.*

*Your mother wants the boys to live with her. But
I won't allow that. We'll stay together. We have
to. Where we'll go or what we'll do, I don't know
now. I don't know a lot of things anymore.*

And later he wrote . . .

*I feel like the world has changed and keeps on
changing, and I don't fit anymore. The things I
grew up believing in, the things we believed in
together, all seem so out of place now. Without
purpose. I went to the preliminary hearing and
saw the man who killed you. I wanted to kill him. I
wanted to jump over that little fence and throttle
him, bash his head against the floor until it splat-
tered open, and he was Black and all the ugly hate
words filled my mind. Nigger. Black nigger son of
a bitch. And I knew I was wrong, but I couldn't
stop, and I knew that we had taught our kids, that
it's wrong to hate people because of their color.
You can't. You can't; it's wrong, and yet I was
doing it because he had hurt you. Because he had
killed you. And I knew I could forgive him for what
he had done to me . . . but not for what he had
done to you. He had no right to scare you. To hurt
you. To kill you.*

Late in the afternoon the faces of the passersby
were all beginning to blend together, and he started
to write again.

You asked me once what I thought was the worst

crime. I know now. I think I knew then, but I couldn't find the words. The worst crime is . . . to take away a person's human dignity . . . and there aren't laws against most of the ways it's done. There aren't laws against ridicule, or making fun of a person, or hurting someone's feelings . . . I deal only with the monsters. The ones who deny another's human dignity through murder and assault, through kidnappings. If I have a purpose, I guess that's it . . . catching the monsters.

And then, in the morning, back at the window after breakfast . . .

I've come here to kill a man. He's a monster. A total sociopath. He's the hidden cancer that our society has allowed to grow and flourish. He's murdered eight or nine people that I know about. He's committed horrible crimes even beyond that. Prisons found him intelligent. Parole boards found him charming. He was going to kill Patrick . . . our Patrick, because I had become a threat to exposing him . . .

There was more he wanted to write, more he wanted to tell her. . . . How much he missed her. It was such a terrible ache, and yet he felt closer to her than he had in the months that she had been missing. . . . And at the same time, the sense of fear was returning. Fear, and the darkness, crying out. . . . Why were his thoughts fragmenting? Scattering? . . . And then he knew why: There was danger. But where? From what . . . ? The laugh. Behind him in the back of the room, the machine-gun laugh that Davis had . . . the one he'd heard that night when he had prodded him to talk, to boast in the little parking lot across from the Forum. Davis was here, behind him. Unexpected. He was supposed to be on the street, but he was behind him, and the laugh giggled on.

Cody risked a cautious backward glance . . . .

Madness. He wasn't there.

But the voice, the laughter, was. . . . And then he saw him. His hair was reddish and had been shaved back so that he was half bald. . . . He was wearing glasses and had grown a beard. He was laughing and carrying on with the woman who owned the restaurant. He was obviously a frequent and favored customer. She was leading him to a table when she paused to point out the "writer" near the window. Their eyes met . . . and the smile left the red-haired, red-bearded Davis's face. . . . The next moments were chaos. Cody felt he was swimming in oil; everything was in slow motion. He was pulling his Walther . . . Davis, shoving the frightened owner aside, had pulled a .38. He was firing. . . . Flame erupted inside of Cody, once, twice. He was falling, falling, when he managed to fire his own round, and he saw blood erupt from Davis's shoulder as he lurched for the back door.

The restaurant was filled with the sounds of screaming and breaking glass and plates.

Cody somehow found his feet. Inside him was fire. He was dizzy; nausea was overtaking him. He couldn't let him get away. He couldn't let the monster go free. He propelled himself against the wall that led to the back door, and in the moment he did, realized that he had smeared it with his own blood.

His legs seemed foreign to him, but they had to work. He crashed into the glass-paneled door that led to the anteroom between the restaurant and the back door, and he was aware of the sound of glass breaking and that his right hand that was still holding his Walther was now bleeding. And then his body burst outside into the parking lot in time to see a shiny, new, black Ford Bronco spinning its wheels, kicking up gravel as it backed up. Cody couldn't see who was driving, but he had to guess it was the monster, and so he ran for it. Just as the Bronco was pulling forward, he grabbed hold of the oversized side mirror with his left hand, and Davis's frightened face stared at him. Christ, he had scared him. . . . He had two bullets in him and was losing touch with rationality and was probably dying, but at least he had scared the son of a bitch . . . and with some satisfaction Cody discovered just how badly he had hurt him when he realized that the only reason Davis didn't fire his gun was because his shoulder had been ripped open by the bullet from Cody's Walther. . . . The arm it was attached to now hung uselessly at the monster's side. The other arm was, of course, desperately needed for driving, and that's the way Davis was driving . . . desperately. The sudden appearance of Cody startled him into side-swiping another car.

The Bronco dragged Cody for about a hundred feet until it careened out of the alleyway and onto the main road. It must have been going near thirty when Cody finally let go, his body spinning and tumbling into oncoming traffic.

A red, sporty jeep hit its brakes, screeching and spinning, its oversized tires missing Cody's head by inches.

Cody never would have avoided the oncoming mail truck unless Davis's Bronco had been in the way. The mail truck broadsided the back half of the Bronco. The mailman, balding, married, three kids, not wearing a seatbelt, plunged halfway through the windshield.

Davis somehow righted the Bronco and sped forward again, crashing into a parked station wagon before he could spin free and race the wounded vehicle down the street.

Pandemonium . . . from the restaurant . . . from the street . . .

Madness.

Cody was on his feet again, and he could feel life slipping away. But not yet. Not until he had the monster. Suddenly he was aware that he was waving his Walther in the face of the man driving the sporty red Jeep, and then Cody was behind the wheel, racing after Davis. Cars were stopped up ahead. Confusion. . . . A rescue van was trying to get through; siren wailing. The street was blocked. And Cody felt no more pain, only a sense of weakness, a glow ebbing warmth, and a sense of Ann . . . a sense of Ann. . . . He turned the Jeep onto the sidewalk and people jumped out of the way. Sixty, seventy feet later he crashed into displays in front of the hardware store, and then he turned back onto the road, past the blockage. He could see the Bronco far ahead, turning onto the main highway.

Sirens, racing past . . . racing to the shooting, the horrible crash. He didn't know how he kept the Jeep on the road, he only knew he had to. . . . One mile, two miles, and he was weaving across the double line. A van full of people swerved to miss him. Ann was closer now, and he felt a pang of anguish, because he wouldn't see the boys again, and Ann was closer still. . . . Up ahead he saw the black Bronco turn off the highway into a development of million-dollar homes . . . or chalets as they called million-dollar homes here . . . chalets that fronted the golf course and had views of the best ski slopes.

Consciousness was vague now, like the moments between sleep and waking . . . but he couldn't let go of it, not yet. He managed to turn the Jeep into the cluster of million-dollar homes, and the Bronco was there, stopped in the middle of the street. Davis was standing next to it. Gun raised, he began to fire. One, two bullets shattered the windshield of the Jeep. None found their mark, and then he must have been out of ammunition; he was running for the house.

Cody knew that he was going for another weapon, and he knew he didn't have the time or strength to stop the Jeep and follow him inside on foot, so he did the only thing he could. He pressed his foot on the gas and propelled the Jeep across the lawn, up the porch, and crashed in through the front door, shattering glass, splintering wood. Cody was thrown from the driver's seat.

Blood was in his eyes now. The taste of it was in his mouth. Pain had returned with waning life. Like a giant slug, he moved himself across the floor. And then, there he was, Davis. The monster. He had something silver, flashing in his hand. He looked frightened and enraged.

"You bastard, we had a deal. . . . I gave you your son."

Cody fired. The bullet hit Davis in the upper chest near his injured shoulder, and the monster sank to his knees.

"We had a deal," Davis wailed.

Christ, Cody thought, *he doesn't even understand. He has no idea what he's done. He has no conscience.*

Cody fired again. His ears were ringing, and everything around him was turning red, but he hit his mark. His bullet slammed into Davis's crotch, and the madman screamed in pain and horror.

Now they were both on the floor. Bloodied and unable to use their legs, they flayed at each other with their deadly weapons . . . Davis with a straight razor. He swung it and missed Cody by a foot, and Cody in turn emptied his clip into the man who had kidnapped his son . . . one, two, three into his chest, and then finally one through the forehead, just above the eyes.

The man who was capable of a pixie smile was dead.

And once Cody realized that, for a moment he felt like crying, and then the darkness overtook him and Ann was there, beautiful Ann. Ann who he loved so much, and she was holding out her hand to him, smiling, and he reached for her hand and felt warm and good. There was a sense of well-being and no pain . . . and he reached for her and reached for her, but she was always just a fingertip away . . . and then he felt her slipping. She was leaving him, leaving him . . . and instead there were bright white lights above and voices, and pain was returning.

Voices.

"Heartbeat, we're getting a heartbeat.

And there were other voices and sounds, ones he knew. An emergency team was trying to keep someone alive. Someone. They were trying to keep him alive, and he was still reaching for Ann, but she was gone now and he started to cry . . .

Chapter Thirty-One

Another seven weeks passed before the fifty-six foot ketch sailed into Hanalei Bay. Caleb was also out of the hospital now. Cody found him atop the cliff, looking out over the ocean. He told him what had happened in the case, and told him about Ann . . . and how sorry he was about Caleb's family members who had died. He knew that, even when the young Hawaiian's body had mended, he'd never be a cop again.

He told him why Cuaresma had tried to kill him and his family, that he had been under orders from Davis, who was worried that both Cody and Caleb knew too much. Davis thought he could chase Cody off the island by threatening his son. That wouldn't work in Caleb's case, only death would. Murder that was made to look like something else . . . a mini-drug-war.

Caleb in his turn told him that Stephen Auerbach had been arrested for his part in the killing of Caleb's aunt.

And the two men sat in silence for over an hour,

until the sun was moving low on the water and they knew they would have to go down.

"Where will you go?"

"We're heading for the South Seas," Cody told him. "Fiji, New Zealand, Australia . . . eventually around the world."

"Quite a trip."

"Yeah," Cody said.